Praise for

KAREN M. MCMANUS

"McMANUS KNOWS HOW TO PLOT A MYSTERY."
—*EW* on *ONE OF US IS LYING*

"A MUST-READ YA thriller."
—*Bustle* on *TWO CAN KEEP A SECRET*

"One of THE BEST writers in the YA mystery genre."
—*Paste* on *ONE OF US IS NEXT*

"Karen McManus is the
UNDISPUTED QUEEN of YA mysteries."
—*HelloGiggles* on *THE COUSINS*

★ "A MASTERFUL TALE of secrets,
lies, and twisted intentions."
—*Booklist* on *YOU'LL BE THE DEATH OF ME*

★ "THE STRONGEST YET from a master of the genre."
—*Kirkus Reviews* on *NOTHING MORE TO TELL*

★ "A soulful, HIGH-STAKES THRILL RIDE."
—*Publishers Weekly* on *ONE OF US IS BACK*

BOOKS BY KAREN M. McMANUS

You'll Be the Death of Me

Karen M. McManus

DELACORTE PRESS

Text copyright © 2021 by Karen M. McManus, LLC
Cover art used under license from Shutterstock.com and Getty Images

All rights reserved. Published in the United States by Delacorte Press,
an imprint of Random House Children's Books, a division of Penguin Random House LLC,
New York. Originally published in hardcover in the United States by Delacorte Press,
an imprint of Random House Children's Books, a division of
Penguin Random House LLC, New York, in 2021.

Delacorte Press is a registered trademark and the colophon
is a trademark of Penguin Random House LLC.

Visit us on the Web! GetUnderlined.com

Educators and librarians, for a variety of teaching tools, visit us at RHTeachersLibrarians.com

The Library of Congress has cataloged the hardcover edition of this work as follows:
Names: McManus, Karen M., author.
Title: You'll be the death of me / Karen M. McManus.
Other titles: You will be the death of me
Description: First edition. | New York: Delacorte Press, [2021] | Audience: Ages 14+. |
Audience: Grades 10–12. | Summary: Estranged friends Ivy, Mateo, and
Cal witness a murder while skipping school, and the only way they can solve it is by
revealing what they have been hiding from one another—and themselves.
Identifiers: LCCN 2020037625 (print) | LCCN 2020037626 (ebook) |
ISBN 978-0-593-17586-6 (hardcover) | ISBN 978-0-593-17588-0 (library binding) |
ISBN 978-0-593-17587-3 (ebook)
Subjects: CYAC: Murder—Fiction. | Friendship—Fiction. | Secrets—Fiction.
Classification: LCC PZ7.1.M4637 You 2021 (print) | LCC PZ7.1.M4637 (ebook) |
DDC [Fic]—dc23

ISBN 978-0-593-17589-7 (paperback)

Printed in the United States of America
1st Printing
First Ember Edition 2024

For Zachary, Shalyn, and Aidan

IVY

I respect a good checklist, but I'm beginning to think my mother went overboard.

"Sorry, what page?" I ask, flipping through the handout at our kitchen table while Mom watches me expectantly via Skype. The heading reads *Sterling-Shepard 20th-Anniversary Trip: Instructions for Ivy and Daniel,* and it's eleven pages total. Double-sided. My mother planned the first time she and Dad ever left me and my brother alone—for four days—with the same thoroughness and military precision she brings to everything. Between the checklist and the frequent calls over Skype and FaceTime, it's like they never left.

"Nine," Mom says. Her blond hair is pulled back in her signature French twist and her makeup is perfect, even though it's barely five a.m. in San Francisco. My parents' flight home doesn't take off for another three and a half hours, but Mom is never anything but prepared. "Right after the lighting section."

"Ah, the lighting section." My brother, Daniel, sighs dramatically from across the table as he overfills a bowl with Lucky Charms. Daniel, despite being sixteen, has the cereal tastes of a toddler. "I would have thought we could turn them on when we need them, and off when we don't. I was wrong. So very, very wrong."

"A well-lit house deters break-ins," Mom says, like we don't live on a street where the closest thing we've ever witnessed to a criminal act is kids riding bicycles without a helmet.

I keep my eyeroll to myself, though, because it's impossible to win an argument against my mother. She teaches applied statistics at MIT, and has up-to-the-minute data for everything. It's why I'm thumbing through her checklist for the section on *CCY Award Ceremony*—a list of to-dos in preparation for Mom being named Carlton Citizen of the Year, thanks to her contributions to a statewide report on opioid abuse.

"Found it," I say, quickly scanning the page for anything I might have missed. "I picked up your dress from the dry cleaner yesterday, so that's all set."

"That's what I wanted to talk to you about," Mom says. "Our plane is supposed to land at five-thirty. Theoretically, with the ceremony starting at seven, that's enough time to come home and change. But I just realized I never told you what to do if we're running late and need to go straight from the airport to Mackenzie Hall."

"Um." I meet her penetrating gaze through my laptop screen. "Couldn't you just, you know, text me if that happens?"

"I will if I can. But you should probably sign up for flight alerts in case the plane Wi-Fi isn't working," Mom says. "We couldn't get a signal the entire way over. Anyway, if we don't touch down before six, I'd like you to meet us there and bring the dress. I'll need shoes and jewelry, too. Do you have a pen handy? I'll tell you which ones."

Daniel helps himself to more cereal, and I try to suppress my usual low-simmering resentment of my brother as I hastily scribble notes. Half my life is spent wondering why I have to work twice as hard as Daniel at everything, but in this case, I asked for it. Before my parents left, I insisted on handling every aspect of the award ceremony—mainly because I was afraid that if I didn't, my mother would realize she'd made a mistake by asking me, not Daniel, to introduce her. My wunderkind brother, who skipped a grade and is currently outshining me in every aspect of our senior year, would have been the logical choice.

Part of me can't help but think Mom regrets her decision. Especially after yesterday, when my one-and-only claim to school fame was brutally torpedoed.

My stomach rolls as I drop the pen and push my empty cereal bowl away. Mom, ever alert, catches the motion. "Ivy, I'm sorry. I'm keeping you from breakfast, aren't I?"

"It's fine. I'm not hungry."

"You have to eat, though," she urges. "Have some toast. Or fruit."

The thought doesn't appeal even a little. "I can't."

Mom's forehead scrunches in concern. "You're not getting sick, are you?"

Before I have a chance to reply, Daniel loudly fake-coughs, *"Boney."* I glare daggers at him, then glance at Mom on-screen to see if she caught the reference.

Of course she did.

"Oh, honey," she says, her expression turning sympathetic

3

with a touch of exasperation. "You're not still thinking about the election, are you?"

"No," I lie.

The election. Yesterday's debacle. Where I, Ivy Sterling-Shepard, three-time class president, lost the senior-year election to Brian "Boney" Mahoney. Who ran as a joke. His slogan was literally "Vote for Boney and I'll leave you alone-y."

Okay, fine. It's catchy. But now Boney is class president and really will do nothing, whereas I had all kinds of plans to improve student life at Carlton High. I'd been working with a local farm share on bringing organic options to the salad bar, and with one of the guidance counselors on a mediation program to resolve disputes between students. Not to mention a resource-sharing partnership with the Carlton Library so our school library could offer ebooks and audiobooks along with hard copies. I was even looking into holding a senior class blood drive for Carlton Hospital, despite the fact that I faint at the sight of needles.

But in the end, nobody cared about any of that. So today, at exactly ten a.m., Boney is going to give his presidential victory speech to the senior class. If it's anything like our debates, it will mostly consist of long, confused pauses between fart jokes.

I've been trying to put on a brave face, but it hurts. Student government was my thing. The only activity I've ever been better at than Daniel. Well, not *better*, exactly, since he never bothered to run for anything, but still. It was mine.

Mom gives me a look that says *Time for some tough love.* It's one of her most powerful looks, right after *Don't you dare take that tone with me.* "Honey, I know how disappointed you are. But you can't dwell, or you really will make yourself sick."

"Who's sick?" My father's voice booms from someplace in

4

their hotel room. A second later he emerges from the bathroom dressed in travel-ready casual clothes, rubbing his salt-and-pepper hair with a towel. "I hope it's not you, Samantha. Not with a six-hour flight ahead of us."

"I'm perfectly fine, James. I'm talking to—"

Dad approaches the desk where Mom is sitting. "Is it Daniel? Daniel, did you pick something up at the club? I heard there was a rash of food poisoning over the weekend."

"Yeah, but I don't eat there," Daniel says. Dad recently got my brother a job at a country club he helped develop in the next town over, and although Daniel is only a busboy, he makes a fortune in tips. Even if he *had* eaten bad shellfish, he'd probably drag himself into work anyway, if only to keep adding to his collection of overpriced sneakers.

As usual, I'm an afterthought in the Sterling-Shepard household. I half expect my father to inquire about our dachshund, Mila, before he gets to me. "Nobody's sick," I say as his face comes into focus over Mom's shoulder. "I'm just . . . I was wondering if maybe I could go to school a little later today? Like, eleven or so."

Dad's brows shoot up in surprise. I haven't been absent for a single hour of my entire high school career. It's not that I never get sick. It's just that I've always had to work so hard to stay on top of classes that I live in constant fear of falling behind. The only time I ever willingly missed school was way back in sixth grade, when I spontaneously slipped out of a boring field trip at the Massachusetts Horticultural Society with two boys from my class who, at the time, I didn't know all that well.

We were seated close to an exit, and at a particularly dull point in the lecture, Cal O'Shea-Wallace started inching toward the auditorium door. Cal was the only kid in our class with two dads, and I'd always secretly wanted to be friends with him because he was funny, had a hyphenated last name like me, and wore brightly patterned shirts that I found oddly mesmerizing. He caught my eye, and then the eye of the kid next to me, Mateo Wojcik, and made a beckoning motion with one hand. Mateo and I exchanged glances, shrugged—*Why not?*—and followed.

I thought we'd just linger guiltily in the hallway for a minute, but the outdoor exit was *right there*. When Mateo pushed it open, we stepped into bright sunshine, and a literal parade that happened to be passing by to celebrate a recent Red Sox championship. We melted into the crowd instead of returning to our seats, and spent two hours wandering around Boston on our own. We even made it back to the Horticultural Society without anyone realizing we'd been gone. The whole experience—Cal called it "the Greatest Day Ever"—created a fast friendship between the three of us that, at the time, seemed like it would last forever.

It lasted till eighth grade, which is almost the same in kid years.

"Why eleven o'clock?" Dad's voice yanks me back into the present as Mom twists in her chair to look at him.

"The post-election assembly is this morning," she says.

"Ahh," Dad sighs, his handsome features settling into a sympathetic expression. "Ivy, what happened yesterday is a shame. But it's no reflection of your worth or ability. That wasn't the first time a buffoon has been handed an office he doesn't deserve, and it won't be the last. All you can do is hold your head high."

"Absolutely." Mom nods so vigorously that a strand of hair

nearly escapes her French twist. But not quite. It wouldn't dare. "Besides, I wouldn't be surprised if Brian ends up resigning when all is said and done. He's not really cut out for student government, is he? Once the novelty wears off, you can take his place."

"Sure," Dad says cheerfully, like being Boney Mahoney's cleanup crew wouldn't be a mortifying way to become class president. "And remember, Ivy: anticipation is often worse than reality. I'll bet today won't be nearly as bad as you think." He puts a hand on the back of Mom's chair and they smile in unison, framed like a photograph within my laptop as they wait for me to agree. They're the perfect team: Mom cool and analytical, Dad warm and exuberant, and both of them positive that they're always right.

The problem with my parents is that they've never failed at anything. Samantha Sterling and James Shepard have been a power couple ever since they met at Columbia Business School, even though my dad dropped out six months later when he decided he'd rather flip houses. He started here in his hometown of Carlton, a close-in suburb of Boston that turned trendy almost as soon as Dad acquired a couple of run-down old Victorians. Now, twenty years later, he's one of those recession-proof real estate developers who always manages to buy low and sell high.

Bottom line: neither of them understand what it's like to need a day off. Or even just a morning.

I can't bring myself to keep complaining in the face of their combined optimism, though. "I know," I say, suppressing a sigh. "I was kidding."

"Good," Mom says with an approving nod. "And what are you wearing tonight?"

"The dress Aunt Helen sent," I say, feeling a flicker of enthusiasm return. My mother's much older sister might be pushing sixty, but she has excellent taste—and lots of discretionary income, thanks to the hundreds of thousands of romance novels she sells every year. Her latest gift is from a Belgian designer I've never heard of before, and it's the most fashionable thing I've ever owned. Tonight will be the first time I've worn it outside my bedroom.

"What about shoes?"

I don't own shoes that do the dress justice, but that can't be helped. Maybe Aunt Helen will come through on those when she sells her next book. "Black heels."

"Perfect," Mom says. "Now, in terms of dinner, make sure you don't wait for us since we're cutting it so close. You could unfreeze some of the chili, or—"

"I'm going to Olive Garden with Trevor," Daniel interrupts. "After lacrosse practice."

Mom frowns. "Are you sure you'll have time for that?"

That's my brother's cue to change his plans, but he doesn't take it. "Totally."

Mom looks ready to protest, but Dad raps his knuckles on the desk before she can. "Better sign off, Samantha," he says. "You still have to pack."

"Right," Mom sighs. She hates to rush when it comes to packing, so I think we're done until she adds, "One last thing, Ivy—do you have your remarks for the ceremony all ready?"

"Yeah, of course." I'd spent most of the weekend working on them. "I emailed them yesterday, remember?"

"Oh, I know. They're wonderful. I just meant . . ." For the first time since we started speaking, Mom looks unsure of herself, which almost never happens. "You're going to bring a hard copy with you, right? I know how you—I know you can get nervous in front of a crowd, sometimes."

My stomach tightens. "It's in my backpack."

"Daniel!" Dad barks suddenly. "Turn the computer, Ivy. I want to talk to your brother."

"What? Why?" Daniel asks defensively as I spin the laptop, my cheeks starting to burn with remembered humiliation. I know what's coming.

"Listen, son." I can't see Dad anymore, but I can picture him trying to put on his stern face. Despite his best efforts, it's not even a little bit intimidating. "I need you to promise that you will not, under any circumstances, mess with your sister's notes."

"Dad, I wouldn't— *God.*" Daniel slumps in his chair, rolling his eyes exaggeratedly, and it takes everything in me not to throw my cereal bowl at his head. "Can everyone please get over that? It was supposed to be a joke. I didn't think she'd actually read the damn thing."

"That's not a promise," Dad says. "This is a big night for your mother. And you know how much you upset your sister last time."

If they keep talking about this, I really *will* throw up. "Dad, it's fine," I say tightly. "It was just a stupid prank. I'm over it."

"You don't sound over it," Dad points out. Correctly.

I turn my laptop back toward me and paste on a smile. "I am, really. It's old news."

Based on my father's dubious expression, he doesn't believe me. And he shouldn't. Compared to yesterday's fresh humiliation, sure—what happened last spring is old news. But I am not, in any way, shape, or form, *over it.*

The irony is, it wasn't even a particularly important speech. I was supposed to make closing remarks at the junior class's spring talent show, and I knew everyone's attention would be wandering. Still, I had the whole thing written down, like I always do, because public speaking makes me nervous and I didn't want to forget anything.

What I didn't realize, until I was standing onstage in front of the entire class, was that Daniel had stolen my notes and replaced them with something else: a page from Aunt Helen's latest erotic firefighter novel, *The Fire Within*. And I just—went into some sort of panicked fugue state where I actually *read* it. Out loud. First to confused silence as people thought I was part of the show, and then to hysterical laughter when they realized I wasn't. A teacher finally had to rush the stage and stop me, right around the time I was describing the hero in full anatomical detail.

I still don't understand how it happened. How my brain could have frozen while my mouth kept running. But it did, and it was mortifying. Especially since there's no doubt in my mind that it represents the exact moment when the entire school started thinking of me as a joke.

Boney Mahoney just made it official.

Dad is still lecturing my brother, even though he can't see him anymore. "Your aunt is a brilliant creative force, Daniel. If you have half the professional success that she does someday, you'll be a lucky man."

"I know," Daniel mutters.

"Speaking of which, I noticed before we left that she sent an advance copy of *You Can't Take the Heat*. I'd better not hear a word of that tonight, or I'll—"

"Dad. Stop," I interrupt. "Nothing is going to go wrong. Tonight will be perfect." I force certainty into my voice as I meet my mother's eyes, which are wide and worried—like they're reflecting all of my recent failures. I need to get back on track, and erase that look once and for all. "It'll be everything you deserve, Mom. I promise."

2

MATEO

Here's the thing about powerhouse people: you have no idea how much they take on until they can't do it all anymore.

I used to think I did plenty to help around the house. More than my friends, anyway. But now that my mother is at maybe half her usual capacity, facts have to be faced: Former Mateo did jack shit. I'm trying to step up, but most of the time I don't even think about what needs to be done until it's too late. Like now, when I'm staring into an empty refrigerator. Thinking about how I worked five hours at the grocery store last night and never considered, even once, that maybe I should bring home some food.

"Oh baby, I'm sorry, we're out of almost everything," Ma calls. She's in the living room doing her physical therapy exercises, but the whole first floor of our house is open concept, and anyway, I'm pretty sure she has eyes in the back of her head. "I haven't made it to the store this week. Can you grab breakfast at school?"

Carlton High cafeteria food is crap, but pointing that out would be a Former Mateo move. "Yeah, no problem," I say, shutting the refrigerator door as my stomach growls.

"Here." I turn as my cousin Autumn, sitting at the kitchen table with a half-zipped backpack in front of her, tosses me a PowerBar. I catch it in one hand, peel back the wrapper, and bite off half.

"Bless you," I mumble around the mouthful.

"Anything for you, brousin."

Autumn has lived with us for seven years, since her parents died in a car crash when she was eleven. Ma was a single parent by then—she and my dad had just divorced, which horrified her Puerto Rican family and totally unfazed his Polish one—and Autumn was her niece by marriage, not blood. That should've put my mother low on the list of people responsible for a traumatized preteen orphan, especially with all the married couples on Dad's side. But Ma's always been the adult who Gets Shit Done.

And unlike the rest of them, she wanted Autumn. "That girl needs us, and we need her," she told me over my outraged protests as she painted what used to be my game room a cheerful lavender. "We have to take care of our own, right?"

I didn't like it, at first. Autumn acted out a lot back then, which was obviously normal but still hugely uncomfortable for ten-year-old me. You never knew what would set her off—or what inanimate object she'd decide to punch. The first time Ma ever took us shopping, a clueless cashier told my cousin, "Look at that beautiful red hair! You and your brother don't look anything alike." And Autumn's face froze.

"He's my *cousin*," Autumn said tightly, her eyes getting big and shiny. "I don't have a brother. I don't have *anybody*." And then she drove her fist into the candy display next to the register, scaring the life out of the cashier.

I scrambled for the fallen candy while Ma put both hands on Autumn's shoulders and pulled her away from the display. Her voice was light, like there was no meltdown happening anywhere near us. "Well, maybe now you have a brother *and* a cousin," she said.

"A brousin," I said, stuffing the candy bars back in all the wrong spots. And that made Autumn choke out a near laugh, so it stuck.

My cousin tosses me another PowerBar after I've polished off the first in three bites. "You working at the grocery store tonight?" she asks.

I take a huge bite before answering. "No, Garrett's." It's my favorite job; a no-frills dive bar where I bus tables. "Where are you headed? Waitressing?"

"Murder van," Autumn says. One of her jobs is working for Sorrento's, a knife-sharpening company, which means she drives to restaurants all over greater Boston in a battered white van with a giant knife on one side. The nickname was a no-brainer.

"How are you getting there?" I ask. We only have one car, so transportation is a constant juggling act in our house.

"Gabe's picking me up. He could probably drop you off at school if you want."

"Hard pass." I don't bother hiding my grimace. Autumn knows I can't stand her boyfriend. They started going out right before they graduated last spring, and I thought it wouldn't last a week. Or maybe that's just what I hoped. I've never cared for Gabe, but I took what Autumn calls an "irrational dislike" to him the first time I heard him answer his phone by saying "Dígame." Which he still does, all the time.

"Why do you care?" she asks whenever I complain. "It's just a greeting. Stop looking for reasons to hate people."

It's a poser move, is my point. He doesn't even speak Spanish.

Gabe and my cousin don't fit, unless you think of it in terms of balance: Autumn cares too much about everything, and Gabe doesn't give a crap about anything. He used to head up the party crowd at Carlton High, and now he's taking a "gap year." As far as I can tell, that means he acts like he's still in high school, minus the homework. He doesn't have a job, but somehow still managed to buy himself a new Camaro that he revs obnoxiously in our driveway every time he comes to pick up Autumn.

Now, she folds her arms and cocks her head at me. "Fine. By all means, walk a mile when you don't have to out of sheer spite and stubbornness."

"I will," I grumble, finishing my second PowerBar and tossing the wrapper into the garbage. Maybe I'm just jealous of Gabe. I have a chip on my shoulder, lately, for anyone who has more than they need and doesn't have to work for it. I have two jobs, and Autumn, who graduated Carlton High last spring, has three. And it's still not enough. Not since the one-two punch we got hit with.

I turn as Ma enters the kitchen, walking slowly and deliberately to avoid limping. Punch #1: in June she was diagnosed with osteoarthritis, a bullshit disease that messes with your joints and isn't supposed to happen to people her age. She does physical therapy nonstop, but she can't walk without pain unless she takes anti-inflammatory meds.

"How are you feeling, Aunt Elena?" Autumn asks in an overly bright tone.

"Great!" Ma says, sounding even more chipper. My cousin learned from the best. I clench my jaw and look away, because I can't fake it like they do. Every single day, it's like getting slammed in the head with a two-by-four to see my mother, who used to run 5Ks and play softball every weekend, strain to make it from the living room to the kitchen.

It's not like I expect life to be fair. I learned it's not seven years ago, when a drunk driver plowed into Autumn's parents and walked away without a scratch. Still sucks, though.

Ma makes it to the kitchen island and leans against it. "Did you remember to pick up my prescription?" she asks Autumn.

"Yup. Right here." Autumn roots through her backpack, pulling out a white pharmacy bag that she hands to my mother. My cousin's eyes briefly meet mine, then drop as she reaches into the backpack again. "And here's your change."

"Change?" Ma's eyebrows shoot up at the thick stack of twenties in Autumn's hand. Those pills cost a fortune. "I wasn't expecting change. How much?"

"Four hundred and eighty dollars," Autumn says blandly.

"But how . . ." Ma looks totally lost. "Did you use my credit card?"

"No. The co-pay was only twenty bucks this time." Ma still hasn't made any move to take the money, so Autumn gets up and drops it onto the counter in front of her. Then she sits back down and picks up a scrunchie from the table. She starts pulling her hair into a ponytail, cool and casual. "The pharmacist said the formulary changed."

"Changed?" Ma echoes. I stare at the floor, because I sure as hell can't look at her.

"Yeah. He says there's a generic version available now. But don't worry, it's still the same medication."

Autumn is a good actress, but my shoulders still tense because Ma has a bullshit detector like no one I've ever met. It's a measure of how rough the last few months have been that she only blinks in surprise once, then smiles gratefully.

"Well, that's the best news I've had in a while." She pulls an amber bottle from the pharmacy bag and unscrews the top, peering into it like she can't believe it's the same medication. It must meet her approval, because she crosses to the cabinet next to the refrigerator and pulls out a glass, filling it with water from the sink.

Autumn and I both watch her like a hawk until she actually swallows the pill. She's been skipping doses for weeks, trying to stretch the latest bottle much further than it's meant to go, because our finances suck right now.

Which brings me to Punch #2: my mother used to own her own business, a bowling alley called Spare Me that was a Carlton institution. Ma, Autumn, and I all worked there, and it was fun as hell. Until six months ago, when some kid slipped on an overwaxed lane and got hurt to the point that his parents went full lawsuit. By the time the dust settled, Spare Me was bankrupt and my mother was desperate to sell. Carlton developer extraordinaire James Shepard scooped it up for nothing.

I shouldn't be mad about that. *It's business, not personal,*

Ma keeps telling me. *I'm glad it was James. He'll develop a good property.* And yeah, he probably will. He's shown Ma plans for a bowling alley–slash–entertainment complex that's a lot glitzier than Spare Me, but not stupidly out of proportion for the town, and he asked her to take on a consulting role when it's closer to final. There might even be a cushy corporate job for her down the line. Way down.

But the thing is: James's daughter, Ivy, and I used to be friends. And even though it's been a while, I'd be lying if I said it didn't suck to hear about James's plans from him instead of her. Because I know Ivy has the inside track. She hears about this stuff way before anyone else. She could've given me a heads-up, but she didn't.

I don't know why I care. It's not like it would've changed anything. And it's not like I hang out with her anymore. But when James Shepard came to our house with his rose-gold laptop and his blueprints, so goddamn nice and charming and respectful while he laid out how his company was going to rebuild from the ashes of my mother's dream, all I could think was: *You could've fucking told me, Ivy.*

"Earth. To. Mateo." Ma's in front of me, snapping her fingers in my face. I didn't even notice her move, so I must've been lost in thought for a while. Crap. That kind of zoning out worries my mother—who, sure enough, is peering at me like she's trying to see inside my brain. Sometimes I think she'd yank it right out of my skull if she could. "You sure I can't convince you to come to the Bronx for the day? Aunt Rose would love to see you."

"I have school," I remind her.

"I know," Ma sighs. "But you're never absent, and I feel like

18

you could use a day off." She turns toward Autumn. "Both of you could. You've been working so hard."

She's right. A day off would be incredible—if it didn't involve at least seven hours round trip in a car with her college friend Christy. Christy offered to play chauffeur as soon as Ma said she wanted to visit Aunt Rose on her ninetieth birthday, which was great of her, since Ma can't easily drive long distances anymore. But Christy never stops talking. *Ever.* And eventually, every conversation turns toward stuff she and Ma did during college that I'd rather live the rest of my life without knowing.

"Wish I could," I lie. "But Garrett's is short-staffed tonight."

"Mr. Sorrento needs me, too," Autumn says quickly. She doesn't enjoy Christy's monologues any more than I do. "You know how it is. Those knives won't sharpen themselves. We'll call Aunt Rose and wish her a happy birthday, though."

Before Ma can answer, a familiar roar fills my ears and sets my teeth on edge. I cross to the front door and pull it open, stepping onto the porch. Sure enough, Gabe's red Camaro is in our driveway, engine revving while he dangles one arm out of the driver's-side window and pretends not to notice me. He's slouched low in his seat, but not low enough that I can't make out his slicked-back hair and mirrored sunglasses. Would I hate Gabe less if he didn't look like such a massive sleaze all the time? The world will never know.

I lift my hands and start a slow clap as Autumn joins me outside, staring between me and the car with a puzzled expression. "What are you doing?" she asks.

"Giving it up for Gabe's engine," I say, clapping hard enough to make my palms sting. "Seems important to him that people notice it."

Autumn shoves at my arm, disrupting the applause. "Don't be a dick."

"He's the dick," I say automatically. We could have this argument in our sleep.

"Babe, come on," Gabe calls, lifting his arm in a beckoning motion. "You're gonna be late for work."

Autumn's phone rings in her hand, and we both glance down at it. "Who's Charlie?" I ask over another rev of the engine. "Gabe's replacement? Please say yes."

I expect her to roll her eyes, but instead she declines the call and shoves her phone into her backpack. "Nobody."

The back of my neck prickles. I know that tone, and it doesn't mean anything good. "Is he one of them?" I ask.

She shakes her head, resolute. "The less you know, the better."

I *knew* it. "Are you making extra stops today?"

"Probably."

My jaw twitches. "Don't."

Her mouth sets in a thin line. "I have to."

"For how much longer?" We could have this argument in our sleep, too.

"As long as I can," Autumn says.

She hoists her backpack higher on her shoulder and meets my eyes, the question she's been asking me for weeks written across her face. *We have to take care of our own, right?*

I don't want to nod, but how the hell else am I supposed to answer?

Yeah. We do.

3

CAL

"It's orange," I tell Viola when she puts the doughnut in front of me.

"Well, duh." Viola might be in her forties, but she can roll her eyes as aggressively as any teenager at Carlton High. "That's the Cheeto dust."

I poke uncertainly at one side of the doughnut. My fingertip comes back bright orange. "And this tastes good?"

"Honey, you know our motto at Crave." She puts one hand on her hip and cocks her head, inviting me to finish the sentence.

"The weirder the better," I say dutifully.

"That's right." She pats me on the shoulder before turning back toward the kitchen. "Enjoy your Cheeto-dusted Bavarian cream."

I regard the orange lump on my plate with a mix of anticipation and fear. Crave Doughnuts is my favorite breakfast place in the greater Boston area, but I haven't been in a while. It's hard to find anyone willing to eat this particular style of doughnut unless they're being ironic. My ex-girlfriend, Noemi, is gluten-free and all about clean eating, so she refused to set foot in the place no matter how much I begged. Somehow, that makes it even worse that she ultimately broke up with me at Veggie Galaxy.

"I don't know what's happened to you. You don't even seem like yourself anymore," she told me over a plate of kale and seitan salad last week. "It's like aliens abducted the real Cal and left this shell behind."

"Um, okay. Wow. That's harsh," I muttered, feeling a stab of hurt even though I'd seen this coming. Not *this*, exactly, but something. We'd barely seen each other all week, and then all of a sudden she texted *We should go to Veggie Galaxy tomorrow.* I had a bad feeling, and not just because I hate kale. "I've been a little distracted, that's all."

"It doesn't feel like you're distracted. It feels . . ." Noemi tossed her braids over one shoulder and scrunched her nose up, thinking. She looked really cute, and it hit me with a pang how much I used to like her. Still did like her, except . . . it wasn't that simple anymore. "Like you stopped trying. You're doing stuff because you think you're supposed to, but it's not real. *You're* not real. I mean, look at you," she added, gesturing toward my plate. "You've eaten almost an entire plate full of kale, and you haven't complained once. You're a pod person."

"I didn't realize criticizing your food choices was a prerequisite for being a good boyfriend," I grumbled, stuffing another forkful of kale into my mouth. Then I almost gagged, because honest to God, only rabbits should eat that crap. A few minutes later, Noemi signaled for the check and insisted on paying it, and I was single once again. Sort of. Truth is, Noemi was probably picking up on the fact that I've been interested in someone else for a while, but she didn't have to pummel my self-esteem into the ground in retaliation.

"Take some time for yourself, Cal," my dad said when it happened. Well, one of my dads. I have two of them—and a biological mother I see a few times a year, who's a college friend of my dads and was their surrogate seventeen years ago—but I call both of them Dad. Which is pretty straightforward—to me—but a certain subset of my classmates finds it endlessly confusing. Boney Mahoney, in particular, used to ask me all the time in elementary school, "But how do they know which one you're talking to?"

It's easy. I've always used a slightly different inflection on the word with each of my fathers, something that started so naturally when I was a little kid that I don't even remember doing it. But that's not the kind of thing you can explain to a guy like Boney, who has all the subtle communication skills of a brick. So I told him I call them by their first names, Wes and Henry. Even though I don't, unless I'm talking about them to someone else.

Anyway, Wes is the dad I go to with personal stuff. "There's more to life than romantic relationships," he said when Noemi and I broke up. He's the dean at Carlton College, and I'm pretty sure he spends half his life worrying that I'm going to have a marriage certificate before a bachelor's degree. "Focus on your friends for a change."

Yeah, right. Spoken like a man who's never met my friends, which he hasn't, because my Carlton High circle is one of convenience. We're all people on the fringes of school who drop one another as soon as something better comes along, then go skulking back when it ends. The last time I had real friends was middle school. Wes, who knows way more about my social life than any self-respecting seventeen-year-old should allow, claims it's because I've been a serial dater since ninth grade. And I maintain that it's the other way around. It's the ultimate chicken-egg conversation.

At least my new girlfriend likes the same things I do: art, comics, and calorically dense breakfast food with zero nutritional value. Well, *girlfriend* is probably a stretch. Lara and I haven't defined things yet. It's complicated, but I'm all-in enough that I drove forty minutes in rush hour traffic to eat weird doughnuts with her.

I hope I did, anyway.

Ten minutes later, my doughnut's getting stale. My phone buzzes, and Lara's name pops up with a string of sad-face emojis. *So sorry, can't be there after all! Something came up.*

I tamp down disappointment, because that's how it is with Lara. *Something* comes up a lot. I knew when I got into my car that there was a fifty-fifty chance I'd end up eating alone. I pull my plate toward me and take a huge bite of my Cheeto-dusted Bavarian cream and chew thoughtfully. Sweet, salty, with a strong hint of processed cheese. It's magnificent.

I finish the rest in three bites, wipe my hands on a napkin, and glance at the clock on the wall. The drive back to Carlton against traffic will take less than half an hour, and it's not even eight yet. I have time for one more thing. My messenger bag is on the floor beside me, and I reach into it to pull out my laptop. The browser is already open to my old WordPress site, and with a few clicks I open the first web comic I ever made.

The Greatest Day Ever
Written and illustrated by Calvin O'Shea-Wallace

I showed all my web comics to Lara a couple of weeks ago, and she immediately claimed that this was the best of the bunch. Which was a little insulting, since I was twelve when I drew it, but she said it had a "raw energy" my newer stuff lacks. And maybe she's right. I started it after that day in sixth grade when I skipped a class trip with Ivy Sterling-Shepard and Mateo Wojcik to wander around Boston, and there's a certain exhilaration in every panel that mirrors how I felt about getting away with something so outrageous.

Plus, if I do say so myself, the likenesses aren't bad. There's Ivy with her unusual brown eyes–blond hair combination, her ever-present ponytail blowing in the wind, and an expression that's half-worried, half-thrilled. I might've drawn her with bigger boobs than she had then, or even now, but what do you expect? I was twelve.

Mateo, admittedly, I didn't draw entirely true to life. I was supposed to be the hero of *The Greatest Day Ever,* and him the sidekick. That wouldn't have worked if I'd given him that whole dark-and-brooding thing girls were already swooning over in sixth grade. So he was shorter in web comic form. And skinnier. Plus, he might've had a slight acne problem. But he still had the best one-liners that came out of nowhere.

"Hey! That's you!" I jump at Viola's voice as she reaches

across my shoulder to grab my empty plate. I've paused on a panel that's just me racing through Boston Common in all my red-haired, floral-shirted, twelve-year-old glory. "Who made that?"

"I did," I say, scrolling to a new panel so my face isn't quite so prominent. This one has Ivy and Mateo, too. "When I was twelve."

"Well, isn't that something." Viola fingers the skull necklace that's dangling halfway down her Ramones T-shirt. She was the drummer for a punk-rock band when she was my age, and I don't think her style aesthetic has changed in thirty years. "You've got real talent, Cal. Who are the other two?"

"Just some friends."

"I don't recall ever seeing them here."

"They've never been."

I say it lightly with a shrug, but the words make me feel as flat as Noemi's *You're not real* speech. Ivy and Mateo were the best friends I ever had, but I've barely spoken to them since eighth grade. It's normal for people to grow apart when they reach high school, I guess, and it's not like our friend breakup was some big, dramatic thing. We didn't fight, or turn on one another, or say the kind of things you can't take back.

Still, I can't shake the feeling that it was all my fault.

"You want another doughnut?" Viola asks. "There's a new hazelnut bacon one I think you might like."

"No thanks. I gotta haul ass if I'm gonna make it to school on time," I say, shutting my laptop and slipping it back into my bag. I leave money on the table—enough for three doughnuts, to make up for the fact that I don't have time to get the actual check—and sling my bag across my shoulders. "See you later."

"I hope so," Viola calls as I dart between a hipster couple sporting graphic T-shirts and the same haircut. "We've missed your face around here."

I don't believe in fate, as a general principle. But it feels like more than a coincidence when I step out of my car in the Carlton High parking lot and almost walk straight into Ivy Sterling-Shepard.

"Hey," she says as her brother, Daniel, grunts a semigreeting and brushes past me. That kid's gotten a lot taller since freshman year—some days I barely recognize him loping through school in his lacrosse gear. Nobody should be that good at so many different things. It doesn't build character.

Ivy watches him go like she's thinking the same thing, before turning her attention back to me. "Cal, wow. I haven't seen you in forever."

"I know." I lean against the side of my car. "Weren't you in Scotland or something?"

"Yeah, for six weeks over the summer. My mom was teaching there."

"That must've been awesome." Ivy could have used the distance, probably, after the whole junior talent show debacle. I watched from the second row of the auditorium with Noemi and her friends, who were all doubled over with laughter.

Okay, I was, too. I couldn't help it. I felt bad later, though, wondering if Ivy had seen me. The thought makes my skin prickle with shame, so I quickly add, "This is so weird. I was just thinking about you."

There's never been anything except a friend vibe between Ivy and me, so I don't worry about her taking that the wrong way, like *Damn, girl, you've been on my mind.* I'm a little surprised, though, when she says, "Really? Me too. About you, I mean."

"You were?"

"Yeah. I was trying to remember the last time I missed a class," she says, pressing her key fob to lock the black Audi beside her. I recognize it from middle school, so it's definitely her parents' old car, but still. That's a sweet ride for a high school senior. "It was the day we skipped the field trip."

"That's exactly what I was thinking about," I say, and for a second we share a conspiratorial grin. "Hey, and congrats to your mom."

She blinks. "What?"

"Carlton Citizen of the Year, right?"

"You know about that?" Ivy asks.

"My dad was on the voting committee. Wes," I add, which feels a little weird. Back when we were friends, Ivy always knew which dad I was referring to without me having to specify.

"Really?" Her eyes widen. "Mom was so surprised. She always says statisticians are unsung heroes. Plus there's usually more of a local angle for the award, and with the opioid report . . ." She shrugs. "It's not like Carlton is a hot spot or anything."

"Don't be so sure," I say. "Wes says that crap has been all over campus lately. He even set up a task force to deal with it." Ivy's expression gets alert, because there's nothing she likes better than a good task force, and I quickly change the subject before she can start lobbing suggestions. "Anyway, he voted for her. He and Henry will be there tonight."

"My parents are barely going to make it," Ivy says. "They're in San Francisco for their anniversary, and they had to scramble to rearrange their flights to be home in time."

Sounds like a typically overachieving Sterling-Shepard move; my dads would've just videotaped an acceptance speech from California. "That's great," I say, which feels like my cue to move on. But we both keep standing there, until it gets awkward enough that my eyes stray over her shoulder. Then I do a double take as a tall, dark-haired guy swings himself over the fence surrounding the parking lot. "Well, damn. The stars keep aligning today. There's the third member of our illicit trio."

Ivy turns as Mateo catches sight of us. He gives a chin jut in our direction, then looks ready to continue his path to class until I stick my hand in the air and wave it wildly. It'd be a dick move to ignore me, and Mateo—despite being the kind of guy who'd rather swallow knives than make small talk—isn't a dick, so he heads our way.

"What's up?" he asks once he reaches the bumper of Ivy's car. She looks nervous all of a sudden, twisting the end of her ponytail around one finger. I'm starting to feel a little weird, too. Now that I've summoned Mateo, I don't know what to say to him. Talking with Ivy is easy, as long as I avoid minefields like the junior talent show, or how she got crushed in the student council election yesterday by Boney Mahoney. But Mateo? All I know about him these days is that his mom's bowling alley had to shut down. Not an ideal conversation starter.

"We were just talking about the Greatest Day Ever," I say instead. And then I feel like a loser, because that name wasn't cool even when we were twelve. But instead of groaning, Mateo gives me a small, tired smile. For the first time, I notice the dark shadows under his eyes. He looks like he hasn't slept in a week.

"Those were the days," he says.

"I'd give anything to get out of school today," Ivy says. She's still twirling her ponytail, eyes fixed on the back of Carlton High. I don't have to ask her why. Boney's acceptance speech is going to be painful for all of us, but especially her.

Mateo rubs a hand over his face. "Same."

"Let's do it," I blurt out. I'm mostly kidding, until neither of them shut me down right away. And then, it hits me that there's nothing I'd rather do. I have two classes with Noemi today, a history test I'm not ready for, no hope of seeing Lara, and nothing more exciting to look forward to than burritos for lunch. "Seriously, why not?" I say, gaining enthusiasm as I warm up to the idea. "Do you guys know how easy it is to skip now? They barely even bother to check, as long as a parent calls in before first bell. Hang on." I pull my phone out of my pocket, scroll to *Carlton High* in my contacts, and tap the number that pops up. I listen to the main menu until the automated voice drones, *If you're reporting an absence . . .*

Ivy licks her lips. "What are you doing?"

I press three on my keypad, then hold up a finger until I hear a beep. "Good morning. This is Henry O'Shea-Wallace, calling on behalf of my son, Calvin, at eight-fifty a.m. on Tuesday, September twenty-first," I say in my father's quiet, clipped voice. "Unfortunately, Calvin is running a slight fever today, so we'll be keeping him home as a precaution. He has all his assignments and will complete them as needed for Wednesday."

Mateo grins when I hang up. "I forgot how good you are at imitating people," he says.

"You ain't seen nothing yet," I say, giving Ivy a meaningful look. The kind that says, *If you don't want this to happen, there's still time to stop me.* She doesn't, so I redial the number, this time putting my phone on speaker so she and Mateo can hear. When the message beep sounds, I adopt a hearty baritone. "Hi, this is James Shepard. I'm afraid Ivy won't be in school this morning—she's feeling under the weather. Thanks, and have a great day!" Then I hang up as Ivy collapses against her car, hands on either side of her face.

"I can't believe you did that. I thought you were bluffing," she says.

"You did not," I scoff.

Her answering half smile tells me I'm right, but she still looks nervous. "I don't know if this is such a good idea," she says, digging the toe of her loafer into the ground. Ivy still has the prepster look down cold, but she's moved into darker colors with her black sweater, gray plaid miniskirt, and black tights. She looks better than she did in middle school when she was all about the primary colors. "We could probably pass it off as a prank—"

"What about me?" Mateo interrupts. We both turn to look at him as he inclines his head toward me, eyebrows raised. "You good enough to imitate my mom, Cal?"

"Not since puberty." I dial Carlton High's number one more time, then hold out my phone to Ivy.

She takes a step back, eyes wide. "What? No. I can't."

"Well, *I* can't," I say as the recorded voice starts its spiel up once again. Nobody would believe Mateo's dad calling in for him. That guy has never been involved in anything school-related. "And neither can Mateo. It's you or nothing."

Ivy darts a glance toward Mateo. "You want me to?"

"Why not?" He shrugs. "I could use a day off."

My phone beeps as the voicemail kicks in, and Ivy grabs it. "Yes, hello," she says breathlessly. "This is Elena Wo—um, Reyes." Mateo rolls his eyes at the near slip on last names. "Calling about my son. Mateo Wojcik. He's sick. He has . . . strep."

"Ivy, no," I hiss. "I think you need a doctor's note to come back from strep."

Her shoulders get rigid. "I mean, not strep. A sore throat. I'm getting him tested for strep, but it probably isn't strep. It's just a precaution. I'll call back if he tests positive, but I'm sure he won't, so don't expect to hear from me again. Anyway, Mateo won't be in today, so bye." She hangs up and practically throws the phone at me.

I shoot Mateo a frozen look of horror, because that was a disaster. Whoever listens to it might actually check in with his mom, which I'm sure is the last thing he needs. I'm expecting him to shift into turbo-annoyed mode, but he starts laughing instead. And all of a sudden he's transformed—Mateo cracking up looks less like the guy who brushes past me in the hallway as if he doesn't see me, and more like my old friend.

"I should've remembered you can't lie to save your life," he says to Ivy, still laughing. "That *sucked*."

She bites her lip. "I could call back and tell them you're feeling better."

"Pretty sure that would only make things worse," Mateo says. "Anyway, I meant what I said. I could use a day off." The parking lot has emptied out, and a bell clangs loudly from inside Carlton High. If we're going to back out, now would be the time. But even though none of us says anything else, nobody moves, either.

"Where would we even go, though?" Ivy finally asks when the second bell rings.

I grin. "Boston, obviously," I say, pressing the key fob to unlock my car. "I'll drive."

4

IVY

It takes less than fifteen minutes for me to realize this was a huge mistake.

At first, all I feel is relief as Cal pulls out of the Carlton High parking lot. My thoughts are as bright and sunny as the crisp September weather: *I'm free! I don't have to listen to Boney's acceptance speech! I don't have to endure sympathetic looks from my friends and teachers! Nobody is going to remind me that, even though I'm no longer class president, I can engorge their manhood anytime!* Cal fires up a playlist filled with the kind of alternative pop we both love, and we chat about music and movies and where we should go first.

Then we run out of low-hanging conversational fruit, and when I glance in the rearview mirror to see if Mateo might have something to contribute, he looks sound asleep in the back seat. Or maybe he's just pretending; he used to say that sleeping in cars made him feel sick. Oh God. Is he regretting this already?

Doubts start seeping in: What if the school calls my parents to check on my absence? I can't remember what phone number we have on file. My parents still have a landline, even though we never use it, because it's bundled with cable. If the school calls that, I'm fine—Dad unplugged it years ago to avoid telemarketers—but if they call one of my parents' cells, I'm screwed. Their flight doesn't board until around eleven our time, so there's still plenty of opportunity to catch them, and they'd be beyond disappointed in me.

Even if the school doesn't call, a teacher might say something to Daniel about me being sick. He won't know to play along, and even if he did, let's face it: he wouldn't. He loves watching me squirm. Should I text him anyway and bribe him into silence somehow? What can I offer? Sneakers? Right, like I have hundreds of dollars lying around for whatever limited-edition pair of Nikes he's currently coveting.

Should I text my friends? I pull out my phone, and I already have a message from my best friend, Emily. *Where are you? Are you sick?* Neither of us have missed school since we started hanging out freshman year, so there's no precedent for this, but it's definitely the kind of thing we'd let one another know.

My pulse starts to accelerate uncomfortably. What did Dad say this morning? *All you can do is hold your head high.* This is the opposite of that. This is me slinking away, hiding, letting everyone at Carlton High know that Boney beat me in all possible ways.

It's so hot in here. There's no air. Is the AC even *on*? I stare at the car's dashboard, at my phone, at Cal, out the window, and then twist in my seat to look at Mateo. His eyes are still closed, but he murmurs, "Three . . . two . . . one . . ."

That halts my panicked inner monologue. "Huh?" I ask. "I thought you were asleep."

He opens his eyes and meets mine. "Freak-out."

"Excuse me?" I ask, startled.

"You. Freaking out about skipping school. Right on schedule."

"I'm not freaking out!" I snap. I don't know if I'm annoyed because he was faking sleep the whole time Cal and I were talking, or because he nailed my mental state with his eyes closed. "I didn't say a word."

"You didn't have to." Mateo yawns and rubs a hand across his head, rumpling his dark hair. "I could hear you bouncing around in your seat."

"I was not *bouncing*—"

"Guys, come on!" Cal's voice holds a note of desperate cheer as he exits the highway. "This is gonna be fun, seriously. And we won't get in trouble. Someone would've called by now if there was a problem."

I don't think that's necessarily true. But I don't want to get accused of *freaking out* again, so all I say is "Where are you going?"

"I was thinking we could start at Quincy Market? Lots of parking there, and places to get food and stuff. And the aquarium's nearby if we want to head over there at some point. Check out the penguins, maybe."

"Penguins?" I echo.

"I like penguins." Cal's voice has a wistful, almost uncertain quality to it. "I used to, anyway. I probably still do. That doesn't seem like the kind of thing that goes away, even if you haven't seen a penguin in a while."

I'm still facing Mateo and we exchange looks, briefly united in confusion. "Probably not?" I offer.

I'm not sure that's the right answer, because Cal sighs deeply. "We'll see."

Mateo drums his fingers restlessly against his knee. "I work near there," he says.

"You do? Where?" Cal asks.

"Garrett's. It's a bar."

"You can work in a bar when you're seventeen?" I ask.

"As long as you're not serving alcohol, yeah."

"Kind of a hike from Carlton, though, isn't it?" Cal asks.

Mateo shrugs. "I take the T. And it pays more than anyplace local. It's worth it."

Traffic gets more congested as we approach Faneuil Hall, and while Cal concentrates on the road, I covertly study Mateo. He's wearing a gray Spare Me T-shirt, the logo so faded that I'd never be able to tell what it was if I hadn't seen it on the side of a building for half my life. My chest constricts, and I wish I hadn't been so short with him. "How is your family?" I ask. "What's Autumn up to?"

"Working a lot," he says.

I'm not sure if that involves college, and I don't want to ask in case it's a sore subject. "Is she still going out with . . ." I blank on the name, even though I can see him clearly in my mind's eye. He was one of last year's senior boys who took particular delight in grabbing his crotch every time I walked past him in the hallway after my meltdown at the junior talent show.

"Gabe Prescott?" Mateo looks like he just swallowed a mouthful of rancid meat. "Yeah. Unfortunately."

"What a weird couple," Cal says. "Didn't Gabe get voted *Most Likely to Commit a Felony and Not Get Caught*?" Carlton High did away with yearbook senior superlatives like *Best-Looking* and

37

Most Likely to Succeed years ago, deeming them "unhealthy labeling," so now seniors have their own underground list with categories that change every year. I'm honestly a little afraid of what I might win in the spring. Talk about an unhealthy label.

"No," Mateo says. "He got *Most Likely to Lose a Reality Show.*"

I laugh, because that's actually a good one and probably accurate. But Mateo's expression clearly says *Next topic, please,* so I ask, "And how's your mom doing?"

"She's okay. Been better," he says briefly.

"It really sucks that Spare Me had to close," Cal says. "My dads thought the DeWitts totally overreacted. Patrick didn't even break any bones, did he?"

"He dislocated his shoulder," Mateo says.

"Well, he's playing lacrosse again," Cal says, like that settles the matter.

Oh God. I should've known this would come up, and it's the last thing I want to talk about. Before I can think of a subject change, Mateo asks, "How's Carlton Entertainment Complex coming along, Ivy? The CEC?" His lip curls on the acronym. "That's what your dad calls it, right?"

New subject. New subject. But my mind is an empty canvas. "Okay, I guess," I say casually. "I don't actually hear much about his projects on a day-to-day basis, so . . ."

"I'll bet you hear more than I do, though." Mateo leans forward against his seat belt, dark eyes capturing mine, and I can't look away. I forgot how penetrating his gaze can be, like he's staring into depths of your soul you didn't even know existed. It was unnerving at thirteen, and it's even worse now.

Full disclosure: Mateo was my first crush. I spent half of eighth grade desperately mooning over him while pretending not to, positive that he couldn't possibly feel the same. And then, one time when we were hanging out without Cal, we kissed. Which was the thrill of my life, until we never spoke of it again. I can only assume he regretted it and wanted to go back to being friends, which I tried to tell myself was perfectly fine. But it became miserably awkward pretending not to care, and our trio dissolved for good soon after.

Suddenly, I'd give anything to be sitting in first-period history with Emily, even knowing that Boney's speech is coming up next. I shift back and forth in my seat, then force myself to sit still. That was a little too close to bouncing, and I don't want Mateo noticing that this topic sends me into an emotional tailspin. "Probably," I say. "Is there, um, something in particular you want to know?"

"Not really," Mateo says, slumping back and flicking his eyes toward the window. The sharp planes of his face, tense a moment ago, settle back into weariness. "It's not like it would change anything."

"Oh, sweet," Cal calls out. "That garage has space. I'm gonna park here." I can't tell if he's ignoring the tension in the car, or if he's too focused a driver to have picked up on it. I turn to face front, and Mateo and I sit in silence as Cal grabs a ticket at the entrance and makes his way through four levels of the parking garage, finally finding a spot in the open-air top floor. "We can leave our stuff in the trunk if you want," he says as he cuts the engine and pulls the emergency brake.

I feel nauseated for real now, like I should legitimately be lying in my darkened bedroom taking a sick day. I almost ask Cal if he'd be willing to turn around and take me home, but one look at his hopeful face as he pulls his keys from the ignition squashes that. I'm here, so I might as well grab some coffee before convincing him to cut the day short. "Yeah, okay," I say, pulling a small cross-body bag from my backpack. I slip my wallet, my phone, and my sunglasses inside, then loop it over my shoulder and open the car door.

Awkward silence descends yet again as the three of us throw our backpacks into the trunk and leave the parking garage. Part of the magic of the Greatest Day Ever was that we stumbled into a giant celebration for the Red Sox. It occurs to me now that if we'd had to supply our own entertainment that day, we probably would have turned around and gone back inside.

And we never would've become friends at all.

"So . . . should we get coffee?" I ask. "Is there a Starbucks nearby?"

"I don't know, but . . ." Cal glances around. "There's a place not far from here that I go to with a friend sometimes. It's a little more off the beaten path, if you don't mind a walk."

"Sure." I follow him down the sidewalk while simultaneously pulling out my phone. I quickly scroll through a pile of new text messages as I walk, breathing a sigh of relief that none of them are from my parents or school. I still need to sign up for alerts about my parents' flight, so I do that and see that it's scheduled to board at eight a.m. Pacific time, which is a little more than an hour from now.

I say a quick, silent prayer that my parents never find out that I skipped, so that nothing takes away from Mom's big night.

I should've thought about that before I agreed to call in sick, but it's not too late. I'll grab a coffee, ask Cal to drop me back off at school, and tell the nurse that I was nauseated but feel better now.

And then, magically, I *do* feel better. Having a plan always helps. I take a deep breath and turn back to my messages.

Emily: Helloooooooo, anyone there?

Emily: Bueller? Bueller?

I smile as we pause at a crosswalk. Emily's been on an '80s movie kick lately.

Daniel: Emily keeps asking me where you are.

Daniel: Did you skip or something?

Daniel: M&D are gonna flip.

I stiffen and almost text back, *You'd better not say anything,* but stop myself just in time. Because then of course he would. I'll be back at school before lunch, and that will shut him up. I hope.

I'm about to put my phone away to join Cal and Mateo's conversation when another text flashes across my screen.

Emily: Boney's not here, either.

Emily: ARE YOU TOGETHER.

Emily: Kidding. I know you're not.

Emily: Right?

I frown at my screen. Emily must be wrong about Boney. He's giving his acceptance speech soon, so obviously he's around there somewhere. I start to text her back, but before I can, someone pulls at my elbow. "Ivy," Cal says.

"What?" I look up, realizing I have no idea where we are. The buildings around us are a lot more industrial-looking than they were a few minutes ago.

"There's kind of a massive line," Cal says, gesturing to a café across the street from us. He's right; the line is snaking out the door and down the sidewalk. "Do you want to go someplace else first?"

I want to go home, I think, but for some reason the words won't come. "Like where?" I ask, at the same time Mateo says, "Penguins."

We both turn to look at him, and he points to our left. "Aquarium's that way. Seemed like you really wanted to see some, Cal."

"Oh yeah, right," Cal says, but something in his expression flattens. "We don't have to go right away or anything, though." The light changes and we start automatically across the street, Cal leading the way to who knows where. "I just wanted to— I'm having this kind of miniature personal crisis, I guess. It's not really about penguins."

"Didn't think so," I say, just as Mateo deadpans, "It never is." I snicker, but Cal doesn't join in, so I get myself under control. "Then what *is* it about?" I ask.

He tugs at the hem of his shirt. It's a blue button-down with subtle green polka dots—not nearly as flashy as the bright patterns he used to wear in middle school, but still more interesting than standard Carlton High guy attire. Cal has a colorful fashion sense that he inherited from precisely neither of his dads. Wes and Henry are both crewneck sweater–and–khaki guys who never met a neutral palette they didn't like. "Relationship stuff," he says. "You know how it is. Or maybe not. You guys seeing anyone?"

The question catches me off guard, even though it's a perfectly natural topic for old friends to talk about. For a moment I'm tempted to tell them about Angus MacFarland, a boy I dated in Scotland over the summer. But even I have to admit that he sounds made-up. "Not presently, no," I say.

Mateo doesn't chime in, and Cal prods, "What about you, Mateo? I thought I heard that you and Carmen Costa are a thing."

My stomach gives an uncomfortable little twist. I don't want to hear about Mateo's relationship with Carmen Costa, which is probably perfect because Carmen is great. She even came up to me after the election results were announced yesterday, when most people were treating me like I was radioactive, and told me she'd voted for me.

"Not anymore," Mateo says, and my brows lift in surprise.

"Since when?" Cal asks.

"Summer."

I wait for him to say more, but he stops in the middle of the sidewalk instead, hands on his hips as he gazes around us. The buildings have been getting progressively more run-down and graffiti-covered with every step we take. "Cal, where exactly are we going?" he asks.

"Huh?" Cal blinks, like it hadn't occurred to him to figure out a new destination. "Oh, well . . . I guess . . . there's an art store nearby that I like. Maybe we could stop in?"

"Fine by me," Mateo says. "Ivy?"

"Okay," I say, even though I can think of a lot of things I'd rather do than watch Cal choose between seventeen shades of green pencil. Though I guess after that, I'll feel a lot less guilty about abandoning him.

We start walking again in silence, until my need for information outweighs my need to look cool and unbothered. "So, Mateo. What happened with you and Carmen?"

He shrugs. "Just ran its course. I started working a lot, and she was spending all her time with her friends, so we weren't hanging out. After about a month of that I saw her and she was like, *We might as well be broken up.* I was like, *Yeah,* and she was like, *Maybe we should be,* and I said, *Okay.*" His face is as stoic as ever, and I can't tell if he's putting up a front, or if the whole thing really was that casual.

Cal looks dubious, too. "Really? That was it?" Mateo nods and Cal sighs. "Well, at least she didn't dump you at Veggie Galaxy."

I wait for Cal to add some kind of context to that statement, but before he can, Mateo nods sagely and says, "I tell myself that every day."

I laugh and then notice Cal's glum expression. "Wait, did that happen to you?"

"Yeah," he says. "Right after Noemi told me I was a pod person going through the motions of life." I make a sympathetic noise, and he adds, "It's fine. Gave me a chance to get to know someone I have a lot more in common with. We're not, like, officially dating or anything, but it's . . . good for me." He swallows almost nervously. "I think."

"You think?" I ask. This sounds like the lead-up to the kind of conversation I used to have with Cal all the time: one where he needs advice, but doesn't know how to ask for it.

Before I can press him, though, a blur of tie-dye catches my eye across the street. At first I think I must be seeing things; there's no way it's the same cursed pattern that's been haunting my dreams since last week's class president debate. But when I

44

focus on it and see it's attached to a familiar, blue-tipped faux-hawk, I stop in my tracks and grab hold of Cal's arm, anchoring him in place. There's no denying it.

"You guys, wait," I say, pointing at the figure across the street from us. "Do you see that?" Mateo stops, too, turning with a questioning look. "What the hell is *Boney Mahoney* doing here?"

CARLTON HIGH SCHOOL MEDIA LAB

Two boys are seated at a curved metal desk; the large-screen monitor between them reads CARLTON SPEAKS. The front of the desk is draped with a banner displaying the school mascot, the Carlton High Cougar. The first boy, leaning forward with barely contained energy, is lanky with longish dark curls and the kind of doe eyes that look deceptively innocent; the second boy is broad-shouldered with short locs and posture that would be relaxed if he weren't constantly fiddling with the pen he's holding.

> **BOY #1:** What's up, Carlton High? This is Ishaan Mittal, and . . . (*Glances at the other boy.*)

> **BOY #2,** *setting his pen down:* And this is Zack Abrams. We're supposed to be giving a post-assembly analysis of our new student body president's speech, but we're not doing that because—

> **ISHAAN,** *leaning forward and placing both palms on the desk for emphasis:* Because the kid never showed!

> **ZACK,** *under his breath:* Ishaan, I wasn't . . . I was still setting that up.

ISHAAN, *oblivious:* This morning, Carlton High's controversial new senior class president, Boney Mahoney—

TEACHER'S VOICE, *off camera:* Proper names, guys. And just "new senior class president" is fine.

ISHAAN: This morning, Carlton High's new senior class president, Brian Mahoney, made a mockery of his election by blowing off the entire school—

TEACHER'S VOICE: Less editorializing, please. How about we summarize the election and then talk about student reactions to this morning's assembly?

ZACK: I mean, people were mostly happy they didn't have to listen to Boney.

ISHAAN: With all due respect, Mr. G., the election is old news. Nobody needs it summarized. The burning question that everyone wants answered is: Where the hell is Boney? (*Stares intensely into the camera.*) Yesterday, he pledged to lead us into the future. But today—

ZACK: Today he probably overslept.

ISHAAN: He did promise that if we elected him, he'd leave us alone. What none of us realized, perhaps, is that he meant it literally.

MR. G., *with a long-suffering sigh:* Come on, guys. You know the drill. No curse words, no nicknames, no speculation.

ZACK, *quietly:* No fun.

ISHAAN, *slumping back in his seat:* This show is wasting my talents.

5

MATEO

Ivy looks shocked, then outraged. "I can't believe him!" she says as maybe-Boney disappears around a corner. I didn't get a good look at the guy, but she seems sure. "He's supposed to be giving a speech now!" Her eyes go wide. "Oh my God. Did he abdicate? Am I president now?" She whips out her phone and stares at the screen. "Come on, Emily. You were texting up a storm five minutes ago. Where are you when I need you?"

"Maybe it wasn't even him," I say.

"Oh, it was him," she mutters. "Unbelievable. You can't miss assembly when you're class president. Attendance is mandatory. It's written into the school bylaws, or it would have been, if I'd been elected and the bylaws had passed." She glares across the street, then starts walking with long, determined strides. "Come on. Let's see where he's going."

"Who cares?" I ask, but that's a pointless question. Obviously, she does.

I'm hoping the guy is out of sight by the time we turn the corner, but no such luck. We spot him instantly, and from this angle, I can see that Ivy was right—it's definitely Boney, with his phone in one hand and a backpack dangling from his shoulder. We trail him down another two streets until he stops in front of a loft-style building with a bright green door. He fiddles with something beside the door, then pulls it open and steps inside.

"Hold on." Cal grabs Ivy's arm as she tries to follow. "You can't just walk in. There's a security code."

She blinks at him. "What? How do you know?"

"So . . . this building . . ." Cal runs a hand through his hair, his eyes darting everywhere except at us. "You know that person I mentioned before, the one I've been seeing lately? Her art studio is in here."

"Studio?" I ask. "She has an art studio?"

"Well, it's not actually hers," Cal says. "A friend rents it and lets her work there sometimes. The building's up for sale, so the tenants were supposed to clear out last month, but a few of them are still using the space." Ivy inhales sharply, and Cal's skittering glance finally lands on her. "Don't look so shocked. It's not a big deal. It's fine."

"There's no way it's *fine,*" Ivy says, frowning. "If my dad bought this building, he'd definitely have a problem with former tenants squatting here."

She has a point, but she might be missing a bigger one. "Cal," I say. "Is this girl not in high school?"

"Not technically," Cal says.

"She's in college?" I ask, trying not to sound as surprised as I feel. I never would've pegged Cal for the kind of guy who'd go for an older girl. Or have an older girl go for him.

"Look, can we just . . ." Cal glances around again. "She's actually going to be here any minute. She's always here on Tuesdays, right at ten o'clock. It's, like, routine with her, because she says the light is perfect then. And it's going to be super awkward if she sees me."

"Why?" Ivy asks. "Does she know Boney?" Her voice lowers in sympathy, and she puts a hand on Cal's arm. "Is this a love-triangle situation?"

"No!" He shakes her off. "Can we just—move on? Visit the penguins. We should've started there."

Ivy crosses her arms. "We can do that after I talk to Boney. Give me the code."

"I . . . I don't know it," Cal says, looking over his shoulder. It's such an obvious lie that even I'm not fooled.

"Give me the code," Ivy repeats. "Then you can slink off and hide. Otherwise, I'm going to force you to stand in the middle of the street until your girlfriend shows up and things get, as you put it, *super awkward.*"

Cal makes a strangled sound and chokes out "Five eight three two" as if the numbers are being yanked from his throat. Then he ducks into an alley like some kind of fugitive as Ivy takes off toward the green door.

"Cal, what the hell?" I look up and down the street—no mystery girl in sight—before following him. If this entire situation weren't so weird, I'd laugh at the sight of him pressed into the alcove of a doorway. "What's your problem? Why can't she see you?"

Cal licks his lips nervously. "It's not that, so much. It's more like she can't see you."

"Me?" Now I'm beyond confused. "Why not?"

51

"Or Ivy. I shouldn't have given her the code. I panicked."

"Cal, you're making no sense." Then another thought strikes me, fast and unwelcome. "Shit, you're right. You *shouldn't* have given her the code. It's a terrible idea for Ivy and Boney to talk right now." Boney is known for being a laid-back guy, but he has a temper, too. I've seen him go off on people, and Ivy looks like she's been waiting for an excuse to give him hell.

Yesterday, after the election results were announced, Ivy stalked past me and my ex-girlfriend, Carmen, in the hallway. "I'm worried about that girl," Carmen said, nodding at Ivy. "She seems so stressed. I hope she has some kind of outlet to blow off steam."

Carmen and I are still friends, because our split was almost as chill as I told Cal and Ivy. Except, when Carmen said we might as well break up, I had the feeling she was waiting for me to protest. And I wanted to. But I didn't, because as Autumn likes to say, *I'm incapable of dealing with even the slightest hint of rejection.*

Whatever. Nobody likes rejection. That's science.

I shake the thought off and focus on the problem at hand: the fact that Cal and I are still lurking uselessly in the alley while Ivy and Boney are probably having an epic screamfest in the middle of an abandoned building. "We better go after her," I tell Cal, and start for the street. He doesn't move, and I turn back, exasperated. "Come on. I'm going in, and Ivy's already there, so whatever you're worrying about—deal with it, okay?"

I turn without waiting to see if he'll follow me, and I'm a little surprised when he does. Also glad, since I forgot the security code. The street is still deserted, with nobody in sight as Cal presses 5-8-3-2 on the keypad beside the door.

There's no buzzing sound, but when Cal pulls on the door

handle, it opens. We step into a hallway that's brighter than I expected, thanks to a skylight in the ceiling. The walls are white, the floors wooden and lightly scarred. There are two sets of stairs on either side of us, and it's so quiet that I can hear myself breathe.

"Ivy?" I call. "Where are you?"

There's nothing but silence for a few seconds. Then Ivy's voice—so high and thin that I barely recognize it—floats from somewhere above us to the left. "Upstairs," she says.

"You okay?" I ask, starting up the left staircase with Cal behind me.

"I don't know," she says in the same voice, and now I recognize the tone.

She's afraid.

I pick up my pace, taking the steps two at a time. "What floor are you on?" I call.

"I don't know," she says again. My heart is pounding, both from exertion and worry, and I'm steeling myself for the worst when I reach the fourth floor and catch sight of her hovering at the edge of a doorway. Alone, and from what I can see, perfectly fine.

I lean against the wall to catch my breath. We're in a long hallway with multiple doors on either side, all of them closed except the one Ivy's next to. "Ivy, what the hell," I pant as Cal lags behind me on the stairs, a couple of floors down. "You scared the crap out of me. Where's Boney?"

"I think . . ." She's still staring into the room in front of her, clutching one side of the doorframe like she needs the support. "I think he might be there."

"Where?" I come up beside her and peer into the room. At first, all I notice are the large windows, built-in bookshelves, and a long table strewn with paper, pencils, and brushes. A few easels are scattered here and there, some covered with half-finished drawings. Definitely a studio, and definitely recently used, even though the building is supposed to be empty.

And then I follow Ivy's gaze to a pair of bright purple sneakers jutting out from behind a large rolling cabinet. Somebody's lying there, perfectly still and silent.

Not a flicker of movement, anywhere.

I clear my throat and call, "Boney?" There's no response; no sound at all except for the faint wail of sirens in the distance. Was Boney wearing purple sneakers? I can't remember; all that comes to mind when I try to picture him outside is the tie-dye T-shirt and his backpack. Neither of those are visible from where we're standing. "Are those his—" I start to ask Ivy.

Then something jostles my arm. I turn with a fist raised on instinct, ready to strike, but it's just Cal on his tiptoes, trying to see around me. He stumbles backward, hands up in a gesture of peace, as he asks, "What's going on?"

"Somebody's in there. Somebody who's . . ." I don't know how to finish that sentence. I take a couple of steps into the room so Cal can see what we're seeing, then turn back and look at Ivy. "You haven't gotten any closer than this?"

"No." She finally unfreezes, coming up beside me and twisting her hands together. "I was afraid that . . . I didn't know if somebody else was here, or—"

"Did you see anyone else?" I ask. The sound of sirens is getting closer.

Ivy shakes her head. Color starts to return to her cheeks, and her shoulders straighten as she walks toward the sneakers. "I don't know why I was so spooked, I just—"

Then she gasps, stops in her tracks, and collapses onto the ground.

For a second, I'm too shocked to react. Then I yell, "Ivy!" and sprint toward her, dropping to my knees and pulling her still form toward me. I put one hand against her neck and lift her face toward mine, heart hammering, to check her pulse and her breathing. Both are steady, but her eyes are closed and she's a dead weight in my arms. "Ivy," I say again, like there's any chance of her answering me right now. "What the hell happened?" I look toward the cabinet, wondering if she fainted from shock at the sight of a dead body, but I still can't see anything except the purple sneakers.

Cal crouches beside me and points. "I think that happened."

I follow his gaze and almost laugh, even though there's nothing funny about any of this. There's a syringe lying a few feet away from us on the floor, sharp and deadly-looking. My heart rate starts to return to normal as I say, "Guess somebody still faints at the sight of needles, huh?" I look past the syringe, and catch sight of a phone beneath a nearby easel. "Grab Ivy's phone, would you?"

Cal does and stuffs it into his pocket, his face pale. "Mateo, do you hear that?"

"Hear what?" I ask, seconds before realizing the sound of sirens has gotten louder than ever. All of a sudden, it's like they're on top of us.

"Something's off. Something's wrong." Cal's practically vibrating, bouncing on the balls of his feet with adrenaline-fueled anxiety.

I can't believe I even have to say this, while holding a motionless Ivy and backing away from a maybe-dead guy, but—"A lot of things are pretty fucking wrong right now, Cal."

He ignores me, crossing to the oversized windows and looking down. "The police are pulling up," he reports. "Right in front of the building. How would they even know to be here? Did Ivy call them?"

"I don't think so. She would've said something if she did," I say. "You think the police have the code for the door?"

The sound of shattering glass makes us both flinch. Cal passes a hand across his mouth. "I think they're using a different way in," he says. More glass breaks, and muffled voices reach our ears. "They're gonna be here any second."

"Dude, what . . ." I glance between Cal and the syringe. "What's going on? What the hell are we supposed to do?"

Cal's eyes take up half his face as he says, "I think we should leave."

Now I do laugh, low and harsh. "Great idea. We'll just wave at the police while we carry an unconscious girl past them, and leave poor . . ."

I can't bring myself to say Boney's name. *Maybe it's not even Boney,* I think. *Maybe it's some tortured artist who overdosed and . . .* what, exactly? Flung the syringe away before he collapsed? "Leave this poor guy behind," I finish.

I was in the room once before with a dead person. It was my great-uncle Hector; he was eighty-four and sick enough that we made the trip to the Bronx when I was nine years old to "say our goodbyes," as Ma said. Uncle Hector was in bed, lying motionless with his eyes closed, my aunt Rose clutching his hand with a rosary. And then, suddenly, he was a different kind of still. I could see it even from across the room, and my mother could, too. Ma put her hand on my shoulder, squeezed, and murmured, "That was very peaceful."

There's nothing peaceful about any of this.

"We don't have to pass the police," Cal says. "There's a back staircase at the other end of the hall. It opens into an alleyway behind the building. Totally different street."

That seems like simultaneously the best and worst idea I've ever heard. My brain isn't working properly, and I wish to God that Ivy would wake up and do the thinking for us. "Okay, but . . . shouldn't we tell them what we saw?" I ask.

"Like what? A pair of sneakers and a syringe? They're gonna see the same thing. If whoever's over there can be helped . . ." Cal crosses back toward the room's entrance and pauses on the threshold, his voice dropping into a near whisper. "They'll help him. We can't. All we're gonna do is get into a shitload of trouble because we're *not supposed to be here.*"

And just like that, he's gone.

I hesitate for half a beat, looking from Ivy's face to those goddamn purple sneakers, until the voices below me start getting way too close for comfort. I think about what might happen if I stay. I didn't do anything wrong, but unlike Cal, I can't count on cops giving me the benefit of the doubt. Getting found like this—holding an unconscious girl in the same room where somebody might've just died—could get me arrested or worse. Even if it doesn't, the last thing I need is police poking around in my life, questioning me.

Or my family.

My eyes linger on the syringe on the floor, and I make up my mind. Cal's right: there's nothing we can do to help anyone except ourselves. I hoist Ivy a little higher in my arms and run after him toward the back stairs, as quickly and silently as I can.

6

CAL

In the studio, my entire being had a single, simple goal: *get away.*
So once I bolt through the back door, into a deserted street with
no police and no other people in sight, relief floods through me.

For about five seconds. Then all I can think is *Now what?*
Mateo bursts out of the door after me, carrying a still-unconscious
Ivy. The parking garage is a good half mile away, and Boney . . .
Jesus.

Boney Mahoney might've died back there.

I've known Boney since kindergarten, long enough to remember how he got that ridiculous nickname. It was in second
grade, when we all had cubbies in the classroom labeled with
our names. We'd made the labels ourselves, with Magic Markers
on construction paper. One day Kaitlyn Taylor tripped while
she was carrying a cup of water, sending its contents splashing
over Boney's *Brian Mahoney* label. The marker ran so badly that
all you could read was the initial of his first name and the end

of his last name. Everyone called him B. Oney after that, which naturally morphed into Boney, and it stuck.

Besides him quizzing me about my dads, the longest conversation we'd ever had was during Kenny Chu's birthday party at a rock climbing gym in fifth grade. It's the only party Boney and I ever went to together, because Kenny's mom made him invite every boy in class. We were both standing on one of the big cushy mats, waiting for our turn, when Boney looked around and said, "Why do you think they have gyms where you can climb rocks, but not where you can climb trees?"

I'd never thought about it before. "Maybe because it's hard to grow trees inside," I told him.

"You could make them. It's not like these are real rocks," Boney pointed out.

"True," I said. "Someone should get on that."

He cocked a finger at me, eyes narrowed. "If you invent it when you grow up and become a millionaire, I get half." No surprise there; Boney was always looking for ways to make money. In fifth grade, he was best known for buying cheap candy and selling it to us during lunch at a huge markup. Which I bought, obviously, because candy.

Once we got to high school, he turned into Boney the burnout, and I barely thought about him. I'd almost forgotten about Boney the junior entrepreneur, with his tree-climbing gyms and his overpriced candy. My eyes sting, and I blink harder.

Mateo leans against the side of the building, Ivy cradled against his chest, and glances at me like he's expecting maybe I had a plan beyond crashing through the back door. I don't. All the decisiveness I had upstairs deserts me in an instant. The only choice I can make now is whether to hurl or pass out. Both seem like solid options, but my stomach decides for me. It seizes, and I bend over to vomit into a patch of grass.

"Okay," Mateo says when I stand and shakily wipe my mouth. "We need to regroup."

He has that Determined Mateo look I remember from the tail end of our friendship, when his dad hit the road to "find himself" as a roadie for a Grateful Dead cover band. Like Mateo had finally realized he'd been letting a useless person dictate half his life, so he was going to have to step up and . . . oh. Oh, okay. I've become the useless person that Mateo has to compensate for, and I both recognize and accept that in an instant. I'm relieved, actually. All I want is to follow someone else's lead for a while.

Mateo strides toward the sidewalk, Ivy still in his arms, and looks both ways into the deserted street. An engine roars suddenly, way too close for comfort, and we barely have time to exchange panicked glances before a car careens around the corner. But it's just some guy on his cell phone, who doesn't even spare us a glance as he speeds past. As soon as he's gone, Mateo starts moving again, half jogging across the street before he ducks into an alley between two buildings. I follow nervously, too shell-shocked to ask questions, as he winds through the narrow passageway.

It feels good to keep moving. When I focus on putting one foot in front of the other, I don't have to think about what happened back there. Not just in the building, but in Lara's *literal studio*. Her latest drawing half-finished on the nearest easel, as though she'd just been working on it. Which she should have been on a Tuesday morning. It's her only day off, her best chance to create, and she's always said she can't concentrate at home.

So why wasn't she there?

And why was Boney? Because that had to be Boney, right? Even though none of us had the guts to look beyond the sneakers, we saw him go in.

But we never saw him come out.

My stomach starts rolling again, and I force my attention back onto the sidewalk in front of me. I have enough presence of mind to wonder whether eventually, we'll run into someone who demands to know why Mateo is carrying an unconscious girl. Seems like minimum responsible adult behavior on a city morning, but the only person we pass is a drunk old man slumped against the side of a building.

Mateo turns another corner, then pauses at the edge of a large metal door. "Keys are in my right pocket," he says. "Can you get them?"

"I . . . what?"

"Get my keys," he says, his voice edging into impatience. "My hands are kinda full."

"I know, but . . . where are we?"

"Garrett's," he says. "Back door. They don't open till five, so it should be deserted."

I stop asking questions and extract the keys as quickly as I can. "It's the big, round one," Mateo says. I find the right key, and fit it into the lock with shaking hands. It turns easily, and I pull the heavy door open as the sound of sirens starts up again. I startle so badly that I would've dropped the keys if they weren't dangling from the lock. Mateo ducks inside with Ivy and I follow suit, slamming the door closed behind me.

We're in a dim, musty-smelling room piled high with cardboard boxes and what look like empty kegs. There's only one other door besides the one we just came in, and it opens into

61

a small stairwell. I follow Mateo upstairs and find myself in a room dominated by a bar on one end and two pool tables at the other. One side of the room is all windows, but they're covered by shades that let in only a faint, yellowish light. The tables nearest them have bench seating covered with faded red cushions, and that's where Mateo finally deposits Ivy.

Once she's down, he shakes his arms out and rolls his neck and shoulders a few times, then carefully straightens an edge of her skirt that rode up during the transfer. Ivy murmurs something but doesn't wake.

"Is she . . . shouldn't she be conscious by now?" I ask. The last time I saw Ivy pass out from her needle phobia was in seventh grade, when somebody found a discarded syringe on the soccer field at school and started waving it around during gym. My memory from that time is a little hazy, but I could swear she woke up within minutes.

"I don't know," Mateo says. "She was pretty freaked out." He leans over her, pressing his fingertips against one side of her neck. "Pulse seems normal. Breathing's normal. Maybe she just needs a little more time."

"You know Ivy," I say. "She can probably use the rest." Mateo gives me a tight-lipped smile in recognition of the weak joke. Back when we hung out with Ivy, she never slept more than five hours a night. I'd miss texts from her after I went to bed, and then a bunch more before I woke up the next morning. Now that I think of it, I feel kind of nostalgic for the weird, random facts that used to strike Ivy while everyone else was sleeping.

Did you know it would only take one hour to drive to space?
THERE ARE PINK DOLPHINS (YouTube link)

Cal you have to get a friend for Gilbert. In Switzerland it's illegal to own only one guinea pig because they get lonely.

She had a good point about Gilbert. My guinea pig was a lot happier after my parents agreed to let me buy a second one. Except then George died, and Gilbert was so inconsolable that he died three days later—so. Not sure it was a win, in the end.

I gaze around the dim room, nervously biting the inside of my cheek. I've never been in a bar before, which is the sort of thing I'd mention under different circumstances. "So this is where you work, huh?"

"Yeah," Mateo says. "The owner doesn't usually show up till around two, so I think we're okay for a while." He crosses over to the bar and ducks behind it, grabbing a couple of glasses that he fills from a small sink. He hands one to me, then sits down at a table close to Ivy. I lower myself into a chair across from him and take a long sip. My mouth tastes slightly less horrible when I'm done.

"You okay?" Mateo asks.

"I don't know," I say weakly. "You?"

"Same." Mateo shakes his head, then drains half his water in one gulp. "That was a nightmare, back there."

"I know." I wipe a hand across my mouth. "Not really what I had in mind when I suggested we re-create the Greatest Day Ever."

"We should've gone to the fucking aquarium," Mateo says.

I can't help it: despite everything that just happened, I snort out a laugh. A semihysterical one, sure, but it's better than crying. "Cosigned," I say.

Then Mateo's expression shifts. It's still tense, but more

focused, like he's getting ready to peer into the hidden depths of my brain. It's a look I remember well from his mother—which is ironic, since he always hated it when she gave it to him.

I know exactly what's coming next.

"Cal," he says. "Who's the girl?"

"Huh?" I drink my water, stalling for time.

"Your friend. The one who works there." Mateo's tone sharpens when my glass is half empty and I'm still chugging away, studiously avoiding his gaze. "Was that by any chance her studio we were standing in?"

"Yeah." The word slips out before I can stop it. *Damn it.* I can't run my mouth here. I need to think. And I need to talk to Lara. I pull out my phone as I add, "But she wasn't there."

"Just because we didn't see her doesn't mean she wasn't there," Mateo points out, and I wish he'd stop being so reasonable for once in his life. "You said she's there every Tuesday, right?"

"Usually." My fingers fly across my phone as I fire off a text to Lara. *Are you at the studio?*

"So why wouldn't she have been there today?" he asks.

"I don't know." I'm staring at my phone, willing her to respond as fast as humanly possible, and my heart takes a giant leap when gray dots appear.

No, couldn't make it today.

I exhale a long breath. I'm beyond glad to hear that, but . . . *Why not?* I text back.

Decided to take a ceramics class! More gray dots, and then a picture of a glazed green bowl sitting beside a kiln appears.

Relief floods through me for a few blissful seconds, then recedes almost as quickly as it came. Because that still doesn't explain why Boney . . . or whoever that was . . . was there.

But I can't ask that via text. *I need to talk to you,* I write back. *Now. In person.* She doesn't respond right away, and I add, *It's urgent.*

"Cal," Mateo says. When I look up, he's still wearing that *I'm going to x-ray your brain* look. "Are you texting her?"

"Yeah. She says she wasn't there." I know that's not enough to stop further questions I can't answer yet, so I stare around the bar for some kind of distraction. There's a large, wall-mounted television to our left, and I point to it. "Hey, can we turn that on?" I ask. "Maybe whatever happened back there made the news."

Mateo gives me a look that says *This discussion isn't over*— also inherited from his mother—but gets to his feet. "Yeah, I guess. Check your phone, too." He crosses over to the bar, reaching into the wooden cubby behind it to pull out a remote. I'm too nervous to navigate to Boston.com while he fires up the television, though. Somehow, it feels better to wait for information to hit me than to go looking for it.

The screen bursts to life with the volume way too loud, and we both wince until Mateo lowers it. It's on the local sports channel, so Mateo clicks until he lands on a guy in a shirt and tie with the words *Breaking News* scrolling beneath him in red. "He's in front of the art studios," Mateo says, returning to our table with his eyes glued to the screen.

My heart plummets. Somehow, seeing the building on television makes this nightmare scenario much more real. "Shit. Do you think—"

"Shhh," Mateo says, raising the volume back up a notch.

". . . police are actively looking for information related to a tip that both they, and producers here at *The Hawkins Report,* received shortly before the body of an unidentified young man was discovered in this very building," the reporter says.

Oh God. *The body.*

The words hit me like a punch to the gut. Ever since we left Lara's studio, I've been telling myself that we can't be sure what we saw. Maybe that guy was just passed out, or sleeping. Playing a joke. None of those possibilities made much sense, but I clung to them anyway. "So that means . . . if we saw . . . if the body was . . ." My throat closes on Boney's name, refusing to give it up.

"Unidentified," Mateo says quickly. But not like the word brings him any real comfort.

The reporter levels his gaze at the camera. "This anonymous source stated that they became concerned after seeing a young, blond woman inject the man with a syringe, after which he immediately became unresponsive," he continues. "The building, which is not currently occupied, does not have security cameras enabled, so the public is being asked to call with any information related to a blond woman, described as attractive and possibly in her early twenties, who may have been in the area during this time."

Two things happen at once. Mateo pauses the television, freezing the reporter's face on-screen, and there's a sudden gasp to my right. When I turn, Ivy is sitting straight up, her hand on her chest and her pale ponytail spilling over one shoulder. She stares at me, then at Mateo, then down at the booth she's been passed out in since we got here.

"What. Is. *Happening?*" she demands.

7

IVY

At first, I have no idea where we are. I don't remember anything, except leaving school this morning with Cal and Mateo. Both of them are staring at me like I just sprouted a second head—which would be unfortunate, since the first one is pounding painfully.

And then, with a sickening rush, I remember *everything*.

"Oh my God." I jump to my feet, my heart in my throat. "What did we . . . why are we . . . *where* are we?" I gaze around wildly until my eyes land on a wall full of fluorescent beer signs. I'm pretty sure I'd remember those if I'd ever been here before. "What is this place?"

"Sit down before you pass out again. I'll get you some water," Mateo says.

I start to protest that I'm fine, but I'm already swaying with too much residual wooziness to pull it off. I collapse back into the bench behind me as Mateo heads toward some kind of counter. *A bar,* I realize when he lifts one side. We're in a bar. One where Mateo is moving around with familiar ease. "Is this Garrett's?" I ask.

Cal, who's been sitting silently all this time, gives me a small, crooked smile. "Well, your brain's still working. That's good news. Do you remember why you fainted?"

"There was a syringe," I say with a shudder. "I saw it before I could—"

"Here." Mateo sits across from me and puts a glass of water between us. "Drink this first. Give yourself a minute."

I do, partly due to raging thirst, and partly because it's nice, at this particular moment in time, to feel like someone's taking care of me. But there are too many questions crowding my mind to stay quiet for long. And with Mateo and Cal both looking so grave, I have to ask the most important one. "What happened to the guy on the floor?" I burst out.

Mateo and Cal exchange glances. "We don't actually know," Cal says. Mateo picks up my empty glass, grabs two more on a nearby table, and brings them back to the bar. "We didn't get a chance to check. After you passed out, things got complicated. Well, more complicated."

"More complicated?" I echo. "How so?"

Cal drums his fingers on the table in front of him. "All of a sudden the police showed up with, like, sirens blaring. Next thing we knew, they were breaking down the door and storming up the stairs and we just—you know." He slides a finger under his collar and tugs it away from his neck. "We figured they had the situation under control, so we . . . left."

I blink at him. "You left," I repeat.

"Yeah." Cal licks his lips. He's ghost pale, making the light dusting of freckles across his nose and cheeks more pronounced than usual. "Through the back entrance."

I can't help myself; I'm on my feet again, pacing the scarred wooden floor. "You didn't talk to the police first?" I ask.

"No," Cal says.

"Let me get this straight." My voice rises. "So what you're telling me is—the two of you decided to *flee a crime scene?*"

Cal just licks his lips again, and I turn toward Mateo. He rests his forearms on the counter, looking like a world-weary bartender ready to listen to whatever tale of woe I'm about to spin. "How could you possibly think that was a good idea?" I ask accusingly.

Mateo's jaw ticks. "Look, it was an intense situation. The cops were coming, and we had no idea why. We had to make a fast decision, and those of us who were *still conscious* made it. Sorry if it's not what you would've done, but we couldn't exactly consult you."

A protest dies on my lips as I meet his tense gaze and realize I'm not being fair to him. Back in middle school, when the three of us used to wander through the Carlton Mall, Mateo was the only one who'd ever get followed around by security. A guard even searched his backpack once. Mateo just stood there, stone-faced and silent, while the guard pulled out battered notebooks, pens, a bunch of hopelessly tangled earbuds, and a hoodie before handing it all back without an apology. So I can understand—better late than never—why he didn't want to stay in that studio. Still, I can't stop pacing, stalking an agitated path between Cal's table and the bar. "Okay, but we should at least tell someone that we saw Boney go in—"

And then I stop, because I'm at the edge of the bar, and

there's no missing the way Mateo's shoulders stiffen at the mention of Boney's name. All my nervous energy drains away in an instant, replaced by cold tendrils of dread. "What?" I ask.

"The guy we saw . . ." Mateo swallows hard. "Whoever it is, he's dead."

It feels like the floor just vanished from beneath my feet. I sag against the counter, gripping its edges, willing myself to stay upright. "It was Boney."

"How do you know?" Mateo asks.

"The sneakers," I say heavily. "They're his."

When I was standing frozen in the doorway, I wasn't sure. But now, as I think back to Boney mounting the auditorium stage for our debate last week . . . I am. I remember seeing a flash of bright purple on his feet, and I remember how deeply it annoyed me. The pettiest part of me—the part that knew I was going to lose the election, and lose badly—wondered, *Why does everything about him have to be so extra?*

I was furious with him yesterday, and this morning. When I saw him heading into that building, I couldn't wait to tell him off. A whole speech formed instantly in my head as I barreled across the street, and I wouldn't even have needed notes. I bury my head in my arms, pressing my burning forehead against the cool bar for a few seconds of comforting darkness.

But as soon as I feel Mateo's hand on my elbow, I lift my head. I can't let myself cry, because if I start now, there's no telling when I'll stop. And some instinct deep inside me is pushing down the tears, urging me to keep a clear head.

"Ivy," Mateo says gently, and I recoil as if he yelled at me. *No.* I absolutely cannot accept any tenderness from Mateo right now. That way lies a breakdown.

"How do you know?" My voice is thick, pushing past the lump in my throat, and I have to swallow a few times until it sounds normal. "How do you know he died?"

"We saw . . ." Mateo gestures over my head and I turn. For the first time I notice the television in the corner, and I do a double take at the sight of a familiar face paused on-screen.

"Why is Dale Hawkins on?" I ask.

Mateo ducks under the bar and heads toward the table where Cal is sitting. "Is that who that is?" he asks.

"Yeah," I say, following him. "My parents know him. And I do, sort of. We've been to some of the same fundraisers." Dale used to be a reporter for one of the Boston networks, but after a contract dispute he left for a local cable station and started his own news program—although as far as my dad is concerned, Dale uses the term "news" very loosely. "More like sensational-ized infotainment," Dad always says.

He might not be entirely objective. Dale has done a few un-flattering features about Dad's work, always taking the angle of *Corporate bigwigs steamroll local business.* "There's never any nu-ance," Dad complains. "He goes for cheap sentiment every time, the hypocrite." It irritates Dad to no end that Dale Hawkins, who lives in Carlton, too, tore down an old bungalow to build his giant McMansion.

The shot on-screen looks familiar; I've seen Dale stand in front of a run-down building with that deeply concerned look on his face every time he reports on Shepard Properties. But the graf-fiti over his right shoulder, coupled with the green door behind him, stops me cold. He's in front of the building we just left.

My nerves start snapping even before Mateo confirms, "He's reporting on what happened at the studio." He picks up a remote and aims it at the television. "Hold on. I need to rewind." After a couple of seconds Dale Hawkins springs to life, his expression grave as he reports, "We're now live in a quiet industrial area north of Faneuil Hall, which this morning became the scene of a troubling and mysterious tragedy."

Mateo, Cal, and I watch the segment in silence, until we get to the part where Dale says, *The public is being asked to call with any information related to a blond woman, described as attractive and possibly in her early twenties, who may have been in the area during this time.* Then Mateo hits pause again, saying, "That's as far as we got before you woke up."

"Okay," I say, wondering if I'm imagining the way his eyes seem to be resting on my hair. "Keep going."

There's not much left, though—just Dale Hawkins reciting phone numbers before signing off with the annoyingly intense, lingering gaze into the camera that he's known for. Then we're all quiet for a few beats, until Mateo decides to state the obvious.

"So," he says. "Blond woman."

I twist my ponytail over my shoulder, running its ends through my fingers. Both of the boys are quiet, waiting for me to speak. "He can't mean . . . he couldn't have been talking about me, right?" I finally say.

Neither of them respond. "I'm not in my twenties," I argue, glancing between Cal's troubled face and Mateo's impassive one. I hate how impossible Mateo is to read; right now, he could be agreeing that I fit the description, or thinking that *attractive* is a stretch. Which is so far off the point that I give myself a mental slap.

Mateo shrugs. "A lot of people suck at guessing ages."

"Yeah, but . . ." Dale's words keep circling in a loop through my brain. "Even if someone saw me in the doorway, they couldn't have thought I was *injecting* Boney. I never got anywhere near him." I'm suddenly, belatedly, and overwhelmingly grateful to Mateo and Cal for getting me out of there before the police arrived. I don't remember anything useful, and if I'd been found in the room after a tip like that—well, the horrible irony of me being questioned about a drug-related death right before my mother's award ceremony wouldn't have been lost on anyone.

"Maybe they saw you going upstairs and got confused," Mateo says.

"Do you think . . . is there any way Boney could've done that to himself? Like an overdose?" Cal rubs his temple and glances my way. "I mean, we were just talking about this, right? Drugs are everywhere, even in Carlton."

"But we're not *in* Carlton," I point out. "Why would Boney go to Boston at ten o'clock in the morning to get high? He could've done that a lot closer to home."

I turn toward Mateo to see if he agrees, but his eyes are on the floor. "Did you see anyone else in the building?" he asks in a low voice.

I shake my head. "No."

"Or hear anyone?" he presses.

I'm about to say *No* again, but then I pause, thinking. I was full of adrenaline when I charged through the front door, determined to find Boney and tell him off. I had no idea where he was, but somehow I went straight to him. How did I do that? What made me turn left, and go up four flights of stairs? "Maybe," I say, tugging harder at my ponytail. "I think I did hear . . . *something*. A noise that drew me upstairs. Movement, or footsteps." My memory becomes clearer, my voice more certain. "It sounded like someone was there."

"Good thing you didn't run into them," Mateo says grimly.

A chill runs down my spine at the words. I glance at Cal, but his head is down, staring at his phone, and all of a sudden my mind is clear and I realize what has been obvious the whole time. "Wait a minute," I say, my voice so sharp that he looks up. "That girl. The one who uses the studio. Is she blond?" Cal blanches, and I want to smack my own forehead for not thinking of her sooner. "She is, isn't she?"

"She wasn't there," Cal says quickly.

"Is. She. *Blond?*" I bite out.

Cal grows paler still. We're exploring heretofore unknown levels of pastiness, with no end in sight. "She . . . I . . . I have your phone," he says.

It's an obvious attempt at changing the subject, but it still makes me pause. "What?"

Cal digs into his pocket and pulls out a last-generation iPhone in a thick black case. "You dropped it when you fainted, but we found it. Here."

I take the unfamiliar case gingerly. "This isn't mine," I say, unzipping my bag and pulling out my own phone in its rose-gold plaid case. "Mine is right where I left it. So this is . . ."

"Shit," Mateo says, taking it from my hand. "This must be Boney's."

Cal gulps. "Or whoever killed him."

We stare at the phone in silence for a beat. "That is . . . it's evidence," I say haltingly. "We need to return it."

Mateo's brow furrows. "To the scene of the crime? How do you suggest we do that?"

"We could—mail it, maybe? With a note?" I suggest.

Cal stands abruptly, his chair scraping noisily behind him. "I need the bathroom," he says.

Mateo points over his shoulder. "Left of the television."

"Thanks. Be right back."

I watch Cal leave, waiting until I hear the sound of a door swinging shut before I turn to Mateo and hiss, "What is going *on* with him?"

"I don't know," Mateo says. "But something is definitely up with that girl. He refuses to talk about her. Won't answer the simplest questions."

He's still holding the black-cased phone, and I know I should keep pressing him about getting it back to the police. Or offer a theory about what's happening with Cal. But I can't bring myself to do either of those things. I'm too nervous, too confused, and too plain exhausted. Instead, I gaze at the row of bottles behind the bar and say, "Am I the only one who could use a drink right about now?"

Mateo laughs, flashing the dimples that only appear when he's caught off guard. When I was thirteen and my crush was at its most intense, I used to live for pulling that smile out of him. "Ivy Sterling-Shepard. Booze before noon? You've changed."

"Extenuating circumstances," I say. I'm not sure if he takes me seriously—or if I even *am* serious—but he crosses over to the bar and ducks beneath it.

"What'll it be?" he asks, sweeping a hand in front of the bottles.

"Maker's Mark," I say.

"A whiskey girl, huh?" His lips quirk. "You're full of surprises."

"I only want a little," I say. I'm not much of a drinker, and definitely not a social one by Carlton High standards. But ever since Daniel and I each turned sixteen, our parents have let us sample whatever they're having, because they think forbidding alcohol will only make us want it more. Their strategy worked, for the most part, since Daniel has no interest and I dislike everything except the smooth, spicy whiskey my father favors.

"Don't worry. You're getting the bare minimum, or Garrett's going to notice."

He's not kidding. When he returns with a single shot glass, amber liquid barely covers the bottom. "I thought you'd have some, too," I say when he hands it to me.

"Better not," he says. I feel a sharp pang of guilt, because he's obviously worried about his boss noticing. I should probably give the glass back, but Mateo would refuse to take it, and it'd turn into a whole production and . . .

And the whiskey is already gone.

Warmth suffuses my chest, filling me with the same comforting sensation I get when I'm hanging out in our family room with Dad. Him at his desk, working, and me curled up in a chair, reading. Safe and sound. Then the feeling disappears as I think about Boney's parents, and how this morning must have felt like any other day. They probably went off to work like parents always do, rushed and preoccupied, never imagining the news they'd get a few hours later.

I briefly squeeze my eyes shut as pressure builds behind them. *You can't,* I remind myself. Breakdowns are for later, when we're out of this mess. I breathe deeply for a few beats, then ask Mateo, "What should we do now?"

"I don't know," he says, turning the black phone over in his hand. "You're right, we need to get this to the police somehow. If it's Boney's, maybe there's something in his messages, or his calls, that would explain why he was at that building."

"See if you can open it," I urge. "I bet he has a really basic passcode. Try 1-2-3-4."

Mateo does, tapping at the screen, and shakes his head. "Nope."

"Try his name," I suggest. But before Mateo can, Cal emerges from the restroom. He's carefully rolling up his sleeves, a classic Cal move when he's about to say something that he knows isn't going to go over well.

"So." Cal clears his throat. "I have to go for a little bit."

"Go?" Mateo and I say in unison. "Go where?" I add. When Cal doesn't answer right away, my temper starts to rise. "You can't just leave, you know. We're in a *situation*."

"You're not the boss of me," Cal mutters, like the sulky four-year-old he turns into whenever someone tries to talk him out of doing something stupid.

"Are you seeing *her*?" I demand. "The blond with access to a murder den?"

"I never said she was blond," Cal says defensively.

I snort. "You didn't have to. Does she know Boney?"

"She . . . look, it's complicated. I can explain, but I need to talk to her first." Cal pulls his phone from his pocket. "She's not far from here, so I'm going to head over there, and then I'll come back and we can figure out what to do next. The Haymarket T stop is near here, right?"

He starts to move, but I spring up and block his path. "You can't be serious," I protest, but before I can gather steam, Mateo puts a hand on my arm.

"It's all right, Ivy. Let him go."

"What?" I gape at him, and Cal takes the opportunity to skirt around me.

"We're all stressed," Mateo says. "It'll only get worse if we start arguing with one another." He picks up my empty shot glass and heads for the bar, ducking beneath it so he can rinse the glass out in the sink. Cal follows him, and for the first time I notice a doorway behind the bar area leading to a small set of stairs. "I'm sure Cal has a good reason for leaving."

"I do. I do," Cal says, sidling past Mateo. "I'll be back in an hour, tops. Probably less. I'll, um, knock three times on the door so you'll know it's me."

Mateo suppresses a sigh as he dries the glass. "Just text us, Cal."

"Roger that," Cal says, hurrying down the stairs. He disappears, and a moment later, I hear the creak of hinges and the slam of a door.

I stand with my arms crossed, feeling helpless and wordless. Well, I have words, but I find myself unable to say them. Mateo is my kryptonite, and not only because I had a crush on him years ago. "So we're just going to wait here, then?" I ask, unable to keep a note of resentment from creeping into my voice.

Mateo finishes drying the shot glass, then carefully folds the bar towel and places it under the counter. "Of course not," he says. "We're going to follow him."

8

MATEO

Cal's bright red hair makes him easy to track. Ivy and I catch up to him a few blocks from Garrett's, passing a familiar area that hosts a farmers' market on weekends. My mother is a city person at heart, born and raised in the Bronx, and she used to take me to downtown Boston all the time when I was a kid. Usually it was just the two of us, or the three of us once Autumn came. But occasionally we'd be joined by my dad and, twice a year, by Ma's entire extended family when they came to visit.

My grandmother liked to use the time as a recruiting trip. At some point in the day, she'd always look around and sniff, "Cute, but not a real city. You must miss that, Elena."

Ma was the only Reyes kid who'd ever left New York, accepting a softball scholarship to Boston College and never looking back. My grandmother managed to limit her complaints when Ma was married, but after the divorce happened and my dad hit the road, her phone calls got more frequent. And now, with

Spare Me closed and Ma's osteoarthritis diagnosis—even though she hasn't told my grandmother how bad it is—we hear from her almost daily. "Let us help you," she urges. "Come home."

Ma's reply never changes. "I *am* home. My children were born here." She always says that, *my children,* like there's no difference between Autumn and me. And my grandmother has never questioned that, even though Autumn isn't a blood relative. Gram feels the same way.

I might secretly think my grandmother has a point—family support would take the pressure off me and Autumn, not to mention get her away from Loser Gabe—but there's no way in hell I'm going against my mother. So anytime Gram or one of my aunts or uncles reaches out to me privately, I give them the same response Ma does. *We're doing fine.*

"What is your deadbeat father doing to help?" Gram asked the last time she called.

"Extra child support," I said, which is true. She doesn't need to know it's only fifty bucks a check. Dad keeps claiming he's looking for work nearby so he can move back to Carlton and help out more, but that's not something I plan on mentioning to my grandmother. She'd know as well as I do that it's nothing but empty talk.

"Oh, Mateo," she sighed before she hung up on that call. "You're as stubborn as she is, aren't you? You'll be the death of me."

Thank God she has no idea what's happening now, or that could get literal.

Ivy's been quiet as we walk, seemingly lost in her own thoughts, until both our phones start to buzz simultaneously. Hers is in the bag she has slung over her shoulder, and while she roots around for it, I pull mine out of my pocket. There's a pileup of texts waiting for me, from Carmen and my friend Zack:

Zack: *Where are you? Boney Mahoney is fucking DEAD.*

Zack: *Stabbed in the heart or something.*

Zack: *Idk, rumors are flying.*

Shit. How do people know already? The news didn't mention Boney's name, did it? Unless there's already been a follow-up report since we watched.

Zack: *Me & Ishaan are doing a special version of Carlton Speaks during lunch.*

Zack: *Going rogue. Don't tell anyone.*

Zack and another guy in our class started up a YouTube series last spring to report on school happenings as part of their media technology elective, and it was popular enough that they kept it going. They're supposed to run everything past a teacher before posting, though, and no way would speculation about Boney be an approved topic.

Carmen: *Hey, are you ok???*

Carmen: *Not a good day to miss school. Boney did, too, and everyone's saying he got murdered in Boston (crying emoji)*

Carmen: *Ivy's not here, either, which is a weird coincidence.*

When I look at Ivy, she's staring wide-eyed at her screen. "So," she says in a high, tight voice. "Emily says the news released Boney's name, and all hell's broken loose at school. People are *highly interested* in the tip about the blond woman. And the fact that I'm not there. Can you believe that? People are actually gossiping that I . . . that I might have *murdered* Boney over a student council election!"

"Nobody's saying that," I protest as another text crosses my phone.

Carmen: You wouldn't believe what people are saying about her.

"Oh, really?" Ivy gestures at my buzzing phone, brows raised. "None of your friends have brought me up?"

"Nope," I lie, pocketing my phone before she can grab it. "Stop checking your texts, okay? We're almost at the T—you won't get reception there anyway. By the time we get wherever Cal's going, people will be talking about something else." I don't believe that for a second, but if Ivy starts spinning out now, there's a good chance she'll never stop.

"I can't! What if—ohhh. Oh, okay." An expression of intense relief crosses her face as she holds up her screen. "My parents' plane just took off."

"Their plane?" I ask as Haymarket station comes into sight.

"They were in San Francisco for the weekend. Twentieth-anniversary trip. And tonight, my mom's getting the Carlton Citizen of the Year Award at Mackenzie Hall, and I'm supposed to introduce her. So this *cannot* be happening." Ivy stuffs her phone into her bag with a determined expression. "I have six hours to fix it before they land."

We maneuver ourselves into a solid surveillance position on the train—in a separate car from Cal, but close enough that we can see him through the glass door. He's standing with his back to us, shoulders hunched, and there's something so defeated about his posture that I feel a surge of protectiveness for the guy. Back when we used to hang out, Cal was this really open, friendly, carefree kid. I don't know who he's meeting, but if she's making him look like this, I already don't like her.

Then again, maybe I just never knew Cal all that well. A

lot of things that seemed simple and straightforward back then probably weren't.

Ivy and I are standing, holding the bar above us, and she's clenching it so tightly that her knuckles are white. "I guess he's going to Cambridge," she says when we pass through North Station and Cal doesn't budge. There are only two more stops on this line: Science Park and Lechmere in East Cambridge. She shuffles her feet and adds, "So . . . should we talk about things?"

"What things?" I ask warily, wondering if she managed to read my thoughts. My brain might keep getting stuck in the past, but that doesn't mean I want to revisit it with her. The more time I spend alone with Ivy, the more sure I am about that.

"You know." She lowers her voice. "Stuff like . . . what to tell people. About where we were today, and . . . everything."

Everything. Right. It's only just started to sink in how much *everything* we have to deal with. My friends, who have no idea where I am, are going to expect an answer soon. Autumn might check in, and what am I supposed to tell her? We don't keep secrets from one another, even when she's doing stuff I'd rather not know about. Which is always, lately.

The whole situation makes my head hurt. "One thing at a time, okay? Let's figure out what's going on with Cal and worry about the rest later." I'm not sure how much I even care about what Cal's up to, to be honest, but he's a problem that can be solved. Not like whatever happened to Boney.

"But what if we—"

"I said *later*, Ivy," I say, my voice rising along with my temper. This isn't eighth grade, when I'd do whatever the hell Ivy wanted just because she asked.

"Okay, okay," Ivy mutters, moving away from me as a few

passengers idly glance our way. She doesn't look happy, but oh well.

The train rumbles aboveground at Science Park, and I watch the Museum of Science come into view outside my window. It's one of the Carlton school system's favorite field trip destinations, so I've been at least a half dozen times. The last time, in seventh grade, I was teamed up with Ivy and Cal for an interactive exhibit where one of the stations tested physiological responses to pictures of different animals. If your pupils got bigger, or your heart rate sped up, that meant you were afraid of that animal.

Ivy and I had fear reactions to stereotypically intimidating creatures—a hissing snake and a snarling crocodile—but Cal only got them when he looked at a rabbit sitting in a flower patch. Ivy couldn't stop laughing about it. "You're scared of bunnies, Cal," she teased.

"I am not!" he protested. "The test is broken."

"Worked for us," I said while Ivy continued to crack up.

Then she looked thoughtful. "It's a good thing the human race has evolved past the hunter-gatherer stage, isn't it? You wouldn't last a day in the wild, Cal. You're afraid of the wrong things." That's Ivy for you; she has this way of making observations that seem like throwaways, but end up being weirdly deep enough that you think about them years later. Wherever Cal is headed, I can almost guarantee that it's bad news and he doesn't realize it.

Cal doesn't get off at Science Park, and a minute later a voice over the speaker calls out, "Lechmere, last stop." Ivy and I sway in place until the train comes to a loud, grinding halt. The doors open, and we funnel onto the open-air platform with the rest of the passengers. We hang back from Cal as he follows the crowd through the turnstiles toward the street and waits at a crosswalk for the light to turn. At this point there's nowhere for Ivy and me to hide, and all Cal would need to do is turn his head to see us. But he doesn't. Not at the crosswalk, not on the street, and not as we trail him down the sidewalk until he stops at a squat, blue brick building with a sign that reads *Second Street Café*.

"Here we go," Ivy murmurs as Cal ducks inside.

I've never been here before, but it's a good spot for stealthily following someone. The space is large and industrial, dominated by exposed pipes in the ceiling and abstract paintings on the walls. Some kind of bluesy music plays in the background, mingling with the buzz of the crowd. Cal pauses, scanning the room, then makes his way toward a corner table. A blond girl wearing a baseball cap is sitting there, and she lifts her hand in greeting.

"I knew she was blond," Ivy says through clenched teeth. "I *knew* it." Then her expression changes from annoyance to puzzlement. "Wait. Is that . . ."

The girl tilts her head, giving me a good view of her face, and a couple of things stop me in my tracks. One, we know her. And two, *girl* is the wrong age category. "Yup," I say.

Ivy pauses beside me. "Why is he meeting *her*?" she asks, clearly confused. "Is this a school thing? Or do you think she knows Cal's mystery girlfriend? Or maybe—" Then Ivy's jaw drops as Cal grabs both of the blond woman's hands in his, twining their fingers together. He presses a kiss to her knuckles and she pulls away, but not like she's shocked by Cal making an unexpected move. The look on her face doesn't say, *What are you doing?* It says, *Not here.*

What. The. Hell.

I sink into an empty table and Ivy drops next to me. The

impatience I felt toward her on the train vanishes, and all I can focus on is the odd couple in front of us. "Was Cal just holding hands with our *art teacher*?" she asks.

Yeah, he was. Our young, crazy-hot art teacher. Ms. Jamison started working at Carlton High two years ago, right after she graduated from college, and she made an instant impression. Most of our teachers are middle-aged, or straight-up old. The only female teacher who people have ever thought was even a little bit attractive before Ms. Jamison showed up was Ms. Meija. She's one of the Spanish teachers, at least thirty, and looks like someone's mom on a TV show. Good, but not *I'm going to take this class even though I don't have to* good.

Ms. Jamison looks that kind of good. Art has never been so popular.

I've never spoken to her. The closest I came was last August, when my dad was in town on break from his roadie gig and decided to take me back-to-school shopping. I didn't need or want anything but figured I'd humor him and save the receipt so I could return everything later. So we were in Target, and he was looking at lava lamps like I was going off to college and needed to furnish a dorm room, when Ms. Jamison walked by. She was checking something on her phone and didn't notice us, but Dad definitely noticed her.

"I have a sudden need for towels," he said, watching her head down that aisle.

"No," I said shortly. That's how roughly sixty percent of conversations with my father go: me trying to shut down something embarrassing and/or obnoxious. It's made worse by the fact that ever since I turned fifteen and got taller than him, he's treated me like his wingman.

"Why not?" Dad asked, already pivoting our cart.

"She teaches at Carlton," I hissed. "Autumn takes her class." Thank God that stopped him, because Ms. Jamison came back into the main aisle then and would've bumped into us otherwise. She smiled politely at my father, glanced at me with a spark of recognition that didn't catch—I'd gotten a lot taller over the summer—and kept going.

I thought I'd dodged that bullet until Dad loudly said, "They didn't make them like that when *I* was in school." That earned us a lingering backward look from Ms. Jamison before she finally, mercifully, disappeared from view. To this day, I couldn't tell you whether she was angry or amused. All I knew was that I was horrified, and I've avoided Ms. Jamison's classes like the plague ever since.

I'm the exception, though. Half the guys in school take it in the hopes of getting friendly with Ms. Jamison, and at least a few of them—the jocks, mostly—brag that they've done more than that. But they're the kind of guys you can't take seriously, so I've never paid attention to them. Plus, last winter Ms. Jamison got engaged to Carlton High's lacrosse coach, Coach Kendall, who's the human equivalent of a golden retriever. Cheerful, friendly, and liked by everyone. From what I've seen of the two of them together, they look happy.

But now here's Cal—*Cal,* of all the damn people—leaning as far forward as the table will let him, looking like he's two seconds away from kissing her.

"This is messed up," Ivy says.

"No kidding," I say. "And why is she even here? Shouldn't she be at school?"

"There's no art on Tuesday. Budget cuts, remember?"

I resist the urge to roll my eyes, but just barely. It's typical Ivy to believe everyone pays attention to stuff like that. "Do you take her class?"

Ivy shakes her head. "I haven't taken an elective since freshman year. Too busy trying to keep up with . . ." She catches herself and finishes with "classes," but I'm pretty sure she was about to say *Daniel*. He tested off the charts on some kind of gifted exam when Ivy and I were still friends, and she got really intense about school after that. Like she could level whatever playing field she thought the two of them were on through sheer force of will. "Do you?"

"Huh?" I got lost in thought, and have no idea what she's asking.

"Take Ms. Jamison's class."

"Nope," I say briefly. No way am I getting into *that* backstory. "Autumn did, though, and she liked her. Said Ms. Jamison was always really encouraging."

Ivy folds her arms and glares at Cal's table. "Oh, I'd say she's *encouraging*, all right," she says darkly.

"Do you think Cal's parents know about this?" I ask.

"Are you kidding? They'd die. Especially Wes," she says.

"Why especially him?" From what I remember, Henry was a lot stricter.

"Because he's the dean at Carlton College. *Hello?*" Ivy waves a hand in front of my face when I don't react. "Do you not watch the news?"

"You know I don't."

"Well, Carlton College just fired a professor for sleeping with a student. It was a whole thing, and Wes was interviewed a bunch of times. If people knew his son was sneaking around with a teacher, he'd look like a hypocrite. Or a clueless, uninvolved parent. Neither is great for the dean of a college."

Suddenly, Cal flattening himself against an alley doorway makes a lot more sense. "No wonder Cal freaked out this morning," I say.

Ivy chews her lip. "He said she wasn't at the studio, right?" I nod. "But he *also* said she works there on Tuesdays. She's blond, and she knows Boney. That's three strikes. Plus a bonus fourth strike for"—she waves her hand toward Cal's table—"all *that*. It's a good thing we followed him. He clearly has no objectivity when it comes to this woman, so he's not going to ask any of the right questions."

"You want to move closer? Try and listen in?" I ask.

"We could," Ivy says. "And we should. But I had something else in mind, too."

YOUTUBE, CARLTON SPEAKS CHANNEL

Ishaan and Zack wave at a phone camera from what looks like the front seat of a car.

ZACK: Hey, this is Zack Abrams and Ishaan Mittal, coming to you live from (*glances around*) Ishaan's car. Which, not gonna lie, could be cleaner.

ISHAAN: You're the one who wanted to record here. I voted for Angelo's Pizzeria.

ZACK: Too noisy. Anyway, we ducked out of lunch to bring you a Carlton Speaks special report on what everyone at school is talking about today: the shocking death of our classmate, Carlton High senior Brian "Boney" Mahoney. The news reports don't have much detail yet, but it sounds like Boney died in an abandoned building in Boston.

ISHAAN: He didn't just die. He was *killed*. By a blond chick.

ZACK, *glaring at Ishaan:* You're getting ahead of the story. That part's not even confirmed yet. (*Looks back at the camera.*) Anyway. Boney was elected senior class president yesterday, and was supposed to give his acceptance speech at ten o'clock this morning. We were all in the auditorium, waiting. *(Dramatic pause.)* But Boney never showed up.

ISHAAN, *crowding into the camera:* You know who else didn't show up?

ZACK: Not yet—

ISHAAN, *loudly:* That's right, a blond chick. The one he beat.

ZACK: Damn it, Ishaan, you always ruin my intro.

ISHAAN: You were taking too long. Anyway, it's weird, right? Ivy Sterling-Shepard never misses a single day of school until today, when the guy who totally humiliates her dies? And nobody's heard from her. Not her brother, not her best friend—

ZACK: I'm not sure we should be saying names here. This is all just speculation, obviously, but—

ISHAAN: But that girl is intense. Like, the kind of intense that snaps one day and goes off the deep end. You can see it, right?

ZACK, *after a beat:* Well. It's not like you *can't* see it.

9

CAL

I don't know why I grabbed her hands, under the circumstances. A combination of habit, probably—even though it's only been a few weeks since we started meeting up outside of class—and the desperate need for some kind of comfort.

I can tell I've annoyed her, though, so now I feel even worse. "Sorry," I say, leaning back and fiddling with her discarded straw wrapper. She's drinking something pink and iced, and gives me a small smile as she takes a sip.

"It's all right. Just a very public spot, you know?"

I know. And I know how this looks—all of it.

I never thought I'd be involved with an older woman, or an almost-married woman, or a teacher. It's not like it was planned. I've had a crush on Lara ever since I first took one of her classes last year, but I never imagined anything would come of it. Especially once she got engaged. But when senior year began, I asked her advice about college art programs, and we started talking a lot more. Then she gave me her number, in case I had any questions outside of class. I sat in my room for three hours that night, composing messages until I finally got up the nerve to send one.

We ended up texting for almost two hours, and every day after that. It went from being about college applications, to art in general, to pop culture, and then about hopes and dreams and plans for the future. I got kind of obsessed with her, I guess. I thought about her nonstop, even when I was with Noemi, and I filled my phone with songs about unrequited love. Earlier this month, I was listening to one of them when she called me for the first time.

"Hello?" I croaked, my heart in my throat.

"Hi, Cal. I was just thinking about your face."

"Excuse me?" I was positive I'd heard her wrong.

"It's so interesting," she said. "Such wonderful angles. I'd love to draw you sometime."

That's how I ended up at her studio the first time. She uses it on occasional weeknights, too, so I told my parents I had a study group at the library and took off for Boston. I don't think I've ever felt so alive as I did that night, every nerve humming while I sat beside her on a wooden bench as she sketched. She kept putting down her pad and pencil so she could touch my cheek or my chin, making slight adjustments to my pose. Nothing else happened then, or since, but it feels like it's only a matter of time.

I'm not clueless. I know she's engaged, and my teacher, and older. Only by seven years, though. My aunt and uncle have a ten-year age difference, and nobody cares. I mean, yeah, they met when Uncle Rob was thirty-five and Aunt Lisa was forty-five, and they didn't work together or anything like that, so I get that it's different. But are people supposed to abandon potential soul mates just because of a few socially constructed complications?

Not that my dads would ever see it that way. Like I said, I tell Wes an abnormal amount of stuff—but not this. Even if I'd been tempted, I'd have known better after Carlton College fired that professor for sleeping with his student.

"They're both adults, though," I'd said, thinking about Lara and my own eighteenth birthday coming up next spring.

"There's a power differential between teachers and students," Wes pointed out. "It's why we have a policy in place." Then his lips thinned. "Even if we didn't, I will *always* question the judgment and motives of an adult who gets involved with a teenager. Wrong is wrong."

I know that's what everyone would say. And it's how I feel when I pass Coach Kendall in the hall, and he gives me a cheery greeting even though I don't play any sports and he barely knows me. *Wrong is wrong,* I think. But then I get a text from Lara that makes my entire body flood with warmth and happiness, and I wonder, *Is life really that black-and-white?*

Lara breaks into my thoughts by clearing her throat. She adjusts her baseball cap over her blond waves, and I realize I've probably been staring dopily for a good thirty seconds. I tend to do that. "So what's going on, Cal?" she asks. "Why the urgency, and more importantly, why aren't you in school?"

Ugh. I hate when she talks to me like I'm just a random student. "I skipped with a couple of friends," I say. Her eyes pop, and I quickly add, "Don't worry, they're not here. I ditched them in Boston so I could meet you, because . . ." Then I trail off, not sure what to say next. She's acting so normal, like she has no clue about what happened to Boney. And granted, the news just broke and it's her day off, but . . . he died in her studio. *That's what you lead with, Cal,* I think, but the words won't come. Instead, I find myself asking, "Where were you this morning?"

Lara's brow creases with mild impatience. "I told you. I took a ceramics class."

"But you said . . . last night, when we talked about getting breakfast today, you said you'd be going to the studio after."

"Right," she says, sipping her drink. "Then a spot opened up last minute, so I took it."

I wait a beat to see if she has more to add. I'm starting to feel uncomfortably warm, and roll my shirtsleeves up higher. "Well, as it turns out, I was at the studio this morning, and—"

"Hold on," she interrupts, frowning. "You were at the studio? Cal, you can't do that. I'm sorry I disappointed you this morning, but you can't just come looking for me. Especially with your friends in tow. What were you thinking?"

"I wasn't looking for you," I protest. Although . . . maybe, in some corner of my brain, I was. Is that why I suggested getting coffee near the studio, or stopping by the art supply store? Because I was hoping to catch a glimpse of her? I push the thought away and add, "That's not my point. My point is that Boney Mahoney was there, too."

Lara blinks, confused. "Who?"

"Boney Mahoney. Brian, I mean. Brian Mahoney, from school."

It feels weird to admit now, even to myself, but when I first saw Boney walking through that door this morning—I was

95

jealous. All I could think was that he was there because Lara had asked him to be. *Boney's not her type,* I thought, but then it hit me that nobody would ever consider me her type, either.

Before I could get too moody about it, though, everything went straight to hell.

"Oh, sure, okay," Lara says, but she still looks puzzled. "What about Brian?"

I take a deep breath. I can't believe I have to be the one to tell her, but—"He died this morning."

"Oh my God. Really?" Lara's hands fly to her cheeks, her eyes widening. "Oh, how awful. What happened?"

I swallow hard. I don't know how to deliver the rest of the news, except to blurt it out. "I'm not sure yet, but from what they're saying on the news, he was killed. Injected with some kind of drug, maybe. In your studio."

"Killed?" Lara whispers, every drop of color draining from her face. "In my . . . in the building?"

"Not just the building. Your actual studio." My eyes search her face, looking for a flicker of—what? I'm not even sure—before I add, "And somebody called in a tip about a blond woman injecting him."

Lara passes a trembling hand over her mouth. "Please tell me you're making some kind of sick joke."

If I were capable of being mad at her, that would've done it. "No," I say tersely. "I wouldn't joke about something like this."

"I didn't mean . . . I'm just . . . I can't." Lara presses a palm to her cheek, then reaches beneath the table for her bag. She hauls it into her lap and starts scrambling through it, tossing it onto the bench beside us after she extracts her phone. She unlocks it, scrolls for a few minutes, and gets even paler. "Oh my God, this is . . . I can't believe this. You're right, Brian is . . . oh my God, Cal. You were there? What happened?"

I try to explain the situation as succinctly as I can, but I end up having to repeat myself a few times before she grasps it fully. She's completely still the entire time except for her eyes, which keep flicking between me and her screen. Then she drops the phone onto the table, and buries her face in her hands.

I watch her for a few minutes, searching for a sign that her reaction isn't genuine. None of this looks good for Lara. I know that, but I also can't think of a single reason why she'd hurt Boney. "So . . . ," I finally say tentatively. "You were in a ceramics class the whole time? Because that tip about the blond woman—"

Lara's hands drop from her face, her expression hardening. "Had nothing to do with me. I was at the adult education center on Mass Ave until"—she glances at her watch—"about ten minutes ago."

Before I can respond, there's a loud crashing noise to our left. We both jump, and I turn to see a waiter rushing toward a busing station near the front of the room, shooing customers away. Lara twists in her chair, looking almost relieved at the distraction. "People always pile those too high," she says.

"Yeah," I agree, even though I don't give a crap about a few broken dishes. "Lara, what about your friend? The one who lets you use the studio? Would he . . . do you think he could've had anything to do with this?"

"He . . . no. He's been out of town, and . . ." Her eyes suddenly widen. "Cal. Wait. You said you were there with friends, right?" I nod. "Who were they?"

"Ivy Sterling-Shepard and Mateo Wojcik."

"What?" For a second, she looks confused instead of distraught. "The ones from your old web comic? I thought you said you don't talk to them anymore."

We don't have time for the Greatest Day Ever parking lot reunion story. "Sometimes I do," I say vaguely. "They felt like skipping, too, so . . . we did."

"Huh." She's quiet for a moment, absorbing that, then says, "Do they . . . you didn't tell them about me, did you?"

"No," I say, and her face blooms with relief.

"Oh, thank God. Thank you for that, Cal." She grabs both my hands in hers and squeezes tightly before releasing them. "I know I have no right to ask this of you, but—can you please keep this to yourself? I have to talk to my friend about what happened. It's very delicate, since we're not supposed to be using the building. And the fact that you and I spent time there recently is . . . awkward, under the circumstances."

"Yeah, okay," I say, feeling a weird mixture of relief and disappointment. Part of me was hoping she'd come up with a solution to this mess that doesn't involve me continuing to lie to everyone I know, while the rest of me knows there isn't one. "It's just . . . I don't know if we did the right thing by leaving, you know? And it was my idea, because . . ." *Because I wanted to protect you.* It's not the only reason—I was also panicked and confused and afraid of somehow getting arrested—but it was a big one.

Lara reaches out to squeeze my hands again. "It doesn't sound like you could have done anything to help Brian. And honestly, I think you and your friends being there would only have been a distraction for the police. They need to focus on whatever evidence is in the room, not on people who were in the wrong place at the wrong time."

Like Boney, I think. My eyes start stinging then, and I blink so rapidly that Lara says, "Oh Cal, it's going to be all right. Here, let me get you a tissue." I'm still blinking, my vision cloudy, when her voice suddenly changes. "What the hell? Where's my bag?"

I wipe my eyes and try to focus on the table next to us. "Wasn't it there?" I ask, my gaze sweeping across the empty bench where I saw it last. "Did it fall or something?" I lean for a closer look under the table, but the floor is empty, too.

"Oh my God. Did someone take it?" Lara's face floods with color as she jumps to her feet and looks around frantically. "Excuse me," she says to an older woman having a cup of tea by herself two tables over. "Did you see a red bag anywhere? Like a tote bag, about this big?" She holds her hands a foot apart.

"I'm sorry, I didn't," the woman says. "But I just got here."

"Who steals another person's bag in the middle of a coffee shop?" Lara asks, putting her hands on her hips as she glares around us. "My keys are in there! How am I supposed to get home?" Then she seems to realize how much attention she's drawing to herself, and takes a deep breath. When she speaks next, it's in a much calmer voice. "Okay. First things first. I'm going to check with the cashier up front, on the off chance that one of the waitstaff thought it belonged to someone else."

I grasp that straw with all the enthusiasm I can muster. "That's probably exactly what happened," I say, falling into step behind her as she weaves her way through the room toward the cash register. The line is six people deep, but Lara sidles right up to the counter and waves at the guy taking orders. He's a few years older than me, arms covered in elaborate tattoos, and he smiles when she catches his eye.

"Excuse me, sorry to bother you," Lara says breathlessly. "I'm not ordering, but I seem to have misplaced my bag, and I was wondering if anyone might have turned it in?"

I expect the guy to shake his head, but he pauses with one hand on the register. "What does it look like?" he asks.

"Red leather, brown strap? The front pocket has a gold clasp."

"Sounds familiar." The guy reaches beneath the counter, and pulls out her missing bag with a flourish. Lara exhales in relief as he hands it over. "Some girl said she grabbed it by mistake," he says.

"Oh, thank God." Lara unzips the front pocket and pulls out her wallet first, then her keys, before dropping them back inside. "Safe and sound. Thank you so much!"

"Anytime." The guy grins, happy to play the hero, even though he didn't do anything except happen to be on point for the lost and found.

"Whew, that gave me a scare." Lara slings the bag over her shoulder and puts her hand over her heart, leading me away from the line to a less crowded space near the restrooms. "What an absolute nightmare of a morning. Cal, I feel terrible leaving you, but I need to figure some things out. Then we'll see where we land, okay?"

"What does that mean?" I ask.

Before she can answer, her phone rings in her hand. She looks down and holds up a finger. "Hang on, this is my friend who used to rent the studio. I'd better take it. Please don't say a word to anyone until we talk again, all right? Everything will be okay, I promise." I nod, and she quickly pecks my cheek before turning away with her phone to her ear. "Dominick? Dominick, is that you? I can barely hear you. I'm going to find someplace quieter." She heads for the café exit, and I slump against the wall. I can't decide if I actually feel worse after talking with Lara, or just no better.

Wrong is wrong.

I don't know what to do next. Do I head back to Garrett's? Are Mateo and Ivy even still there? What am I supposed to say to them if they are? I move sluggishly toward the exit, then trudge back to Lechmere station on autopilot, scrolling through my phone. The last text message I have is from Lara agreeing to meet; there's not a single person at Carlton High who got in touch to share the news about Boney. Who am I kidding? My so-called friends probably haven't even noticed I'm not there.

When I insert my CharlieCard into the station turnstile and step through, there's already a train waiting with open doors. I climb the train's steps and scan the half-full compartment, selecting a window seat toward the front. Then I settle onto the hard plastic chair and gaze at the bright fall day outside, my mind churning and full of questions that seem impossible to answer.

"Hey, Cal."

Somebody pokes my shoulder. I turn, and nearly slide off my seat in shock when I realize it's Ivy. She and Mateo are sitting side by side behind me, and for a second I'm so happy to see friendly faces that it doesn't occur to me to question why they're here. Then Ivy speaks, and wipes the half smile that's forming on my lips right off.

"So we followed you," she says.

10

IVY

"You did what?" Cal sputters as the doors close and the train lurches forward. He twists fully in his seat, his gaze darting between me and Mateo. "Followed me where?"

"The café," I say. "To your . . . meeting." I wait a beat for him to respond, and when he doesn't, I add, "With Ms. Jamison."

Cal stares at the ground. "So you spied on me," he says flatly.

I guiltily cut my eyes toward Mateo. That's not all we did. Not even close, but now doesn't seem like the time to bring that up. "We were worried about you," I say.

"It's no big deal," Cal says, unrolling his sleeves. You'd think he'd know by now it's a dead giveaway that he's being sketchy. "I was supposed to meet somebody, but she didn't show, and I ran into Ms. Jamison instead. We ended up talking about my midterm project."

Mateo and I exchange incredulous glances. I have to admit, I wasn't expecting Cal to deploy such deep denial, and it renders me momentarily speechless. "Dude, come on," Mateo says, stepping in while I blink at Cal. "We saw."

"Saw me talking about school," Cal says stubbornly. Mateo gives me a helpless look like, *Well, I tried my best. Back to you, Ivy.*

"Cal, you don't seem to understand what we're telling you," I say. "It's not like we just caught a glimpse of you and Ms. Jamison through the window. Remember that big potted fern next to your table?" I get a blank look in return, of course, because he was too busy staring into Ms. Jamison's eyes. I could've tap-danced past them in a clown costume and he wouldn't have noticed. "We were sitting behind it and heard your entire conversation. We know it's her studio, and we saw the two of you holding hands." Cal winces like he'd been hoping we'd shown up after that part. "She's your mystery girl. So please stop pretending you left us to stew in a bar for an hour after our classmate died so you could talk about a *school project.*"

Cal has the grace to blush. "Okay. Sorry," he mumbles. "It's just really complicated. Nobody knows about me and her, because . . ."

I can't help myself. "Because there shouldn't *be* a you and her," I blurt out. "She's your teacher and she's way too old."

Cal's face shutters in an instant. "We haven't even done anything."

"*She* has," I say. Even without knowing specifics, I know she's crossed a line.

His jaw tightens. "I knew you wouldn't understand."

My patience, already stretched thin, snaps. "Do you think her fiancé would?" I ask.

I try not to focus too much on my brother's extracurricular activities, as a general technique for preserving my self-esteem, but I've gotten to know Coach Kendall over the years. He's one of my parents' favorite people at Carlton High, and he's been coming to our Christmas open house since Daniel and I were freshmen. He brings the same thing every year—clumsily decorated cookies—and always asks me for an update on student council activities. Unlike most adults, his eyes don't glaze over when I answer.

He doesn't deserve this, is my point.

"You might think you're in some kind of real relationship, but you're not," I continue when Cal doesn't reply. "Not even close."

"Oh, really? Is it not even close?" Cal asks with a bitter laugh. "Well, I guess you'd know, wouldn't you?" His mouth tightens, and my stomach starts to sink. I know that look; I've pushed him too far. Cal almost never gets truly mean, but when he does—watch out.

He unfolds his arms and starts clapping softly. "Ivy Sterling-Shepard, ladies and gentlemen. Queen of relationship advice. Remind me, when was your last boyfriend?" Dread inches up my spine as his eyes flick toward Mateo and he adds, "Was it in eighth grade, when you planted one on Mateo and he never mentioned it again? Can't blame him. He probably didn't want to hear about it in excruciating detail like I did for two months straight."

Oh my God. I can't believe he went there.

My face flames with years of pent-up humiliation. Mateo goes rigid beside me as Cal stands abruptly and glares down at us. "Go to hell, both of you. I'm finding a new seat, and then I'm getting off at Government Center and going home. You can

104

take the T back to Carlton for all I care. And if you tell anybody about Lara . . ." His lips thin and he lifts his chin toward me. "I'll tell them I have no idea what you did to Boney before we got there, Ivy."

My jaw drops as Cal turns away and heads for the back of the train. His burn of an exit is spoiled when the train lurches again and almost sends him flying, but he manages to right himself and sink into a seat as far away from us as possible. Mateo and I remain seated in total silence, which is exactly as awkward as it sounds.

Well. I started this mess by going off on Cal, so it looks like I have to speak first. "Um, so obviously that little blast from the past isn't relevant to the matter at hand—" I start.

Mateo breaks in. "What did he mean, never mentioned it?"

No, no, no. We do not have to relive this, or attempt to rewrite history. "Mateo, it's fine. Don't worry about it. It was so long ago. I don't even think about that anymore."

Lies, all lies. I thought about it as recently as the ride over, when the train was crowded and we had to stand holding the bars above us. I kept swaying into Mateo's arm, which has gotten a lot more defined than it was before high school, and felt echoes of the buzzing nerves that were my constant companion that summer. There's no question that Mateo is even better-looking now than he was back then, and he's been the strong, steady rock keeping me from melting down all morning. It would be easy to rekindle that crush under different circumstances.

I sneak a glance at Mateo, who's frowning. "Yeah, me nei-ther," he says. Which: ouch. "But it's not like I never mentioned it. I left you that note."

My breath catches. "What note?"

"At your house. With a pack of Sugar Babies." My eyes widen, and he huffs out a short laugh. "You never got those?"

"No," I say. Sugar Babies, my God.

Memories start flooding back, and suddenly it's like I'm thirteen years old again, walking with Mateo to my house from the corner store downtown. Cal wasn't around that day; I can't remember if he was busy, or if I hadn't invited him. Mateo had bought a bunch of candy and was already digging into it. "Skittle?" he asked, waving the open bag.

I made a face. "You know I hate Skittles."

"You're missing out. Give the red ones another shot. They're a lot better than Sugar Daddies."

"Sugar *Babies,*" I corrected him. It was a constant source of amusement to Mateo, back then, that the only candy I liked was a hundred years old and had a perverted name.

"Ivy Sterling-Shepard," Mateo said, shaking his head. He'd started using my full name when we were joking around, and it always gave me a little thrill. There was something almost flirty about it. "Why can't you ever try something new?"

"I try new things all the time." That was such a blatant lie that we both laughed.

"Come on." He held out a red Skittle. "Expand your world."

"Fine," I sighed, plucking it from his palm and popping it into my mouth. I grimaced the entire time I chewed the gritty, fake-fruit sweetness. "Thanks, I hate it," I finally said, swallowing. "Give me Sugar Babies any day."

"You're so random. You know you're the only person in the world who still eats those, right?" Mateo asked. We turned off the main road and onto a path leading into Bird Park, a shortcut to my house. It was late afternoon on a Saturday, and the usually bustling park was nearly empty. "They probably keep a single factory open just for you." He finished the last of his Skittles and dropped the crumpled bag into the larger plastic bag holding the rest of his haul, then rooted around for more. "Can I interest you in a Red Hot?"

"Ew. No," I said. We reached the swing set at the edge of the playground, and I hoisted myself onto one of the rubber seats. *The way-up one,* Daniel and I had called it when we were little. It was so much farther from the ground than the other swings, a kid couldn't dream of getting into it without an adult to help. Even now I had to jump, setting the swing in motion with the effort. "I've tried enough new things for one day," I added.

Mateo dropped his candy bag on the ground and then suddenly he was in front of me, steadying the swing's chains with his outstretched arms. "Are you sure?" he asked.

In the swing I was almost the same height as him, but not quite. His hands were just above mine on the chains, and our knees were nearly touching. My cheeks grew warm as I met his dark, questioning eyes. We'd had little moments like this for weeks, where we'd be talking like normal and then, without warning, the energy between us would shift into something new. I never knew what to do with that pulsing, buzzing feeling.

Until now. "No," I said, and then I leaned forward and kissed him. One of his hands released the chain to curl around the back of my neck, pulling me closer. He smelled like Tide detergent and cherry Skittles, which I no longer hated even a little.

As first kisses go, it was pretty great. Afterward we were both shy and embarrassed, but we couldn't stop smiling, either. I thought for sure it was the start of something, not the end. Until we never talked about it again.

At least, I thought we didn't.

"Sugar Babies?" I repeat now. The train rattles into Haymarket and comes to a stop, its doors opening with a loud hiss. "You left some for me?" Mateo nods, and I say, "I never got them. Where did you put them?"

"Inside the porch."

Our house has a screened-in porch that we never lock, leading to our actual front door. So if something was left there, the only person who would've taken it and not told me is . . . "Daniel," I say tightly. "I bet he snagged the candy and tossed the note. That *asshole*."

"Wow." Mateo shakes his head. "Well, that explains a lot. You don't usually, you know. *Not* talk about stuff."

"I would have at least thanked you!" *After jumping around for joy,* I think. Ugh, this is terrible. My entire high school experience could've been different. "I kept wondering why you acted like it never happened."

"*You* could've said something," Mateo points out.

He's right. I absolutely could have, if I weren't a writhing mass of angst and self-doubt back then. That was the year my parents finally decided to get Daniel tested for being gifted. I knew about it, of course, but Mom and Dad were very matter-of-fact about the results to our faces. I didn't understand how exceptional my brother was until I accidentally eavesdropped on my parents during one of my late-night refrigerator raids a few weeks later.

I was halfway down the stairs when I heard my mother

say, "It's a big responsibility, guiding a child this bright." There was the sound of shuffling paper, and then my mother added, "Sometimes I look at these results and wonder where on earth he came from. We're no slackers, James, but Daniel is . . ."

"Extraordinary," Dad finished. His voice held a note of wonder, like he'd just learned magic was real, and a hot spike of jealousy ran through me. I hadn't known, until right then, how much I would have liked my father to talk about me like that.

"He needs more of a challenge in school, obviously," Mom said. "No wonder he's been acting up this year. The poor thing is bored out of his mind, and with a mind like his—boredom is dangerous. But he's also still a kid. We shouldn't overschedule him, or isolate him from his peers. And of course, there's Ivy to consider." I held myself even stiller on the stairs, barely breathing as she added, "Ivy can't be made to feel less than."

I know it's the opposite of what my mother wanted, but as soon as she uttered the phrase, I felt exactly that.

And it continued all year. I could see through my parents' casual facade whenever they talked about Daniel skipping eighth grade to start high school with me, or when brochures started arriving about summer programs at MIT. Daniel was *extraordinary*, and I was *less than*. So when I thought Mateo was pretending our kiss had never happened, I was disappointed but not surprised. It felt inevitable.

The train continues to rattle along as Mateo waits for a response, but I can't give him that one. "What did the note say?" I ask instead.

"Huh?"

"You said you left a note, with the Sugar Babies? What did it say?"

"Oh. I asked if you wanted to get king-sized ones at the *Infinity War* premiere."

He'd asked me out. In such an impossibly cute way that I want to bang my head against the window. Not to mention, I ended up seeing *Infinity War* with Daniel, of all goddamn people. My extraordinary brother, thief of Sugar Babies and dreams.

"I would have," I mutter, slumping in my seat. I want to ask Mateo why he didn't follow up, but I'm pretty sure I already know. He might not have been having my crisis of confidence back then, but it's still excruciating to think that you put yourself out there and got nothing back. No wonder we stopped talking shortly after that.

"Next stop, Government Center," the conductor calls, and that snaps me back to the present. The last two stops were a blur, and we're running out of time before we lose Cal. "Oh no," I say, turning in my seat. "Do you think he's really leaving without us?"

"Looks like it," Mateo says as Cal stands.

I glance at the pile of notifications on my phone, and my heart drops. *Emily: Principal Nelson says the police are coming to school later.*

I know exactly what my classmates are going to tell them; and meanwhile, our only link to an *actual* suspect—one who's blond, knows Boney, and works in the studio where he died— is about to take off. "If we separate now, we're screwed," I say, getting to my feet.

Mateo, politely, doesn't point out that *I'm* the only one who's screwed. He just moves his legs into the aisle so I can slide past him.

I consider my options as I make my way toward Cal. I'm

still upset about what he said to me. I might not have the moral high ground all the time, especially lately, but I definitely had it for *this* argument. I want an apology, but if I lead with that, he'll blow me off. And maybe . . . it's possible . . . that I could have handled the conversation better.

You can be right in principle and still wrong in approach, Mom used to tell me when I'd get frustrated that other kids in student government wouldn't follow my lead. *Nobody likes to feel steamrolled.* I'd always brush her off, because I didn't understand the point of mincing words or wasting time when you knew what had to be done. Even when Boney beat me out for class president, I told myself that the problem wasn't me, it was my classmates. And him.

If I hadn't been such a sore loser, would today have gone differently? Would Boney have taken the election more seriously, and come to school today?

I blink rapidly to clear my stinging eyes before tapping Cal's arm. When he turns with a cool frown, I speak in a rush. "Cal, don't go, okay? Can we take a breather? I shouldn't have said what I did about you and . . ." He stiffens, and I swallow Ms. Jamison's name. "I shouldn't have said that. And maybe we shouldn't have followed you, but we were scared and worried and didn't know what else to do. I realize it was sneaky, though, and . . ."

Nope; I can't do it. I can't bring myself to say *I'm sorry* when the only thing I'm sorry about is getting yelled at by Cal. So I finish with "I won't do it again."

He's still frowning, eyes on the floor, but there's something less rigid about his posture. Maybe what I said earlier started to sink in while he was sitting by himself. Cal's an emotional, romantic guy, but he's also smart. He has to know on some level that what's happening with Ms. Jamison is wrong. Maybe he just needs someone to talk to about it.

"Could we get some food, maybe?" I ask. I never did eat breakfast, so my last meal was dinner last night. I can't tell if I'm light-headed from that or from the sheer stress of today, but I'm definitely starting to fade. "I think we're all hungry, and tired, and probably not thinking as clearly as we could be. I know I'm not."

Cal stares at the ground for a few beats longer. When he finally meets my eyes, his are regretful and more than a little relieved. "Yeah, okay," he says. "Now that you mention it, my blood sugar is probably pretty low." I smile, relief filling my chest, and Cal flushes. "So, um, listen. You and Mateo . . . I don't know why I brought that up, after all this time."

I'm not the only one who has trouble apologizing. "It's all right," I say. "Cleared the air." I turn toward Mateo, who's gotten up from his seat and is leaning against it, watching us. I signal for him to come over, and he starts heading our way as the train pulls into Government Center. "Where do you want to eat?" I ask.

"I have a place in mind," Cal says. He manages an almost smile as the train's brakes squeal. "Just promise me one thing, okay? No more surprises."

"Absolutely," I say.

I've already broken that promise, but we'll deal with that later.

11

MATEO

Cal takes us to some weird-ass doughnut place where nothing is regular-flavored. When we walk inside, we're immediately hit with a giant display of doughnut pictures, and they all look like they were put together by a toddler on a sugar high. I don't like doughnuts as a rule, and I like them even less when they're covered with cereal, meat products, or, in one case, a whole cayenne pepper. I'm staring at the pepper doughnut in fascinated horror when Cal passes me on his way to the cash register.

"I wouldn't start with that one," he advises, getting in line behind an older guy. Cal's mood shot up when we got here, so even though it's past lunchtime and I'd kill for real food, I guess we're getting doughnuts.

I scan the menu like it's the most interesting thing I've ever seen, because it's still too awkward to look at Cal. He and Ivy are making small talk about the menu, but all I can think is *What the hell happened back there?*

Cal is the last person I ever thought would get involved with a teacher, much less *that* teacher. I'll say one thing for Ms. Jamison—she looked genuinely shocked when all the Boney stuff came out. But apparently she's a good enough actress to fool the school and her fiancé, so who knows what she was really thinking.

While I watched them at the café, it hit me for the first time how lonely Cal must be. He doesn't have a brother or cousin at home like Ivy and me, and he hasn't mentioned any friends all day. I'm starting to think he's turned into the kind of guy who'd do whatever someone says and not ask questions, just so he could feel like he's part of something.

And I think Ms. Jamison knows that.

"What are you ordering?" Ivy asks, gazing around us. The whole place has a cartoony vibe; the tables are orange, the floors are multicolored tile, and a giant chandelier sprouting from the ceiling is hung with a dozen plastic doughnuts. The mirrored wall beside us has a funhouse effect that makes my head look like it's split in two, which is almost exactly how it feels. "I'm thinking about the blueberry cake doughnut," she continues. "It might have nutritional value, and there's nothing weird on top."

"I don't know," I say, my eyes straying out the window. There's too much visual stimulation everywhere else. Including Ivy.

I'm almost as rattled by our conversation on the train as I was about Cal and Ms. Jamison. It's like I have to rearrange my whole perception of Ivy to fit what actually happened when we were in middle school, instead of what I believed. I meant what I said on the train; it's not like I spend time thinking about that kiss. Not anymore. But Ivy was the first girl I'd ever asked out, and it stung that she ignored me. If I'm being honest, the memory of that made me more impatient with her earlier than I would've been otherwise, and it's probably why, as Autumn likes to remind me, I bail at the first sign of rejection. Not just from girls, but anyone or anything. I've been like that for so long that I never really thought about how or why it started.

And now I know: it started with a misunderstanding. I don't know what to do with that.

Shove it down, Autumn's voice says in my head. She and I have a running joke about my dad; how any time something happens that he doesn't know how to handle, he just—doesn't. He shoves it so far down in his mental space that it might as well not exist. Which is one of the many reasons he's never seemed like much of an adult. It didn't occur to him, for example, that he should give Autumn a home when his brother died, or take a break from living his roadie dreams once Ma got sick.

As jokes go, it's not actually funny, but it's still solid advice for now. "I'll probably get the same thing you are," I tell Ivy.

"My treat," Cal says. Guess we're forgiven. "If you want, we could—"

"Well, hello there, Cal!" The woman behind the cash register interrupts him with a big grin. She's middle-aged with streaked blue hair, wearing a Ramones T-shirt and cat's-eye glasses. "Back so soon? What are you doing here in the middle of the day?"

Ivy shoots me a nervous look at their familiarity as Cal says, "Hi, Viola. Just getting a snack. I'll have two blueberry cakes and one hazelnut bacon, please."

"Coming right up," Viola says, turning to the rows of doughnuts behind her.

Ivy leans into Cal and hisses, "Why did you bring us

someplace where they know you?" Her eyes are huge and re-proachful. "We haven't figured out our stories. You might end up telling people that you were really home sick all day!"

"Viola's cool," Cal says, digging into his pocket for his bank card. Ivy looks unconvinced, and he adds, "Really, don't worry about it. She's anti the Man. Not a fan of authority figures at all. You wouldn't believe how many health violations this place gets."

"Seriously?" Ivy asks in a loud whisper. "Then why are we eating here?"

"Hang on," Cal says. He pays for the doughnuts and accepts a white paper bag from Viola, who gives Ivy and me a curious look. Almost like she thinks she knows us, but can't remember where from.

"Come back soon, Cal," she says. "And bring your friends."

"I will," Cal says, snatching a bunch of napkins from the counter before turning toward the door. He holds it open for Ivy and adds in a low voice, "Not health violations because it's dirty or anything. They're just really creative with their toppings. Sometimes it's not technically food, so the city throws a fit."

"Do I even want to know?" I ask as we step onto the side-walk.

"Probably not," Cal says, handing us our doughnuts and a couple of napkins each. I take a huge bite of mine and it's better than expected; moist and packed with fresh blueberries, along with some kind of lemony cream. I'm hungry enough that I eat the entire thing before we've even reached the crosswalk. Ivy, who's barely taken two bites of hers, notices.

"Want some?" She waves her doughnut with a small smile, and something tugs at my chest. It's been comfortable being low-key annoyed with Ivy all these years, telling myself I dodged a bullet because she's an overly intense pain in the ass, and not even all that cute. That last one's not true, though, and the first one?

True, but it never bothered me.

"Nah, that's okay," I say. "I'll get something else later." The sugar must be working its magic, because the headache I've had since we entered Ms. Jamison's studio is finally starting to fade. I pat the left pocket of my jeans and add, "Listen, you guys. We still need to do something about Boney's phone."

"Oh, right." Ivy scans our surroundings as we walk. "The studio's not far from here, is it? What if we keep going in that general direction and just—leave it nearby? And then call in a tip. With a pay phone, maybe? Do they still have those?"

Cal looks worried. "I don't think we want to go back there," he says.

"Not *back* there," Ivy corrects. "*Near* there."

"And then what?" I ask. I'm finally thinking clearly enough that it occurs to me that I could just . . . go home. I have a reported absence, and no reason anyone should doubt it. There's nothing I can do for Boney except figure out a way to hand over his phone. Ivy and Cal might have things they need to explain to the police, but I don't.

And I can't take the chance of winding up in front of them.

"Why is it so crowded?" Cal asks. I blink, pulling my thoughts back to the present, and realize he's right. The sidewalk has gotten progressively more congested, to the point that we suddenly find ourselves stuck behind a knot of people.

Ivy cranes her neck. "Is that a news camera?" she asks.

I'm the only one tall enough to see over the crowd. As I take in the scene in front of us, I catch sight of the reporter we saw

117

on TV this morning at Garrett's. He looks like he's doing some kind of person-on-the-street interview, microphone extended toward a guy in a Patriots baseball cap. "It's what's-his-name—Dave something?" I say. "That reporter you know."

"Dale Hawkins?" Ivy freezes, eyes wide. "Oh no. We need to leave."

As soon as she says the words, a bunch of things happen one after the other. The people in front of us move away, the interview concludes, and Dale Hawkins's gaze shifts from the guy in the Patriots hat, to the camera, and then to the crowd. Where it lands directly on Ivy.

Recognition dawns on his face, and Ivy doesn't hesitate another second. She spins on her heel and takes off in the opposite direction, ponytail flying.

"Hey!" Dale Hawkins calls. Cal starts running after Ivy, looking over his shoulder the whole way, and I try to melt into the background. Dale strides forward a few steps, the camera guy in tow, but people are milling around too much for him to get very far before Ivy and Cal disappear around a corner. I duck behind a streetlight that does nothing to hide me, probably looking even more ridiculous than Cal did this morning, as Dale gazes after them.

"I know that girl," he tells his camera guy. Oh hell.

He doesn't spare a glance for me, though. Within minutes he's interviewing an old woman, and another small crowd of pedestrians gather around him. "In my day, this kind of thing didn't happen," the woman says loudly.

The urge to go home hits me again, harder than ever. What did Ivy say I had this morning? A sore throat? Sure, that'll work. I pull out my phone to find Carmen's last text, so I can tell her

I've been home sick all day. Carmen is one of those social connector types who knows everyone; within half an hour, my story will be set. Ivy and Cal will understand. Maybe they can figure out how to disappear from this mess, too.

Besides, it's not like the three of us are some kind of team. Not anymore. We don't owe one another anything.

Then a message from Ivy flashes across my screen. *We're back at the doughnut place.*

Before I can figure out how to explain that I'm cutting my losses and going home, she adds, *I'm going to show Cal what we found at the café.* I grimace, because there's no way that'll go well, as Ivy adds, *I need to move things along in case Dale Hawkins recognized me.*

I briefly debate telling her that he definitely did. But that'll freak her out, and for what? The guy already turned his attention someplace else. Instead, I type, *I gotta bail.* Then I delete it, because that's too abrupt even for me.

I need to leave . . . No. Not much better.

Look, I'm sorry, but . . .

With a sigh, I give up and stuff my phone back into my pocket. The least I can do is tell them in person.

I get to Crave Doughnuts just as Ivy's about to go all-in.

She and Cal are sitting side by side in a booth, a weird quirk of theirs that I've never understood. Why sit next to somebody when there's only two of you? I drop down across from them and she's saying, "So, Cal," her voice barely above a whisper, even though the place is deserted except for the cashier who served us before. "I should preface this by saying that I realize this was a sneaky thing to do and also, technically, illegal. But I think we should look through it with an open mind in case there's any information that could help us understand this mess."

"Huh?" Cal's face is a total blank, and I don't blame him. I know what Ivy's talking about, and I still found that confusing.

She reaches into her bag and pulls out a small black notebook with the words *Day Planner* embossed in gold on the front. "We took this from Ms. Jamison's bag in the café," she says. "And I think we should see what's in here."

"You did what?" Cal blinks as she opens the planner. "Hold up. Is that . . . did you . . . are you guys the ones who took her bag at the café?"

"Temporarily," Ivy says, giving him a wary look. He seems more shell-shocked than angry, which is an improvement over the train.

"But how . . . I would have seen you!" Cal says.

"I grabbed it after Mateo knocked a bunch of dishes over. Remember that?" Ivy says. "Then I took it into the bathroom and looked through it, and saw this." She taps a page in the planner. "My dad has one like it, and he puts his entire life in there. So I figured, why not take a look?"

"Why not take a look?" Cal repeats disbelievingly. "Maybe because it's stolen property?"

"I did mention that as a flaw in the plan," Ivy reminds him.

"What *plan*?" Cal asks, his voice rising. "What's the point of this?"

"Shhh," Ivy hisses. Viola looks up, seems to decide that we could use some privacy, and opens a door behind her. I catch a glimpse of kitchen appliances before she slips inside and closes the door.

"Cal, listen," I say, because chances are good Ivy's only going to make things worse if she keeps talking. "You're right. It was a bonehead move." I don't look at Ivy when I say that, but I can hear her light snort of indignation. "But it's already done. And you can't blame us for thinking Ms. Jamison knows more than she's saying. Bottom line is, Boney died in her studio."

"It's not *her* studio," Cal points out. "She borrows it from a friend. So do other people. And there are new owners, so . . ." He puts up his hands at Ivy's epic eye roll. "I'm just saying, lots of people have access to that space, and—"

"Do any of them know Boney?" Ivy interrupts, and that shuts him up.

I glance at the planner in Ivy's hand. Now that it's right in front of me, I have to admit that I'm curious. "Come on, Cal, let's just take a look. If there's nothing there, then we're assholes."

"You're already assholes," Cal mutters, but he doesn't try to grab the planner, or take off. It seems like all the fight's drained out of him, and I think I was right earlier: the guy is lonely as hell. If he wasn't, he wouldn't keep going to the mat to defend Ms. Jamison. Ivy and I might be assholes, but right now, we're the only friends he has.

"All right then," Ivy says, flipping a page. "I'll start at the beginning."

I can't see much from where I'm sitting, and Cal's not looking, so for a few minutes it's just Ivy turning pages and muttering to herself. She's obviously not finding anything interesting, or she'd be waving it in our faces.

"Exciting reading?" Cal finally asks, almost sounding amused.

"Her handwriting is incomprehensible," Ivy complains. "It's like she's intentionally making this difficult." She flips a page, and something rectangular slips out of one side. "Hmm," she says, pulling it out the rest of the way.

"What is it?" I ask.

"Looks like a card," Ivy says, holding the front toward me. It's a painting of flowers overgrowing a building. "Pretty," she says, flipping the card back toward her and Cal. "Looks impressionist."

"The Garden at Bougival," Cal says. "By Berthe Morisot. It's Lara's favorite painting."

Ivy raises her eyebrows, like she's clocking his use of Ms. Jamison's first name, but all she says is "Let's see if there's anything inside." She opens it, clears her throat, and reads, *"Love you so much, angel. Let's make it happen, D."* As soon as the words are out of her mouth, her cheeks turn pink and she darts a glance at Cal. "Um," she says. "So that's . . ."

Cal looks nauseated. "Probably from Coach Kendall."

Ivy gives him a tight smile. "Coach Kendall's first name is Tom," she says.

"Maybe it's a nickname. Or the card is old," Cal says. "Like from college or something." His face is—God. He really shouldn't be surprised at the possibility that Ms. Jamison has more than one guy on the side, but he clearly is, and it sucks to watch.

"Maybe," Ivy says, looking supremely unconvinced. She closes the card and slips it back inside Ms. Jamison's day planner. "Let's file that away for—"

"Hang on," I interrupt as something catches my eye. Loose paper is poking out of the back of the book, and I grab hold of its corner and pull. It's a thin sheaf of paper, stapled in one corner and folded twice. I unfold it and read the heading: "*Carlton High Senior Class Roster.* Alphabetical order, looks like. Zack Abrams, Makayla Austin . . ."

"Let me see," Ivy says. She plucks it from my hand and scans the first page. Then she flips to the second, and sucks in a sharp breath. "Boney's name is circled."

"It is?" Cal and I both lean forward, and Ivy flips the paper between us. Sure enough: *Brian Mahoney* is ringed with bold red ink. "That's weird," Cal says, his mouth tightening.

Ivy takes the roster back and turns the page. There's another name circled near the bottom, but I can't read it upside down. "*Charlie St. Clair,*" she says with a perplexed frown. "Why would Ms. Jamison circle him?"

I stare at the sheet of paper. Charlie isn't a guy I cross paths with often at Carlton High. He's a jock, and he has an older brother who throws a lot of parties and is friends with Loser Gabe. He has a surfer-guy vibe, complete with an ever-present puka shell necklace, even though he's spent his whole life in landlocked Carlton.

I never thought there was much more to Charlie St. Clair than that. And I wouldn't think so now, either, if the name *Charlie* hadn't flashed across Autumn's screen this morning while we were standing on the porch having our ears assaulted by Loser Gabe.

Is he one of them? I'd asked.

The less you know, the better, she'd said.

I'm not sure what it means that there's suddenly a connection between Boney, the woman whose studio he died in, and someone named Charlie. Maybe nothing.

Maybe everything.

"Is Charlie into art?" Ivy asks Cal. My poker face must be working, because neither of them are paying any attention to me.

He shakes his head. "I don't think so. I've never had a class with him, anyway. Is he friends with Boney?"

"No," Ivy says with the firmness of someone who's held enough class offices to know the school's social dynamics by heart.

"Okay, well, that's random." Cal taps the edge of the paper. "This page ends with Tessa Sutton. Is there another one?"

"Yeah," Ivy says, flipping again.

There's only a quarter page of names, the last of the alphabet. I see another red circle right away, but once again, I can't read the name. Ivy and Cal exchange startled glances, though, so it must mean something to them.

"Who is it?" I ask.

Ivy turns the paper so it's facing me. *"Mateo Wojcik,"* she says.

12

CAL

The sun slips behind a cloud outside, darkening our corner of Crave Doughnuts as Ivy pins Mateo with her gaze and asks, "Why would Ms. Jamison circle your name?"

"No clue," Mateo says.

He looks like he means it, but the thing about Mateo is—unlike Ivy, the guy can lie. Or he could, anyway, back when we used to hang out. Ms. Reyes is one of those super-involved moms who's always up in your business, and Mateo was constantly blocking her. We weren't trying to get away with much—just normal kid stuff, like watching movies we shouldn't and eating too much junk—but he'd never get caught.

"She circled you, Charlie, and *Boney*," Ivy points out.

"Yeah. I saw." Mateo shrugs. "I don't know why."

I should say something, but I can't focus. I'm still fixated on the "D" card that was in Lara's day planner. It wasn't addressed to her by name, but I can't convince myself that it wasn't hers.

Whoever gave it to her knows her well enough to be familiar with her favorite painting, which isn't nearly famous enough to be sold in every random card store the way that, say, Monet's *Water Lilies* are. You'd have to really search for it. It's the kind of thing I would have done, if it had ever occurred to me to send Lara a card.

Love you so much, angel. Let's make it happen. Half of my brain is making excuses for why those words probably don't mean anything, and the other half is frantically analyzing who D might be. There's something pressing against the edge of my subconscious, whispering that I already know the answer, and it's frustrating as hell because I *don't*.

At least, I don't think I do.

I glance at the list in Ivy's hand; there's not a D to be found in any of the circled names. Still . . . Boney, Charlie, and Mateo all have what Lara would probably call "interesting faces." My jealousy from this morning flares up again as I imagine Lara sketching Boney in her studio. And maybe Charlie, and . . . ugh.

Please not Mateo.

"Oh my God," Ivy says in a low whisper, eyes huge. "What if this is her *kill* list?"

"*What?*" I blink, startled, then flush when I realize what completely different tracks our minds were running along.

Ivy tilts her head toward Mateo, oblivious to my confusion. "Why are you on here? What does Ms. Jamison have against you?"

"Nothing," he says. "I told you, I've never even taken her class."

"There must be something," she insists. "Some connection between you and Charlie and Boney. Are you and Charlie friends? Or acquaintances, or—anything?"

"No," Mateo says. My eyes flick between them like I'm watching a ping-pong match, and I get the same feeling that the D card gives me: I'm missing something. "Maybe the list doesn't mean anything," Mateo continues. "Maybe it's some kind of school thing, and it's just a coincidence that Boney's name is on there."

Ivy frowns. "I don't see how that's possible. Because it's not only the list. It's also the fact that she's a blond woman, and she uses the studio on Tuesdays—"

"But she wasn't there," I protest, even though I'm no longer sure who I'm trying to convince. Ivy and Mateo, or myself? "She had a ceramics class."

"A ceramics class," Ivy repeats, her voice flat.

"Yeah. That's what she told me."

"Oh, is that what she told you?" Ivy's lip curls. "Well, I guess that's that, then. We'll just take her word for it, since she's such an honest person."

"She *showed* me." I pull out my phone and scroll to the picture of the green bowl, holding it up to Ivy. "She texted this from her class, when we first got to Garrett's."

"Pssh." Ivy barely glances at it. "She could've had that saved on her phone. Or grabbed it off an image search."

"Why would she lie about something that's so easy to check?" I counter.

Ivy arches her eyebrows. "And *did* you check?"

"I don't mean *me*," I say defensively. "Since when am I in charge of alibis?"

She opens her mouth to answer, but a ringing phone cuts her off. The sound is coming from somewhere in our booth, but it's not mine. Ivy doesn't reach for her bag, so it's clearly not hers, either. We both look toward Mateo, expectant.

He pales as he reaches into his pocket and pulls out a black case that's . . . *ohhh*. My pulse quickens as I recognize the phone I took from Lara's studio, thinking it was Ivy's.

The one that probably belongs to Boney.

"Answer it!" Ivy says. Mateo just keeps holding the phone gingerly, like he's afraid it's going to explode. I pluck it out of his hand as Ivy leans against me for a look at the caller's name. She gasps, and I almost drop the phone.

Charlie.

I swipe to answer and say, "Hello?" I don't mean to do it, exactly, but somehow the word comes out in Boney's signature drawl.

"Boney!" A voice, pitched high and panicky, floods my ear. "Holy shit, man, I never thought I'd be this glad to talk to you. People have been saying you're *dead*. What the hell happened over there? Did the guy ever show?"

"Um." I have no idea what to say next. Ivy mouths something I can't understand, and I wave her away so I can think. "Um, is this Charlie St. Clair?" I ask.

For a few seconds, all I can hear from the other end is ragged breathing. "Why are you asking me that?" Charlie asks in a more normal tone, and now I recognize him. Even when he's freaking out, he sounds like the turtle in *Finding Nemo*.

"Yeah, so, here's the thing. This isn't Boney—" I start.

"Shit!" Charlie interrupts with a strangled half scream, and abruptly hangs up.

"Charlie, wait!" I say into the dead phone. Then I lower it, hoping I can somehow get him back, but now that he's disconnected, Boney's screen is locked again. "Damn it," I say, frustration mounting as I fruitlessly swipe at the screen. "He's gone."

"Let me see," Ivy says. I hand her Boney's phone, and she

says, "Mateo, you tried 1-2-3-4 as a passcode, right?" He nods. "Anything else?"

"No," Mateo says.

"Maybe his name." Ivy mutters *B-O-N-E-Y* as she presses the keypad, then frowns and shakes her head. "No luck. Cal, what did Charlie say?"

I replay our short conversation word for word, as best I can remember. I'm positive that I have at least one part right: Charlie asking, *Did the guy ever show?* I try to say it neutrally, like it doesn't mean anything, even while my brain flashes with additional context.

The guy. Not "she." Not Lara.

I don't want to push that onto Ivy and Mateo. If I do, they might think I only heard what I wanted to hear—or worse, that I'm lying. But relief is already coursing through me at the thought that Boney wasn't there to see Lara. She might've lied to me about a lot of things, but she didn't lie about that.

"I thought you said Boney and Charlie weren't friends," I say to Ivy.

"They're not," she says. "I'm sure of it. Anyway, it sounds like that call was specifically about this morning, doesn't it? Like Charlie knew Boney was going to be at the studio to meet someone. But it doesn't seem as though he's told anyone else, because no one at school is gossiping about it. Plus, both of them had their names circled by Ms. Jamison, so . . . I think we need to talk to Charlie. He's the only person who might be able to make sense of all this. Since the *third* name on the list insists that he can't." She shoots Mateo a sideways look. "Unless that's changed? Have you thought of anything that might be useful?"

"No," he says.

Ivy doesn't press him, and I don't understand why. It's not like she let me get away with anything when it came to Lara. I know Ivy had that huge crush on Mateo years ago, but that can't be the only reason she's so careful around him.

She picks up her phone and glances between us. "Do either of you have Charlie's number?"

"No." Mateo and I say it in unison this time.

"Hmm," she says. "Maybe my brother does. They hang in the same circles, and used to play some of the same sports before Daniel decided to concentrate on lacrosse." She swipes at her phone and grimaces. "Oh God, I have so many texts from Daniel. He's *loving* the gossip." She lowers her voice in an imitation of her brother, reading from her screen. "*Are you a murderer y/n. Should I tell M&D you might be a murderer y/y. Have you fled the country?* So hilarious, Daniel. This is all such a fun joke."

"You sure you want to talk to him right now?" Mateo asks.

"No," Ivy says, stabbing at her phone. "But I don't know anyone else who might have Charlie's number. I'm not going to tell him anything."

She's barely finished texting when her phone rings. "Is it Daniel?" I ask, surprised. "Isn't he in class now? It's past lunch, right?"

"Yeah. It must be anarchy over there." Ivy squeezes her eyes shut briefly. "I hope I don't regret this." She accepts the call and presses the phone to her ear. "Hi."

I scrunch closer to her and hear Daniel ask, "What—and I cannot stress this enough—the *fuck* is going on with you?"

Ivy rubs her temple. "I can't get into that right now. Do you happen to know Charlie St. Clair's number?"

"Excuse me?" Even though it's faint, I can hear the outraged sarcasm in Daniel's voice. "Let me get this straight. You skip school the day Boney Mahoney gets murdered, you match the description of the suspect, you won't answer anyone's texts all day—and now you want *Charlie St. Clair's phone number?*"

"Yes," Ivy says. "Do you have it?"

"Are you out of your mind? Tell me what's going on."

"So you *don't* have it?"

"Maybe I do, but I'm not giving you anything without an explanation," Daniel says peevishly. Ivy rolls her eyes and mouths *He doesn't have it* as her brother's voice takes on a warning tone. "Anyway, that guy's trouble. Stay away from him."

"Why is he trouble?" Ivy asks.

"He just is."

Before Ivy can respond, her phone buzzes. She lowers it to read the text on her screen, and I look down, too.

Emily: Charlie St. Clair just up and LEFT SCHOOL. Walked right out. Everyone here is falling apart.

Emily: I'm going to keep texting you updates, whether you answer me or not.

Emily: Please answer me.

Ivy makes a worried sound and puts the phone back to her ear. Daniel kept talking while we were reading Emily's texts, but I couldn't make out anything he said. "Okay, well, I guess there's nothing left to discuss," Ivy interrupts. "Except, by the way, you were a jerk for taking my Sugar Babies from the porch in eighth grade." Daniel squawks something else, and Ivy adds, "Don't give me that. You know what you did."

"Sugar Babies?" I ask as she disconnects.

"Mateo left them for me," Ivy says, a pink tinge washing over her cheeks. I glance at Mateo, who's suddenly very interested in the doughnut menu. "At my house, after we, um. Briefly hooked up. I just found out about it on the train when you . . . said what you said."

"Ahh," I say, swallowing hard. When I threw a hissy fit, she means. I'd rather not revisit any of that right now. "So Daniel doesn't have Charlie's number, right? And Charlie took off anyway?"

Mateo frowns. "Took off?"

"Emily said he walked out of school," Ivy says, her tone businesslike once again. "It must've been right after Cal answered Boney's phone." She bites her thumbnail. "I wonder if he went home? Maybe we should try to talk with him in person. The St. Clairs live in our neighborhood, a couple of streets over."

"It's as good a plan as any," I say. Lara hasn't checked in since I left the café, even though she's had plenty of time to figure out . . . what had she said? *Where we land.*

Well, it looks like we're landing with Charlie St. Clair. If Lara wanted something different, she could've let me know before now.

"I'm starving. I need more food first," Mateo says. "Real food," he adds, giving me a look like he was expecting me to recommend a doughnut. Which, to be fair, I was. "There's a McDonald's across the street. You guys want something?"

"No thanks," Ivy says.

My stomach is way too knotted to eat anything else. "I'm good."

"Okay. I'll meet you outside." He stands and picks up

Boney's phone from the table. "We should probably shut this down until we figure out how to get it to the police. They might be tracking it."

Jesus, I hadn't even thought about that. Something new and fun to worry about. "Maybe we can leave it with Charlie," I suggest, glancing at Ivy. She's absorbed in reassembling everything she took out of Lara's day planner, with the single-minded focus of someone who can't deal with another piece of stressful information.

"Yeah, maybe," Mateo says. He leaves as Viola returns from the back room with a cloth in one hand. She starts wiping down the counter, sending the occasional thoughtful look our way. I'm debating whether I should go over and make small talk, like I would under normal circumstances, when my phone rings for the first time all day.

It's Wes, because of course it is. Who else would call me?

I briefly consider letting it go to voicemail, but my dad wouldn't call during a school day unless he either knows I skipped or knows about Boney. Neither of those will get better with age. I swipe to answer and say, "Hey, Dad."

"Cal, hello." His voice fills my ear, rich with concern, and my throat tightens. "I heard about your classmate. What terrible news. Your father and I are both devastated." Wes must've given Henry a heads-up before he called me, because no way would Henry come across this news on his own. He's the opposite of plugged in, and still uses a flip phone. "Are you all right?"

"I'm okay. Just kind of in shock, I guess."

"It's such a tragedy. I can only imagine what his poor parents are going through. How are your friends?"

"Oh, you know." I glance at Ivy, who's slung her bag over her shoulder and is perched at the edge of the booth, watching me. "As well as can be expected."

"Does the school have resources set up for you? Are there people you can talk to?"

"Um . . ." Up to this point, I haven't directly lied to him about being at school, which for some reason feels like an important distinction. "I don't need to talk to anyone, Dad."

"But you should, Cal. Even if you don't think you need to."

"I'll just talk to you when you get home."

"I could come home early. I have a donor meeting, but I can move it."

"No!" I practically yell the word, then force my voice lower. "I mean, thanks, but I think a normal routine is best right now. I'd rather talk tonight."

"But we've got that award ceremony," Wes says.

Oh Christ. The Carlton Citizen of the Year Award, where Ivy's mom is receiving the town's highest honor. I'm sure it won't come up at any point during the festivities that half my classmates think her daughter murdered Boney Mahoney. "After that is fine," I say.

"If you're sure," Wes says doubtfully. "It's no problem to cancel my meeting."

"I'm positive. Meet with the donors. Get that coin." Oh God. What am I even saying? I need to end this call, immediately. "I'd better go, but thanks for checking in."

"Of course. Let me know if you need anything. Love you."

"You too," I mumble. I feel like a complete asshole when I hang up, and Ivy's sympathetic look doesn't make it any better.

"Your dad is so nice," she says, getting to her feet.

"I know," I sigh. Viola tosses me another concerned look, and I give her what I hope passes for a carefree wave. "So long, Viola."

She doesn't look as though she buys it. "Take care."

"We will," I say, and beat a hasty retreat out the door.

Silence falls once Ivy and I are on the sidewalk outside, and I consider how best to fill it. I'm still bothered by our fight on the train; not only about all the harsh things I said, but about the things I *didn't* say. I owe Ivy a different conversation, and even though the thought of it makes me want to throw up, this is probably the time to have it. "So, listen," I say. "About all that stuff I said on the train—"

"It's fine," Ivy says quickly. "I don't want to talk about it."

I glance at her tense face, trying to gauge that response. "Don't want to talk about what?" I ask. "What I said, or about you and Mateo?"

"There *is* no me and Mateo," Ivy says, going red. Which is more of an answer than she probably meant to give.

"You still like him," I say, feeling like an idiot for not seeing it sooner. Of course she does; that's why she's treating him with such kid gloves. "And he . . ." The day unfolds for me differently all of a sudden, as I think about the dozen or so ways that Mateo has taken care of Ivy since we first got to Boston—and not just by literally carrying her, although he did that, too. He's always watching out for her or backing her up, looking at her with a focused, intense expression like whatever she's saying is the most important thing he's ever heard. Even when she's being a gigantic pain in the ass. Wes likes to say that Henry can't talk about his feelings, so you have to pay attention to how he shows them. Mateo is the same way. "He likes you, too."

I expect Ivy to smile, but instead her mouth tightens. "No, he doesn't."

"I think he does. This might not be the right time or place, but—"

"It's not just that. There's other stuff," Ivy starts, then clams up as Mateo emerges from McDonald's, white bag in hand. Instead of heading our way, though, he ducks into the 7-Eleven next door. She relaxes against the wall, adding, "*Now* what is he getting? How much food does one person need?"

"This is Mateo, remember?" I say. "The guy is a bottomless pit. I should've known better than to offer him doughnuts for lunch." Ivy just nods, and I lightly tap her arm with the back of my hand. "So . . . what other stuff?"

"Hmm?" she asks.

"Between you and Mateo."

"Oh." She waits a beat, eyes on the ground. "It's nothing."

"It didn't sound like *nothing*," I insist, suddenly curious. The Ivy I used to know wouldn't avoid this conversation; she'd analyze every last detail until I begged for mercy. But then the door to 7-Eleven opens, and Mateo steps onto the sidewalk. "To be continued," I add.

"Or not," Ivy mutters.

Mateo comes up to us with his McDonald's bag in one hand, and something that's small and yellow in the other. "Better late than never," he says, holding it out to Ivy.

It's a pack of Sugar Babies, and she practically melts into the ground as she takes it.

YOUTUBE, CARLTON SPEAKS CHANNEL

Ishaan and Zack are in Ishaan's car once again.

ZACK: Hey, it's Zack Abrams and Ishaan Mittal, reporting live for the second time today because basically no one is going to class anymore.

ISHAAN: They should just send us home.

ZACK: Seriously. Anyway, we're back with a special guest who . . . Emily, you wanna say hi? *(A dark-haired girl comes into focus from the back seat, her expression serious.)*

EMILY, *flatly:* Hi.

ISHAAN: So, Emily Zhang is the alleged best friend of Ivy Sterling-Shepard—

ZACK: She's not alleged. She's her actual friend.

ISHAAN: Right. I meant to say, Emily is the best friend of alleged murder suspect—

EMILY, *leaning forward:* Okay, this is why I'm here. You guys are being so irresponsible. You can't throw Ivy's name around like this, just because she's absent and she didn't get along with Boney.

ISHAAN: Hey, facts are facts.

EMILY: Well, if you're so interested in facts, you should talk about everyone at Carlton High who's not in school today. Who *else* isn't here?

(Ishaan ducks out of camera view as Zack frowns.)

ZACK: What difference does that make? If they don't, like, have some kind of documented problem with Boney?

EMILY: It's comprehensive reporting. And Ivy doesn't have a "documented problem" with Boney. She lost an election to him, that's all. Anyone would be upset. She probably just took the day off.

ZACK: Would you say it's in character for Ivy to take a day off?

EMILY: Well, no, but—

ISHAAN, *popping back into camera range:* You guys, I just checked our stats. We're doing some serious numbers.

ZACK: Huh?

ISHAAN: Like triple our usual views. No, wait . . . *(Ducks out of view again, then reappears.)* Quadruple.

ZACK: Really?

ISHAAN: We're trending, baby. Okay, not trending, exactly, but almost five hundred people are watching this.

EMILY, *eyes widening:* Oh God.

13

IVY

My thoughts are a messy tangle on the drive back to Carlton. My practical side reminds me that I have much bigger problems to deal with right now than the question of whether Mateo bought the Sugar Babies as a friendly joke, or something more. My inner twelve-year-old doesn't care about that, and is screeching in heart-eye emojis. But my conscience is louder than either of them, and keeps repeating the same thing, over and over and over:

You have to tell him.

It's not like I haven't thought about it, even before this disaster of a day. I've been in knots ever since I got back from Scotland and realized the domino effect of what I'd done last June. I tried to make up for it, in a roundabout way. When I still had distance from Mateo, as someone I hadn't talked to in years, it seemed like that might be enough. But now I know that it was nothing but cowardice—a convenient lie I told myself to avoid doing something that felt impossibly hard.

Shame inches up my spine and makes me squirm in my seat. I've been judging Cal all day, almost relishing the fact that his relationship with Ms. Jamison is so clearly, unequivocally *wrong*. It didn't occur to me, until just now, that focusing on Ms. Jamison's bad behavior has been a highly effective way to ignore my own.

I can't even enjoy my Sugar Babies. I'm trying, because I don't want Mateo to think I'm ungrateful, but they taste like chewy cardboard. He and Cal have been sharing sour gummies for the entire drive and, as usual, Cal is carrying the bulk of the conversation.

"Have either of your parents checked in?" he asks, taking the Carlton exit off the highway. It's just past one-thirty in the afternoon, so we've barely hit any traffic on our way home.

"Mine are on a plane," I remind him. I don't add *for another four hours,* but I'm definitely thinking it. It's okay, though. Four hours is more than enough time to stop school gossip about me from spreading any further. Especially if Charlie can provide the kind of connection between Ms. Jamison and Boney that will send the police after her. For one brief, shining moment, I fantasize that he's already done exactly that, and the next update on Boston.com will be a picture of her in handcuffs.

Sure, it's far-fetched. But if something even close to that happened, then Boney would get the justice he deserves without Cal, Mateo, and me having to tell anyone we'd been inside the studio. This entire day could simply—go away. I'd get home early, take a desperately needed nap, and still have plenty of time to get ready for the award ceremony: shower, straighten my hair, put on makeup, and make sure all the tiny buttons on my complicated Belgian dress are fastened properly. The thought sends a fizzy burst of relief flooding through me, and my Sugar Babies suddenly taste good again.

"My mom's in the Bronx," Mateo says. "Thank God. If she was at work, she would've already left to barge into school and check up on me. You know how she is."

I do, and he's right. She's a total mama bear. Mateo has loomed over her since he was twelve, but I'd still pick her in a fight.

"Where's your mom working now?" Cal asks.

I turn in my seat to face Mateo as he says, "Couple different places, but mostly she's at Jeff Chalmers. You know, the car dealership on Spring Street? She does admin stuff for them."

"Does she like it there?" Cal asks.

Mateo shrugs. "It's a job. It's easy, physically. She needs easy right now." He gazes out the window, like that's all he has to say, but then he adds, "She has osteoarthritis, so she can't move all that well without medication."

"She has *what*?" I almost choke on my last Sugar Baby. I can't imagine Mateo's mother, always so energetic and vibrant, being slowed down by the same disease my grandpa Sterling has. "When did that happen?"

"What's osteoarthritis?" Cal adds.

"Joint disease," Mateo says, the corners of his mouth turning down. "She has a lot of pain and stiffness in her knees. People don't usually get it till they're old, so her doctor's not sure why it happened. He said it might have something to do with an old softball injury, or it might just be bad luck. There's medicine that helps, but she doesn't always . . . take it when she's supposed to." He pauses and lifts his shoulders in another shrug, like he's surprised at himself for telling us. I know I am. It takes a lot for Mateo to open up, especially about family stuff. He's always been fiercely protective of anything related to his mother and Autumn, including their privacy.

Then he meets my eyes and adds, "She was diagnosed in July. Right after Spare Me got sued. *That* was a shitty month."

Oh my God oh my God oh my God. My stomach fills with lead, and it feels heavy enough to sink me through the bottom of Cal's car and splatter me onto the road. For a second, I wish it would.

You have to tell him.

No. I cannot *possibly* tell him now.

"Oh wow, I'm sorry," Cal says earnestly. "Your mom is the best. It sucks she has to deal with that."

"But . . ." The words stick in my throat, and I have to force them out. "But my dad met with her in August, and he never said . . . he didn't mention . . ."

I think back to that night, when I'd been waiting so anxiously at home to see how Dad's meeting with Ms. Reyes went. He'd loved my idea of getting her involved in the new property, and told me that she'd seemed excited about it, too. "Ultimately, it might be a nice change from running a small business," he'd said. "Things must have been tight for a while for her to be so underinsured. She seemed a little worn down."

I'd chalked that up to the stress of the lawsuit, which was bad enough. It hadn't occurred to me that Ms. Reyes might be dealing with health issues, too. Now the multiple jobs Mateo's mentioned offhandedly throughout the day take on a different meaning. It's not that he *wants* to commute into Boston to work at Garrett's; it's that he feels like he has to.

"She doesn't talk about it much," Mateo says. He gives me a small, tired smile that's more of a grimace. "And she was sitting down the whole time your dad was at our house. No reason he'd have guessed anything was wrong."

"Mateo, I am *so* sorry." My voice is shaking, thick with unshed tears, and he looks bemused.

"It's not your fault she's sick," he says.

"No, but . . ." My throat closes and I trail off.

"I'm going to need directions soon," Cal says.

I blink and wipe my eyes. "What?"

"To Charlie's house," he replies, and it's only then that I notice we're in downtown Carlton. We just passed the library where I used to spend my summer days as a kid, and we're coming up on the corner store where Mateo bought the haul of candy he tried to share with me four years ago. "Do I go the same way I would if I were going to yours?"

My brain feels full of staticky white noise, making it hard to think clearly, so I'm grateful when Cal has to pause at a red light. I gaze around us, disoriented despite the familiar surroundings, until memory finally kicks in. "Not quite," I say. "I mean, you could, but it's faster if you turn left after the soccer fields. Then right on Fulkerson."

Cal taps his fingers on the steering wheel. "Any thoughts on what we do next if Charlie's not home?"

No. I might've had thoughts five minutes ago, but now I'm stuck with static brain. "He'll be there," I say. I take out my phone, purely for something to do that doesn't involve banging my head against the dashboard, and see yet another text from Emily.

CALL ME. DO NOT IGNORE THIS!!!

Then she sends me a YouTube link. My finger hovers over it briefly, before I do the exact opposite of what she said and drop my phone in my lap. It's horrible, I know, that I've let almost the entire school day go by without checking in with my best friend. The problem is, I have absolutely no idea what to say. How do I explain any of this? The call with Daniel was already enough of a disaster. Before I put the phone to my ear, a small part of me was hoping to hear concern in his voice. That part now feels like a sucker.

I wonder, sometimes, what my relationship with my brother would have been like if he were the older sibling, and our entire dynamic hadn't been built on him usurping what I thought was my rightful position in the family. When we were little, he was like my shadow, following me everywhere. I never minded, though, because he was funny and imaginative and affectionate in a sweet, goofy way. He used to yell "Best sister in the world!" while trying to tackle me, but it was like getting jumped on by a puppy since he was so small and skinny back then. He outgrew me physically first, and that was okay. That was expected. It wasn't until he started outpacing me at school that the dynamic between us changed.

If Daniel were eighteen instead of sixteen, maybe I'd feel admiration for all of his accomplishments rather than jealousy. Maybe he'd be caring and helpful toward me, instead of relishing my every misstep. And creating a few, just for the hell of it.

Cal is about to go straight when he shouldn't, so I remind him "Right on Fulkerson," and he swerves.

"I knew that," he claims.

"Okay, but slow down," I say. "We need to take a left onto Avery Hill . . . right here."

Cal makes the turn onto Charlie's tree-lined street. It's similar to mine: the homes are stately without being garish, the space between them is wide, and the landscaping is lush. Charlie's house is a deep barn-red, contrasting with the whites and grays of his neighbors. "That's it," I say when it appears around a bend, causing Cal to brake abruptly. Not quickly enough, though, and we sail right past.

"I'll just turn around," Cal says. He does, and parks across the street from Charlie's house. "Now what?" he asks.

There's a distinctive red Jeep in the driveway. "Well, he's home," I say. "Or his car is, anyway. So maybe we should go over there and . . . knock?"

Cal makes a face. "You sure that's a good idea? What if whoever killed Boney is after Charlie now? He seemed pretty panicked on the phone."

"Then he might need help," Mateo says, unclicking his seat belt. "Why don't you guys stay here and I'll talk to him."

"By yourself?" I twist in my seat to look at him, confused and alarmed. "You can't! It might be dangerous."

"I'll be careful. Back soon," he says. Before I can argue further, he shuts the door and walks briskly away from the car.

Cal watches his progress up the St. Clairs' driveway with a thoughtful expression. "Ivy, can we talk about how weird Mateo is being?" he asks.

"Weird how?" I ask.

"Like how he barely answered any questions about being on that list. And now all of a sudden he wants to separate? What's up with that?" Mateo is at the St. Clairs' front door now, alternately knocking and ringing the doorbell.

"He's being brave," I say, and Cal's eyes practically roll out of his head.

"You didn't say that about me when I took off," he reminds me.

I have no good answer for that, so I focus on Charlie's front door. "It doesn't look like anyone is home," I say just as Mateo twists the doorknob. The door opens and he steps inside, closing it behind him.

Cal stiffens in his seat and peers through the windshield. "Did somebody let him in?" he asks. "Or did he . . ."

"Go in on his own?" I finish. "I think he did." My heart starts beating uncomfortably fast. I don't know why, but watching Mateo disappear into Charlie's house is the worst feeling I've had in a while—and that's saying something, considering the day we've had.

"Okay then," Cal says, his eyes on the door. "Should we wait?"

"I guess." We lapse into silence and I stare at the dashboard clock, watching its numbers change with agonizing slowness. Cal starts fiddling with the car radio, turning up the volume whenever he lands on a song he likes. Then, within a few seconds of listening, he turns it down and switches stations again.

When five minutes and what feels like forty songs have passed, I can't stand it any longer. "I think we should follow him," I say.

Cal exhales, and I can't tell if it's with relief or frustration. "You really like following people, don't you? That's, like, a *thing* with you."

"Only in certain circumstances," I say, reaching for my door handle. "Are you coming?"

"Of course." He turns off the engine, and I feel a surge of gratitude until he has to get one last jab in. "Wouldn't want you to think I'm not *brave*."

The street is perfectly quiet and peaceful, the only sound around us the occasional chirp of a bird. Charlie lives in the kind of neighborhood that requires dual incomes, so nobody's home in the middle of the day. The only car within sight is his Jeep.

"Hold on a sec," Cal says. He pops his trunk and, to my surprise, pulls out a baseball bat. "Let's bring this along just in case." He holds it carefully, at an angle that makes me think he's never tried to actually hit a ball with it.

"Why do you have that?" I ask as we start toward Charlie's house. I can't picture Cal playing pickup games in his downtime.

"Prop for a new web comic I'm working on," he says. "About a spider who finds a bat left behind in a field and decides to start his own league."

"So it's like Spider-Man but with baseball?"

"No." Cal looks annoyed. "It's nothing like Spider-Man. The spider isn't radioactive, or a superhero, and there aren't any humans. Just different kinds of bugs. Playing baseball."

We step onto the perfect smoothness of the St. Clairs' driveway, which is a welcome change from the cobblestone sidewalks I've been tripping over all day. "How do they lift the bat?" I ask. Cal raises his eyebrows questioningly, and I add, "The bugs. If they don't have superstrength. It would crush them."

"Well, obviously there's a fantasy element," Cal replies.

"Hmm," I say, my eyes scanning the picture-perfect suburban home in front of us. It feels deceptively quiet.

"What do you mean, *hmm*?" Cal asks.

"I don't know. When I think about what you were creating a few years ago, it sounds kind of . . ." I was about to say *basic,* but then we pass Charlie's Jeep, and its windows are so spotless that I can see our reflections in them—including Cal's hurt expression.

Oh no. I've been so busy trying to distract myself from the twin stresses of what Mateo told us about his mom, and whatever might be waiting in Charlie's house, that I almost forgot how nobody needs my unfiltered opinions. "I guess I just really like your older stuff," I finish hastily. "I'm probably biased."

"You sound exactly like Lara," Cal mutters.

I point a warning finger at him. "Do not disrespect me like that."

"Well, she said . . ." Cal trails off as Charlie's front door looms in front of us. "Hold on a sec. Let's think this through. Are we breaking and entering?"

"No. Just entering."

"Still. Do you think this is a good idea? Walking into someone's house?"

The bat dangles in Cal's grip, as though he's about to drop it, so I grab it from him and hold it firmly in one hand. "We have to," I say, and push the door open.

14

MATEO

Charlie can't be all that scared for his life if he doesn't even bother locking his door.

I step into a spacious, empty foyer and close the door behind me. "Charlie? You there?" I call, moving farther into the house. "It's Mateo Wojcik. I need to talk to you." Then I catch sight of the St. Clairs' kitchen through the doorway ahead of me, and freeze in my tracks.

All the cabinets are wide open. The counters and floor are strewn with boxes, bags, and broken dishes. I creep farther into the foyer, every muscle tense, and stop at a set of French doors that lead into what looks like the St. Clairs' living room. It's a chaotic mess: tables upended, cushions pulled apart and tossed onto the floor, lamps and vases smashed. The built-in book-shelves at one end of the room are completely empty. Even the curtains have been torn off the picture window, the rod dangling haphazardly to one side.

The entire place has been ransacked. And if whoever did it is still around, I just announced myself to them.

Obviously, the smart thing to do would be to backtrack out the door and directly into Cal's car. But I can't. Because now I really, *really* need to find out whether Charlie St. Clair—the guy whose name was circled on a list with me and a dead kid, and who just called that kid in a panic—is the same Charlie who popped up on Autumn's phone this morning.

The less you know, the better, she'd said. Not anymore.

I move back toward the kitchen, ears straining. The house is silent except for the quiet hum of central air-conditioning. Up close, the kitchen is an even bigger disaster. There's so much crap on the floor that I'm about to give up on going any farther when I notice a door across from the pantry that's slightly ajar. I pick my way toward it and ease it open, and I catch a faint rustling sound from somewhere below.

There's a set of carpeted stairs leading down. I stand there for a moment, considering just how bad of an idea it is to fol- low the noise. I can hear Autumn's voice in my head as clearly as if she were standing next to me: *Extremely, Mateo. Literally the worst decision of your life.*

Yeah, well, she's one to talk.

I descend as carefully and quietly as I can, my footsteps muf- fled by the thickness of the rug beneath my feet. When I reach the bottom, I'm in what looks like a finished basement that's been torn apart as thoroughly as upstairs. But there's less furniture here, so it's mostly a wreckage of toppled shelves and scattered sports equip- ment. I count four doors spaced evenly throughout the room; one is open, leading to what looks like a laundry area, and the rest are closed. Everything is just as eerily quiet as it was upstairs.

There's a basketball directly in front of me, and I ease it to one side with my foot. It spins harder than I intended, and hits the edge of a metal shelf with a soft thud. *Damn it.*

The faint rustling sound comes again, from behind one of the closed doors. My nerves flare up, and I push them down as I scan the contents of the floor for something I could use to defend myself. There's not much, unless—

"Arghhhhhhh!"

The door flies open and a screaming blur comes at me. All I see is a flash of silver before my skull explodes in pain and I'm on my knees. Another blow lands on my shoulder, weaker than the first. My vision gets hazy as something warm trickles into my eyes. I lunge forward blindly, and my hand connects with the cold metal of some kind of rod. I grab hold of it and pull as hard as I can, grunting in pain when whoever was holding it crashes on top of me. I lose my grip on the rod, and I hear it clatter against the wall. Adrenaline pumps through me hard and fast as I think with a savage kind of triumph, *He's down and unarmed.*

For a few seconds we're a tangle of twisted limbs and flailing fists, throwing punches that don't land hard enough to do damage as we grapple on the floor. I haven't been in a fight in years, but it's like riding a bike, I guess—you don't forget how. I dodge and shift, trying to pin him down while he keeps slipping away.

I still can't see and my head is throbbing. When I feel one of his fingers stabbing into the flesh right next to my eye, a bolt of white-hot anger courses through me. I manage to catch hold of his wrist and bend it sharply backward, causing him to go limp with a scream of pain. I'm on top of him in a flash, blinking furiously to clear my vision, one arm pressing across his neck while the other hauls back in preparation for what I hope will be a knockout blow.

"Stop!" a girl's voice screams behind me. "Mateo, Charlie, stop!"

Charlie? I freeze, then swipe a hand over my eyes. It comes away red with blood, and my vision clears enough to see Charlie St. Clair shove hard at my chest from below. I let myself roll off him and turn to see Ivy a few feet away from me, a baseball bat dangling from one hand. "What the hell?" I rasp. Then I turn back toward Charlie, who's writhing on the floor, clutching his wrist and whimpering. There's a golf club lying a few feet away from him, and Ivy steps over me to pick it up.

"Shit, Charlie, sorry," I say. "I was trying to help you."

"You got a weird fucking way of showing it, dude," Charlie moans. "I think you broke my wrist."

"Sorry," I repeat, wiping my bloody hand on my T-shirt. "But you came after me with a golf club, so . . ."

"Because you *broke into my house.*" Charlie sits up, his wrist forgotten, as he pulls the puka shell necklace away from his neck and presses his fingers to the red marks beneath. I caused those when I was trying to pin him, and if I'd been thinking straight, maybe I would've realized I was dealing with Charlie when I felt the rough edges of the necklace against my forearm. "I thought you were . . ." He gestures around the room. "Whoever did this."

"The door was unlocked. And I said my name," I protest. "I called it out as soon as I got inside."

"I can't hear shit down here. It's soundproof," Charlie says. "Anyway, why would that make me feel better? What the hell are you doing here?" There's something vacant and unfocused about his expression as he looks from me to Ivy, and then over at Cal, who's come up behind us. "And you. And you."

Ivy crouches beside him and takes hold of his wrist. "This doesn't look swollen, but you should probably put some ice on it. And then—oh!" She gasps as she catches sight of my face. "Mateo, you're bleeding. A lot." She reaches out a hand, and I recoil before she can touch me. Now that the adrenaline has drained out of me, the right side of my head feels like it's on fire. "We need to clean that up."

"We need to *leave*," Cal interrupts, his voice tight. "What if whoever did this decides to come back?"

I feel weirdly certain that's not going to happen; like the person, or people, who targeted Charlie's house have already moved on. But before I can follow that thought to its logical conclusion—*moved on where?*—Ivy says, "Good point. We can go to my house."

Charlie's slumped against the wall now, eyes narrowed. "Are you guys even real?" he asks thickly. He extends a hand and pokes Ivy in the arm, frowning. "Huh? Are you?"

Ivy blinks slowly. "Mateo, did you hit him in the head?" she asks.

"I don't think so," I say, although I'm honestly not sure.

"Cal, could you help Charlie get to the car?" Ivy asks. "He seems too disoriented to make it on his own. Stop that," she says to Charlie, who's still poking at her arm. "Mateo, can you walk okay?"

I stagger to my feet. "Sure."

Ivy winces at the spatters of dark red blood I left behind on the light carpet. "Oh God, the rug is a mess."

"Eh." Charlie shrugs, shaking his bangs out of his eyes.

"Trevor Bronson puked in that exact spot last weekend, so, you know. It's seen worse."

"Ew." Ivy springs to her feet, wrinkling her nose at the patch of carpet where her knees just were. "I really wish you hadn't told me that."

Despite everything that just happened, it's such a classic Ivy reaction that I almost laugh. But I can't, because at some point soon—probably once Charlie and I are less bloody—Ivy and Cal are going to start asking questions about why Charlie's house got ransacked. They'll ask, naturally, what somebody might have been looking for.

And I'm afraid that I already know.

Soon after, I'm seated on a stool in Ivy's first-floor bathroom while she roots through the medicine cabinet. She opens an industrial-sized bottle of Tylenol and takes out two, filling a cup from the edge of the sink with water. "How do you feel?" she asks.

"Fine," I say. It's mostly true. My shoulder is a little sore from where Charlie whacked me with the club, but other than that, nothing hurts except my head.

"You're lucky. It could've been a lot worse." Ivy hands me the cup and the pills, and waits for me to wash them down. "Why didn't you leave when you saw what had happened at Charlie's house?"

I buy a little time by finishing my water, but ultimately, there's no good answer. "Why didn't *you*?" I counter.

"Because you were there," she says.

The ache in my chest that only Ivy ever seems to cause returns, making me feel like I lost whatever compass was helping me navigate this conversation. "You were supposed to wait in the car," I grumble. Ivy crosses her arms. I know I should apologize, or thank her, or both. Definitely both. But all I can manage to add is "Where'd you get the baseball bat?"

She takes the empty cup from me. "Cal had it in his trunk."

"So you were gonna—what? Take a swing at someone?"

"Worked for Charlie, didn't it? Up to a point." Ivy opens a door built into the wall behind us, revealing shelves of neatly stacked towels. The bathroom looks almost exactly like I remember from when I used to hang out at Ivy's house, except it's now painted a cream color instead of blue. Ivy pulls a facecloth from the cabinet and turns the tap back on, wetting it and folding it in half before turning back to me. "I'm going to clean your cut now. It might hurt a little."

"Don't worry about it." I force myself not to wince as she starts to dab at my temple. Her hair's come partly out of her ponytail, and when it swings in her face, she makes an annoyed noise and pauses to tuck it behind her ear. I must be feeling better already, because I was a second away from doing it for her. "Thanks for this," I finally say.

"You're welcome." Ivy resumes cleaning, her golden-brown eyes roving across my temple. "This doesn't look so bad after all. There's just one cut, and it's not very deep. The bleeding is already slowing." She steps back to rinse the facecloth beneath the tap, then bends over me again. The return of the cool cloth, and Ivy's light touch, is a relief. "You know, you don't have to do everything on your own."

"What?" My eyes are following hers, and my ears need a second to catch up.

"You can ask people for help. It's not a sign of weakness."

Crap. She thinks I was being noble, going into the St. Clairs' house by myself. Not acting out of self-preservation. I'm torn between wanting to set her straight and wanting to stay the guy she thinks I am. The guy *I* used to think I am.

"I wasn't worried about looking weak," I hedge, shifting restlessly. I should get out of here and check on Charlie instead of leaving him alone with Cal. But with Ivy still swiping gently at my face, I can't bring myself to leave. It feels good, and she's wearing some kind of light, citrusy perfume that smells fantastic, and all I want is to stay cocooned in here for as long as possible and not think about what comes next.

"Well, I hope you weren't worried about me and Cal," Ivy says. "We can take care of ourselves. And we're all in this together, so . . ." She steps back and tilts her head critically. "You have the start of an impressive bruise, but hopefully you won't need stitches. Just keep a bandage on it overnight, at least." She turns for the medicine cabinet once more and pulls out a carton of Band-Aids, adding, "Has the Tylenol kicked in yet?"

"Yeah," I say. Either that, or Charlie didn't hit me as hard as it felt at the time. But I already miss her tending to me, so I add, "You sure you got all the blood off?"

"Positive. Only one thing left to do." Ivy rinses the facecloth in the sink, then wrings it dry and tosses it into a hamper before unwrapping a Band-Aid. She presses it firmly against my temple. "There. Almost as good as new. Don't do that again, okay?" Her hand brushes my cheek, and she leans forward to plant a light kiss on my forehead.

It feels like a signal; or maybe I just think that because I've been hoping for one. "Wait," I say. Her hair's hanging in her face again, and I catch hold of the ends before she can pull back, my eyes locking with hers. "I don't think you're done."

"Sure I am. You're fine," she says, but she doesn't move away. Her lips part, and her lashes flutter as color floods her cheeks. It's one of the great mysteries of the universe why Carlton High guys aren't lined up outside Ivy's door. She's cute from a distance, but up close like this? She's beautiful. "What else could you possibly need?"

"I need . . ." I tuck the hair behind her ear, then trail my hand down until I'm cupping the back of her neck. "You."

Ivy shivers, leaning forward until her soft lips graze mine. It's not enough, though; it's nowhere near enough. I tangle my fingers in her hair and pull her closer for a long, lingering kiss. Any questions that might've been floating around my brain about whether this is a bad idea—and yeah, there were more than a few—disappear at the sensation of her mouth against mine. Kissing Ivy is both familiar and exhilarating, like coming back to a place I wish I hadn't left and finding it's even better than I remember.

"Guys?" Ivy springs backward as Cal's voice floats our way. She doesn't get quite far enough to keep his eyebrows from rising when he pokes his head through the doorframe, but whatever he saw wasn't enough to throw him off course. "Charlie told me what he thinks whoever tore apart his house was looking for, and we have a problem. Wait, let me rephrase that," he adds, anticipating Ivy's inevitable correction. "We have a *new* problem."

She goes still. "Is someone here? Is it the police?"

"No. No one's here," Cal says, leaning against the doorway. Ivy exhales in relief and starts putting the bandages away. "Except the guy we came with. In other words, a very drunk Charlie." He's looking only at Ivy, not me, and dread starts pooling in my stomach.

I knew I shouldn't have left him alone with Charlie.

"A very what?" Ivy asks distractedly. She shuts the medicine cabinet, then does a double take as she catches sight of her reflection in its mirrored door. She tries to put what's left of her ponytail back together, but eventually gives up and tugs the elastic out of her hair, letting it spill over her shoulders.

"Charlie's hammered," Cal says, backing out of the doorway so Ivy can join him in the hall. I get up, too, but Cal still won't look me in the eye. "He was freaked about Boney, and then freaked about his house getting torn apart, so his solution was to break into his parents' vodka." He clears his throat and adds, "Which, I guess, beats overdosing on the Oxycontin that he stole."

Shit, shit, shit. This is bad. This is what I was afraid of when Charlie's name started showing up everywhere. It's the worst possible explanation for how Charlie and Boney are connected.

The less you know, the better.

"Are you serious? No wonder he's been acting so weird," Ivy says. I wait, wordless, until she absorbs the rest of Cal's news. It only takes a second for her eyes to go wide. "Wait, he stole *what*? Did you say Oxycontin? Like . . . opioids?"

"I did," Cal says, folding his arms across his chest. "Charlie told me he found a big stash of Oxy at a party last month, and he's been selling it ever since. Him and Boney." Ivy gasps, and Cal finally lets his eyes settle on mine. They're cool and appraising as he adds, "Along with your cousin. But you already knew that, right?"

15

CAL

I only half believe what I'm saying until Mateo sags against the wall, rubbing a hand across his jaw. "Yeah," he says tiredly. "I did."

"Wait. What?" Ivy asks. Her eyes are so huge, she looks like an anime character. "You've been selling *drugs*?"

"Autumn has," Mateo says. "And I . . . haven't stopped her."

My frayed nerves, already stretched thin from trying to decipher Charlie's babbling while these two were getting cozy in the bathroom, snap at his words. "So all this time, while we've been trying to figure out what happened to Boney, you knew he was a drug dealer?" I ask. "You saw him lying there with a syringe practically dangling from his arm and thought, *Eh, probably not relevant, won't mention it*?"

"I didn't know Boney was involved," Mateo insists. "Autumn wouldn't tell me who she was selling with. She kept saying, *The less you know, the better.*"

My first instinct is to snipe *How convenient*, and I force

myself to swallow the words because I don't know where they're coming from. Do I think Mateo is lying, or am I just angry with him? Both? I need more information before I can decide. "Did you know about Charlie?" I ask, trying to keep my voice even.

Mateo hesitates. "Not exactly. But I saw the name on Autumn's phone this morning, and she acted all sketchy, so I wondered if one of the people she was selling with was named Charlie. Then all of a sudden Boney's dead, and there's this list with his name circled, and Charlie's—and *mine,* which made no sense. So I wanted to talk to Charlie about it."

I glare at him. "But not to us, huh? Even though we straight-up asked if there was any connection you could think of."

"Opioids," Ivy says faintly. "But that's what—oh God, I never told you, did I?" Mateo furrows his brow, confused, until she adds, "That's what my mother's award is about. She was the lead statistician for the governor's report on opioid abuse."

Mateo's shoulders slump even lower. "Shit, I didn't—I had no idea."

I fold my arms. "Would it have changed anything if you did?"

He doesn't reply, and Ivy speaks up again. "Is that why you went into Charlie's house alone?" she asks, her gaze fixed intently on Mateo. "Because you didn't want us to know what Autumn's been doing?"

I almost ask how *brave* she thinks he is now, but manage to bite it back. It's a cheap shot, and she's not the one I'm angry with right now.

Mateo's face turns a dull red. "Yeah. I should've said something, I know. I'm sorry. I wasn't thinking straight." He throws Ivy an apologetic, almost pleading look, and the fact that he's worried about her reaction, when I'm the one who just spent ten minutes trying to coax sense out of Charlie, makes my temper spike even higher.

"Were you thinking straight while you were selling Oxy?" I snap.

"I wasn't the one selling," Mateo says, a hard edge creeping into his voice.

Usually, when Mateo sounds like that, I back down. I'm not a tough guy by any stretch of the imagination. But for the first time all day, I'm not the one who needs to justify himself. It's Mateo's turn, and he's more than earned it.

"Does it matter?" I ask coldly. "You knew. Maybe if you'd bothered to give us a heads-up, we wouldn't have walked into Charlie's ransacked drug den like a bunch of clueless—" And then I freeze, all the rage draining out of me as I'm struck by a single, horrifying thought. "Wait a sec. Charlie said he doesn't keep Oxy at home, so whoever ripped his house apart didn't find what they were looking for. If they're working from the list, they probably moved on to *your* house. Is anyone home?"

"No," Mateo says quickly. "Autumn's at work and my mom's in the Bronx, remember?" He drags a hand through his hair, his expression ragged. "But yeah, my house probably looks like Charlie's right about now. Autumn doesn't keep anything there, either—she says they moved the stash from the shed where they found it to some other location—but I guess it doesn't matter. Whoever's doing this isn't asking questions, they're just . . . they're doing whatever the hell they want." He swallows hard. "Autumn really messed with the wrong people."

"Yeah, she did. And you let her," I say, my anger returning now that I know his family is safe. For now, at least. "Oxy's no joke, Mateo." I don't know much about it, to be honest, but ever since Wes learned about a spike at Carlton College, he's been up late most nights reading about addiction and overdose rates. Sometimes he shares his findings over breakfast, and I can hear his worried voice as clear as a bell as I continue, "People's lives get ruined. Do you even understand how serious this is?"

Mateo's eyes flash, and I brace myself for a scathing response. I want it, actually, and move a little closer so he knows I won't back down. For a second we just stare at each other, shoulders squared and fists curled at our sides like we're about to throw down. Which is ridiculous, because I don't know how to fight and if I tried, he'd kick my ass. I mean, look at what happened to Charlie. He has twenty pounds on me and a golf club, and still almost died.

But right now, I'm mad enough to not care.

Then Mateo drops his head and rubs the back of his neck, looking suddenly exhausted. The dark circles I noticed this morning are more prominent than ever. "Yeah," he says heavily. "I understand."

I blink, and have to literally bite my tongue to keep from spewing more vitriol. I wasn't expecting him to agree with me, and it takes the wind right out of my sails. I was ready to go toe-to-toe with defiant Mateo, but this guy? This guy looks like he hates himself.

Ivy glances tentatively between us. "I have a question," she says quietly, like she's afraid to disrupt the fragile moment of peace. "I don't understand the connection between Charlie, Boney, and Autumn. How did that happen?"

Mateo heaves a sigh. "So, like a month ago, Autumn and Loser Gabe went to a party at this empty house at the edge of Carlton. It was condemned or something, supposed to be torn down soon, totally deserted. Anyway, Gabe was being a dick, like always, so Autumn went outside, and while she was walking around, she heard voices coming from a shed in the backyard. She said a couple guys from school were there, and started acting shifty and weird when they saw her. Turns out they'd found a bunch of Oxy hidden under one of the floorboards, and they were talking about taking it and selling it. One of the guys said he could get eighty bucks a pill." He swallows hard. "And Autumn . . . Autumn wanted in."

That's pretty much what Charlie told me, except a lot less garbled.

"Why?" I ask. It's what I came to find Mateo for; the piece of the puzzle that makes no sense. Even though Charlie and Boney weren't friends, they had friends in common, so I can picture the two of them running into one another at a party. And I can *definitely* picture them stumbling drunkenly across a bunch of hidden drugs and thinking it was a gold mine. Boney used to see dollar signs everywhere, and Charlie's the kind of guy who thinks rules don't apply to him. But Autumn Wojcik? She's always been quiet and serious, and probably made it through four years of high school without a single detention. I could imagine her walking away, maybe, and letting Boney and Charlie drown in their own stupidity. But *joining* them? It doesn't fit. "Why would Autumn want to be part of something like that?"

Mateo's jaw clenches. He doesn't answer right away, and Ivy lets out a strangled little gasp beside me. "Your mom," she breathes.

He nods, his expression pained. "It's like I told you guys in the car—her pills cost a fortune, and our insurance has sucked ever since Spare Me shut down. So most of the time, Ma doesn't take them. Autumn said that if she sold six pills a month, she could pay for the prescription. She said six pills wasn't a lot."

Ivy and I exchange glances as Mateo stares at the floor. "I tried to talk her out of it. Swear to God, I really did. I've been sick about it. But Autumn wouldn't listen. And she wouldn't listen when I told her how much my mom would hate it, or that it could all blow back on Ma and screw up the way people see her. My mom's a Reyes, not a Wojcik. It's different, and Autumn doesn't get that." He exhales a heavy sigh. "She doesn't get a lot of things. Problem is, once my cousin gets an idea in her head, it's like she has tunnel vision. She sees the light at the end, and none of the mess she's making to get there. She said if I wanted to stop her, I'd have to turn her in. And I couldn't do that." His head drops, and I don't think I've ever seen Mateo look so defeated. "There's no way I could ever do that to her. And I didn't think—I never thought something like *this* would happen."

We're all quiet for a few beats, absorbing the aftershock of his words. Ivy looks too devastated to speak, and I have no clue what to say. I guess I can understand the position he was in with Autumn; Mateo's family means everything to him. Ratting her out must have felt impossible, even when she was clearly in the wrong.

I try putting myself in Autumn's shoes: If Wes or Henry were sick and needed medicine we couldn't afford, what would I do? What lengths would I go to? But the parallels are too hard to draw; for one thing, my other dad would be there. Plus, my parents have great insurance, and savings, and all those other things Henry talks about when he's trying to convince me that I should get a business degree alongside an art degree. *You need a safety net,* he always says.

We have that, but Autumn and Mateo don't. Not anymore.

"I get it," I finally say. It's a weak response, I know, but it's more of an olive branch than anything else. A signal that I'm done giving Mateo a hard time. I'm not going to tell him that Autumn did the right thing, but he's not trying to say that, either. She came up with a bad solution to a bad situation, and everyone loses.

"You didn't . . . I mean, your mom . . . ," Ivy says haltingly. She bites her lip, eyes on the highly polished wood of the hallway floor. "We all make mistakes, right? And almost never see the fallout coming. If we did, we'd never do . . . whatever it was that we . . . did." She trails off, and I get the distinct impression that she stopped talking about Mateo after the first sentence.

"Hey, Ivy!" Charlie's voice floats from Ivy's living room, startling me. I almost forgot he was here. "Check it out. They're talking about you on TV."

16

CAL

"Oh God," Ivy says, growing even more pale. "Now what?"

She heads down the hallway with Mateo and me at her heels. Charlie is almost exactly where I left him—curled in one corner of the couch, his eyes half-mast and his expression vacant—except now he has a remote in one hand. The television in front of him is tuned in to Central New England Cable, where Dale Hawkins is standing in front of . . . oh shit.

Carlton High School. Flanked by Emily Zhang, Ishaan Mittal, and Zack Abrams. "What are those three doing there?" I ask. I know Emily is Ivy's best friend, but I've never seen her with either of the other two.

Ivy's mouth is a thin line. "Can you rewind, please, Charlie?"

"Um . . ." Charlie stares at the remote like it's a PhD-level math equation he has no hope of solving, and Ivy snatches it from his hand with a frustrated huff. She restarts the segment from where Dale first appears on-screen.

"Good afternoon, this is Dale Hawkins, continuing with today's special edition of *The Hawkins Report*," he says smoothly. "I'm at Carlton High School, where students are reeling from the news that their classmate, seventeen-year-old Brian Mahoney, was killed this morning. While reporting on that tragic occurrence, I was sent a link to a YouTube video featuring two of the Carlton High seniors standing beside me. These young men claim that one of their classmates, who has a history of bad blood with Mahoney and fits the description of the person of interest police have been seeking, has been missing from school all day."

"No." The last drop of color drains from Ivy's face. "This can't be happening."

The camera pans across the three students standing beside Dale. Emily looks upset, Ishaan looks like he's trying to figure out which side of his face will look better on television, and Zack looks nervous.

"Zack, what the hell," Mateo mutters behind me, and it's only then that I remember the two of them are friendly.

"Tips have been coming into the station all day, and we can't possibly respond to them all," Dale continues. "But this one interested me, because I'm acquainted with the young woman involved. Furthermore—and this is breaking news—my crew and I also happen to have seen her in Boston, not far from the crime scene, less than an hour ago. However, she fled before I was able to speak with her."

"Oh nooooo," Ivy moans.

On-screen, Emily leans forward to interrupt. "Excuse me, but I think it's important to say that the YouTube video wasn't a *tip*. It was gossip."

Dale ignores her and angles his microphone toward Ishaan. "Ishaan Mittal, you're one of the founders of the Carlton Speaks YouTube channel. When did you first begin to question whether Ivy Sterling-Shepard might be involved in what happened to Brian Mahoney?"

"Oh my God." Ivy freezes the screen, like that'll do something to slow the train wreck headed her way. "He said my name. On television. I am so screwed." Her eyes dart wildly around her living room. "I can fix this. I *have* to fix this." Then she flings the remote onto the couch, drops into a chair, and covers her face with her hands. "I have to fix this," she repeats, voice muffled.

Mateo and I exchange glances. "How many people even watch cable news, though?" I say. Nobody answers me, which is probably just as well, since I have no idea and it might be a lot. Mateo puts a hand on Ivy's shoulder and leans down, murmuring something in her ear that I can't hear. She doesn't move a muscle.

"Damn, that was messed up," Charlie says, sounding almost sympathetic. "Except for Emily. She's your ride or die, huh?"

Ivy doesn't respond, and her misery tugs at my conscience. All day, she's been trying to piece together the truth. And I've been either getting in her way, or staying so far out of it that I'm no help at all. Because I wasn't sure I even wanted to know. I'm still not, but I can't just stand around while her life falls apart, either.

"Charlie," I say, turning toward the couch. While Ivy and Mateo were in the bathroom, I was so focused on pulling the drug story out of Charlie that I barely had the chance to ask him anything else. "When I answered Boney's phone, you said, *Did the guy show up?* Who were you talking about?"

169

"A buyer," Charlie says. He steeples his fingers and places them under his chin, forehead creased, like he's making a mighty effort to concentrate. "Some dude called over the weekend about meeting up in Boston for a big order. We all have burner phones, and this one came through Boney's. He wanted, like, twenty times as much as we usually sell. Boney was psyched, but Autumn freaked out."

Mateo blanches. "Well, yeah. That's way too much."

"But Boney went anyway?" I ask.

Way to state the obvious, Cal. Really moving things along.

"He promised Autumn he wouldn't," Charlie says. "But then last night, he told me he'd talked to the guy again and decided to go. He said not to tell Autumn, because she'd just"—he puts up finger quotes—"*hold us back*. He said she's small-time, and we could be big-time."

"Big-time?" I ask, alarmed. "What does that mean?"

Charlie lifts a shoulder. "Not sure. He didn't want to get into it over the phone. He said he'd explain everything once he made the connection."

"The connection?" I echo. "With who? The guy with the giant order?"

"I guess?" Charlie turns his palms up in a helpless gesture.

"Do you know why he went to that specific building?" I ask. "Was that Boney's idea, or the guy he was meeting?"

"The guy," Charlie says. "He gave Boney the address and a code for the door."

I rock on my heels. "Do you have any idea who this guy is?"

"None," Charlie says, sinking lower in the couch. "I felt weird about it this morning, like maybe we should listen to Autumn. If she thinks something's a bad idea, then it probably is. I tried calling her, to ask if we should stop him, but she didn't pick up either of her phones. So I just—let it go." His head droops as he makes a fist and bounces it hard against the armrest of the couch. "Fucking hell. I shouldn't have let it go."

Silence falls as we get lost in our own regrets. I wish, obviously, that I hadn't led Mateo and Ivy to the studio this morning. But more than that, I wish I'd pushed Lara harder for answers when I had the chance. I wish I hadn't been so quick to decide she must be blameless. Because it's getting more and more impossible to believe that she is.

"Hey, Charlie." Mateo finally breaks the silence, taking out his phone and swiping the screen a few times. "I haven't heard from Autumn all day. Have you?" His voice is tight with worry. "Does she know what happened to Boney?"

"I don't think so," Charlie says. "She never called me back. You know how it is when she's driving the murder van."

Before I can react to that, Ivy's head snaps up. "The *what?*" she asks, surprisingly alert for someone who was near comatose last time I checked. Mateo, looking relieved at the sign of life, lightly squeezes her shoulder. "There's a murder van?" Ivy repeats, glaring accusingly at Charlie. "Just what kind of drug business are you guys running?"

"It's a joke," Mateo says quickly. "A nickname. Autumn works for a knife-sharpening company, and there's a giant knife painted on the side of the van, so . . ." He briefly shuts his eyes as Ivy winces. "It seemed a lot funnier before today."

"Jesus," Ivy mutters. She stands up and rolls her shoulders, like she's trying to put herself back into problem-solving mode.

"Did you hear everything we just talked about?" I ask, because it really did seem like she was in another world for a while.

"I heard," she says, patting my arm. "You asked good questions. Except for one glaring omission, but I know that's a difficult topic for you." She turns toward Charlie. "Charlie, did Boney ever say anything to you about Ms. Jamison?"

"The art teacher?" Charlie asks, blinking up at her. "No. Why would he?"

"Because she works in the studio where Boney died," Ivy says. "And we found a list that she'd made with your name, Boney's name, and Mateo's name circled." She waits for some kind of reaction from Charlie, but he still looks confused. "Why do you think she did that?"

Charlie shrugs. "You're the smart one. You tell me."

A trace of color returns to Ivy's cheeks. Without realizing it, Charlie just gave her a much-needed shot of energy. Getting called *smart* is her own personal Red Bull. "Well, now that we understand how you and Boney are connected, it seems like the list must have something to do with the stolen drugs," she says. "But then Autumn should be on it, not Mateo."

"Except Autumn doesn't go to Carlton High anymore," Mateo says. "So her name wouldn't be on a class roster. Maybe only the last name mattered."

Ivy taps her chin. "That's a good point."

Charlie flings one arm over the back of the couch. He looks calm again, as though all the brain cells holding his guilt about Boney have gone back to being comfortably numb. "Or maybe it was a guess," he says. "If you were gonna pick a drug-dealing Wojcik, wouldn't it be *him*?" Charlie waves in Mateo's direction. "The big guy with the bad attitude. Not the cute girl."

"That's . . . also a good point," Ivy says, like it pains her to admit it.

"Yeah, it is," Charlie says, his eyes half-shuttered as he shoots her a lazy grin. "You know, your hair looks really good down. You should wear it like that all the time."

"I . . . thank you?" Ivy says uncertainly.

"You're welcome." Charlie looks her up and down, then pats the seat beside him. "Sit down for a minute. Relax. You're way too tense."

Ivy crosses her arms tightly over her chest. "Personally, I feel like I'm exactly the right amount of tense for the situation at hand," she says.

Charlie squints at her, thoughtful. "Is it weird that I find you kinda hot right now?"

"Okay, listen," Mateo interrupts, clearly not liking the conversational shift. "So what exactly are we saying here? That Ms. Jamison is part of some drug ring? Working with the guy Boney talked to? She figured out who was selling the stolen drugs, and he—what? Tried to buy them back? Or take them back. Or offer Boney some kind of partnership, maybe." His jaw sets. "Whatever it was, it didn't go well for Boney."

"Or the guy," I say. "If he'd gotten what he wanted, Charlie's house probably wouldn't have gotten ripped apart."

"Right," Mateo says, turning to Charlie. "How many pills did you guys take from the shed, total? Autumn wouldn't tell me."

Charlie tugs on his puka shell necklace. "I mean, a lot."

"What's a lot?" Mateo presses. "Dozens? Hundreds? Thousands?"

"Like a hundred," Charlie says. I relax a little, because it could be worse, until he adds, "Bottles."

"A hundred *bottles*?" Mateo starts pacing the room. "Are you kidding me right now? How many pills per bottle?"

Charlie passes a hand over his forehead. "Dude, this is like . . . a lot of math."

I jump in. "Conservatively, let's say twenty per bottle, but it's probably more. At minimum that's two thousand pills, and at eighty dollars a pill, we're talking about . . ."

Ivy wrings her hands. "Hundreds of thousands of dollars," she finishes, her eyes wide and alarmed. "That's a ton of money to lose."

"So we're talking a big-time operation, aren't we?" I say. "Run by the kind of people who'll hunt you down and kill you if you cross them." I can't believe those words just came out of my mouth; at what point, exactly, did this become real life? I'm pretty sure it's Charlie's fault, so I turn to him and add, "How did they figure out it was you guys?"

Charlie heaves a deep sigh. "I don't know, man. Maybe it was the Weasel."

"The what?" Mateo asks.

"The Weasel," Charlie repeats.

"Okay. Sure." Mateo puts a hand over the non-injured half of his face and rubs it vigorously for a few seconds before turning to Charlie with a look of patient forbearance. "I'll bite. Who's that?"

"Dude, no one knows." Charlie sits up with more energy than he's shown since he tried to gouge Mateo's eyes out. "But you know my brother, Stefan? Last year, when he was a senior, he said that any time someone in Carlton tried to have a little drug hustle on the side, they'd get shut down. Like, their supplier would flake out, or the buyers wouldn't show, that kind of thing. Stefan decided there had to be somebody making the rounds at parties and ratting people out. Either a total narc, or somebody who has their own business and doesn't want competition. Stefan calls them the Weasel." Charlie turns toward Mateo and adds, "You know what? Whoever it is, you probably got on their bad side, if they switched your name out with your cousin's. Don't antagonize the Weasel, man!" He starts laughing, like this is all a big joke, and I'm seized with a sudden urge to punch him.

Mateo looks as though he feels the same way. "Let me get this straight. You've known since last year that someone's been keeping an eye on anyone who tries to sell drugs in Carlton—and you decided to do it anyway?" The smirk fades from Charlie's face as Mateo asks, "Did you bother telling Boney and Autumn about this person?"

"What? No. That's—listen, man, that's just Stefan being Stefan, you know? He always says weird *Breaking Bad* shit like that. I mean, come on, the Weasel? It's a joke. I don't take it seriously."

"Maybe you should have," Mateo says in the same cold undertone.

"Okay, but . . ." Charlie's gaze darts around the room, like he's looking for someplace else to cast blame. "But you guys said Ms. Jamison is the one who put the list of names together, so that doesn't fit. She doesn't go to parties, and if she did? People would notice. She'd be a crap Weasel." He nods, seemingly satisfied with his own logic, before adding, "Why do you think she's dealing? Because teachers don't get paid enough, or what?"

"Well, they don't," Ivy says. "But we haven't fully analyzed her motives yet. They could be financial, or they could be more personal. Maybe she got involved with the wrong type of guy." Her eyes slide toward me, eyebrows raised, and she mouths the words we read on Lara's card: *Love you so much, angel.*

"What, Coach Kendall?" Charlie snorts out a dismissive laugh. "Gotta tell you, I don't see it. That guy won't even hand out Tylenol."

"I'm not talking about Coach Kendall," Ivy says. "We think she's seeing somebody behind his back. Somebody with the initial D. Maybe he's Boney's mystery buyer, and she gave him the code to the building."

"Or maybe he already had it," Mateo says, turning toward me. "You said other people have access, right, Cal? Any idea who? Any D names?"

I open my mouth to say no—and then abruptly close it, because the memory that's been poking around the edges of my brain finally hits me full force. Ever since we found the card, I've been thinking of D as a student; someone like Boney, who I'd seen walk into Lara's studio, or like Charlie and Mateo, who were circled on the list in her day planner. Someone like *me*.

The idea made me jealous, and it also made me shortsighted. Because until now, I completely forgot about Lara dismissing me at Second Street Café so she could take a call.

"Yeah," I say. "The guy who used to rent the studio, and let Lara use it? His name is Dominick."

17

IVY

I can't even be mad at Cal for not coming out with the Dominick name sooner. None of us have been our best, most straightforward selves today, and there's no point in losing any more time arguing about it. "How do you know that's his name?" I ask.

"Lara mentioned him when we were at Second Street Café," Cal says. "She took a call from him right before I left."

"Who's Lara?" Charlie asks.

"Ms. Jamison," I tell him before opening Google on my phone and typing *Dominick artist Boston* into the search bar.

Charlie squints at Cal. "Why do you call her by her first name? And what were you doing in a café with her?" Cal turns brick red, and a slow, incredulous grin spreads over Charlie's face. "Wait. Dude. Are you . . . are you and Ms. Jamison . . ." He make an obscene gesture.

"It's not like that," Cal says coldly.

"Sure it's not." Charlie laughs, extending his fist. "Come on, son, give it up. Respect. Didn't think you had it in you."

"Could you dial back the bro, please?" I snap. "It's not cute."

Cal ignores us both until I hold out my phone to display a black-and-white picture of a handsome guy with horn-rimmed glasses. "Dominick Payne," I say. "Local contemporary artist, best known for painting panoramic urban scenes. Do you think this might be him?"

"I wouldn't know," Cal says, leaning over my shoulder as I swipe through other images. "It's not like I ever met the guy, or . . . hold on." I pause at an abstract painting of a cityscape. "I think Lara has a signed print of that in her classroom," he says, rubbing the back of his neck. "She told me . . . she told me it was from a friend."

"Well, there you have it," I say. Even though this is by far the worst puzzle I've ever tried to solve, there's still satisfaction in watching a piece fall into place. "They're connected, and they're both artists, so there's a good chance he's the Dominick she was talking to. The next question is, is he *also* D?"

"And/or a drug dealer," Cal says.

"Right. Mateo, what do you think?" I ask. When he doesn't answer, I look up to see him frowning over his own phone. "Mateo? Did you hear us?"

"Huh?" He glances up, and although I didn't think it was possible, he looks even more drawn and pale than he did when he learned his cousin stole a small fortune in pills. "Oh yeah. Sorry. I did, but I've been trying to text Autumn and she's not answering me. She probably hasn't checked her phone all day and has no idea what's been going on." A muscle twitches in his cheek. "And she needs to. So I guess I'm gonna have to go to her."

"Go to her?" I echo. "How will you even find her if she's driving around?"

"I'll call Sorrento's and ask for her route," Mateo says, looking around my living room until his gaze settles on the door that leads into the kitchen. "You guys still have that breakfast nook?" he asks with a half smile. The built-in bench in front of our bay window was always Mateo's favorite place to eat when he came to my house. I nod, and he adds, "I'll call from there so you guys can keep talking. Can I get myself a glass of water while I'm at it?"

My heart skips as we lock eyes. I'm trying to focus, but even though Mateo looks like the embodiment of this very bad day— bruised face, bloody T-shirt, disheveled hair—I still wish that I could wrap my arms around him and forget everything else. When he kissed me earlier, the horrors of today melted away and for a few blissful seconds, I was exactly where I wanted to be, with the only person I've ever wanted to be with. His confession about Autumn shocked me, but not in the way he probably thinks. I don't judge him for that; how could I? It doesn't change the way I feel about him. I don't think anything will.

But even if I get out of this mess, I can't do anything about it. Mateo might feel the same way now, but he won't once I finally stop lying to him.

"Ivy?" Mateo prompts when I don't answer. "Is that a yes on the water, or . . . ?"

"What? No. I mean yes. I mean, help yourself to whatever." He disappears into the kitchen, and I turn back to Cal and try to adopt a businesslike tone. "Okay, where were we?"

Even though nobody asked him, Charlie picks up the remote and aims it at the television. "Let's finish watching this," he says.

Before I can protest, the screen springs to life and Ishaan Mittal is talking again. "The thing about Ivy is, she's like, super intense," he says earnestly. "And she really wanted to be senior class president. It's the most important thing in the world to her."

"You don't even know me," I mutter, folding my arms as I glare at the screen. Somehow, though, my televised humiliation is slightly less horrifying the second time around. Maybe I've become used to bad news.

Dale Hawkins angles the microphone closer and gives a solemn, respectful nod, like Ishaan's a renowned scientist explaining the cure for cancer. Ishaan plays it up, pausing for effect before he stares directly into the camera. "So when she lost the election to Boney yesterday, she flipped out."

"Excuse me? I did not *flip out*," I yell at the screen, so loudly that I almost miss Emily saying the exact same thing.

"What did I tell you?" Charlie says approvingly. "Ride or die."

"I don't know what happened to Boney this morning," Ishaan continues somberly. "But I can't help but wonder: Did Ivy decide to go scorched earth on him?"

"Scorched earth?" Dale repeats.

"Yeah, you know," Ishaan says. Then he throws his hands over his head while making an explosion sound. Beside him, Emily mouths *Oh my God* and closes her eyes.

Even Dale doesn't seem to know what to do with that, and Zack quickly leans forward. "That is, of course, just one theory," he says.

"And a chilling one," Dale says, recovering. "I'm Dale Hawkins, reporting live for *The Hawkins Report*."

His theme music starts up, and Charlie lifts the remote. "We gotta watch that again," he says as he hits the rewind button.

I ignore him, because once was more than enough to make a few things obvious. One, Dale Hawkins is every bit the hack my father always said he was. Two, Emily is a better friend than I deserve. And three, I should've texted her back way before now.

Better late than never, I think, pulling out my phone.

I'm so sorry I've been out of touch.

I swear I didn't do anything to Boney.

Thanks for being such a good friend.

I'll explain everything later.

As soon as I fix this.

Then, just for the hell of it, I look for Daniel's name among my notifications. My brother has been prolific since I asked him for Charlie's number; I have three missed calls and a long string of texts.

Call me back, or I really will tell M&D.

Do you realize you were ON THE NEWS???

This is going to fuck up Mom's night so bad.

I'm still going to lax after school. Then to Olive Garden with Trevor.

Like you care.

Jesus, Ivy. ANSWER ME.

I feel a sharp stab of guilt—not for Daniel, but for Mom. He's absolutely right that I'm wreaking havoc on her night, and knowing that was the worst part of watching *The Hawkins Report*. But I don't owe Daniel answers; I don't owe him *anything*. As far as I know, he hasn't said a word to defend me all day, and he definitely didn't go to bat for me the way Emily did. The only thing he seems to care about is getting to Olive Garden on time.

"What the hell is he doing?" I turn to see Mateo behind me, staring at Ishaan miming *scorched earth* on-screen.

I suppress a sigh as Cal grabs the remote from Charlie and finally, blessedly, turns off the television. "Never mind. Did you get Autumn's route?" I ask.

"No, Mr. Sorrento wouldn't give it out over the phone," Mateo says, looking überstressed. "I have to go there in person and show ID that proves I'm related to her. It's in Roslindale, so . . ." He turns to Cal. "Can you drive me there?"

"Us there," I say quickly. I'm even less inclined to split up now than I was an hour ago.

Cal hesitates too long for Mateo's liking. "Please," he adds, dark eyes flashing. I don't know what Cal's problem is because I, personally, would be giving Mateo whatever he wanted right now. "I need to know she's okay. And she needs to know what's going on. It's not safe for her to be driving around with no clue."

"Yeah, it's just . . ." Cal tugs at his hair with both hands. "This is a lot. Don't you think? I feel like it's too much. Maybe it's time to go to the police."

"No!" Mateo, Charlie, and I all say it in unison, loud and forceful.

Cal takes a step back, blinking. "But . . . but there's drugs involved, and . . ."

"And you want to get us all arrested?" Charlie asks, flicking white-blond bangs out of his eyes. "No thanks. I'm too pretty for jail."

Mateo snorts. "You're, what, seventeen? And rich. You'll be fine. But Autumn's a legal adult. She could actually go to prison."

"Or I could," I say. "I'm the one who allegedly went *scorched earth*."

Charlie shoots Cal a speculative gaze. "O'Shea-Wallace," he says abruptly. "Your dad's the dean of Carlton College, isn't he?"

"Yeah," Cal says warily. "So?"

"So, Stefan goes there," Charlie says. "He says your dad's really popular."

"He is," Cal says with a note of pride in his voice.

Charlie yawns and stretches his legs out in front of him. "Does he know about you and Ms. Jamison?"

Cal's jaw tightens. "There's nothing to know. We're friends."

"Do you think he'd see it that way?" Charlie asks. "If someone, hypothetically speaking, decided to give him a heads-up that you two were hanging out today?"

Cal blinks. "Are you . . . are you trying to blackmail me?"

"Yup." Charlie nods, matter-of-fact. "Is it working?"

"You can't . . . I'm not . . . your house got *ransacked*," Cal sputters. "How are you going to explain that to your parents?"

"Houses get broken into all the time," Charlie says. "I'll call them, and they'll call the police. Totally separate crime from Boney."

"Except it's *not*," Cal grits out.

I understand his frustration. I really, really do, because I share it. We're doing so many things wrong that it's almost physically painful. But every alternative comes with its own set of problems, and I'm not ready to face any of them. I don't think Cal is, either, so there's a sense of inevitability in the air even before Charlie plays his trump card.

"Dean O'Shea-Wallace's son and his art teacher," he says, leaning forward. "Now, *that* would make one hell of a YouTube video."

Cal blanches, eyes darting around the room like he's searching for an escape hatch, before his gaze settles reproachfully on me and Mateo. Neither of us are doing a thing to stop Charlie's black-mail, and while I know that sucks, I also don't know what else to do. "Fine," he says heavily. "I guess we're going to Sorrento's."

"Cool. And I'm going to Stefan's," Charlie says, getting to his feet. "I'm not hanging around my house to get arrested or murdered or whatever."

Ugh, Cal's going to hate me even more for this, but . . . "You can't drive," I point out. "You're still drunk. We'll take you."

"Sure," Charlie says, then shoots me a sly grin. "You should come with me. Stefan's having a party tonight. Everyone's gonna be there." He clocks Mateo's grim expression and adds, "Including the Weasel, probably."

"Thought you said he's not real," I say, sidestepping the invi-tation to make my way toward our coatrack. I grab one of Dan-iel's hooded sweatshirts and put it on, smoothing it over my top and almost half of my skirt. Then I lift the hood over my head and tuck my hair beneath it. Now that I'm local-news infamous, hiding my face seems like a good idea.

It feels strange to walk outside and see Cal's Honda at a hap-hazard angle in my driveway. I wonder if any of our neighbors drove by and clucked their tongues at the bad parking job. That seems like the kind of thing Carlton people would notice, while missing the teenage drug dealer living under their noses.

"Me and Ivy call back seat," Charlie says as we approach the car.

"No we don't," I snap. Any other day, it might have been flattering that Charlie St. Clair suddenly decided to notice me, because he's cute, popular, and the type of guy who usually looks right through me. But in this particular context, it's just weird and annoying. "I have shotgun," I add, and despite the fact that I know Mateo and I are doomed, I still get a little thrill from how hard he glares at Charlie.

We settle into the car, and Cal inserts his key in the ignition. The dashboard lights up, displaying 2:45 p.m. "Can you believe there's still ten minutes left of school?" Cal asks as the engine roars to life.

"No," Mateo and I say together.

"Where does Stefan live?" Cal asks, firing up the navigation system. Charlie rattles off a Carlton address, and the screen tells us it's only five minutes away.

Cal reaches for the car radio, which is playing so softly that I can barely hear it, and he turns up the volume. Before we'd gone into Charlie's house, Cal's dial spinning had stopped on an old-ies station, and now it's playing a cheesy song called "Afternoon Delight." The poppy, vaguely porn-y chorus fills the car, and it's so ridiculously out of place that, after a few moments of startled silence, all four of us start cracking up. Semihysterically, and for so long that my laughter almost turns into sobs, and I have to press my palm against my mouth to hold them back.

No tears. Not yet.

"Never has a song title been so inappropriate," Cal chokes out.

"Skyrockets in flight, y'all," Charlie snickers. Mateo lets out a snort, but is otherwise silent. When I glance at his reflection in the rearview mirror, his face is stony, like he can't believe he inadvertently trauma-bonded with Charlie.

"Can I ask a favor, you guys?" Cal asks as he turns a corner. "Can we not talk about anything terrifying until we get to the knife-sharpening place, and pretend we're normal people listen-ing to old-school soft rock?"

"Normal people don't do that, but okay," Mateo says.

18

IVY

After we drop off Charlie, we drive in silence to Sorrento's in Roslindale. It occurs to me, as I watch the miles flash by outside my window, that insisting on coming along might not be the best idea I've ever had. It's past three already; by the time we track down Autumn's schedule, and then Autumn herself, it could be close to five o'clock. Which is when I'd been planning to start getting ready for Mom's award ceremony.

The award ceremony is the least of your problems, Ivy.

I shove the poisonous thought away every time it starts to invade my brain, because I desperately need to believe that I can still pull off a perfect night for my mother. I'll make it work. An hour and a half of prep time was overkill anyway. I just won't wash my hair; maybe I'll put it up instead. I could do a French twist like Mom wears, except I don't know how, so I'd have to watch a YouTube video, which I don't have time for, so . . .

My mind keeps running different scenarios, adding and subtracting minutes as though everything that's wrong about today could be solved with the right schedule, until Cal pulls into a parking lot behind a squat, redbrick building. It's full of dingy, mostly dented white vans with giant knives painted on the sides. "Okay, I get the nickname now," he says, navigating into the only empty spot between two of them. "But did it seriously not occur to anyone at this company that their branding is a lot more *serial killer* than *helpful kitchen service?*"

"It's kind of a running joke at this point. I think customers would be disappointed to lose the murder vans," Mateo says, unclipping his seat belt. "Hopefully this won't take long."

I don't want him out of my sight. It's irrational, I know, but Cal's car feels like the only safe place on earth right now. Outside it, we need to pair up. "I'll come with you," I say, tightening the hood of Daniel's sweatshirt around my face.

"Yeah, okay," Mateo says.

My skin pricks as we wind through all the knife-covered vans, which I can't help but feel would make the perfect cover for a sneak attack. But we're the only ones in the parking lot, and reach an awning-covered door safely. Mateo pulls it open to the loud jangle of a bell, and steps aside to let me go in first.

I adjust my hood again as Mateo closes the door behind us and leads me through the vestibule into a narrow hallway. The walls are covered with a dozen framed "Best of Boston" awards, and I make note of the dates as we pass them. The most recent one is from eight years ago, so Sorrento's might be a little past its prime.

"Hold on," Mateo says, pausing to scan the hallway. "I can't remember my way around. I've only been here once before."

I follow his gaze until an older man's head pops out of an

187

open door near the end of the hall, startling me enough that I nearly gasp. "Hello there," he calls.

"Hi, I called about—" Mateo starts, but the man holds up a hand before he can say anything else.

"I'm right in the middle of something, so give me five minutes, okay? Then I'll help you with whatever you need."

He disappears before I can explain that we don't *have* five minutes. "Ugh," I mutter, frustrated. "Should we follow him?"

Mateo stares down the hallway, hands on his hips. "I don't want to piss him off. Let's give him a few minutes. I want to show you something anyway." He digs his phone out of his pocket and unlocks it. "I Googled that Dominick Payne guy while we were driving. You probably did, too, right?"

"Um, yeah," I say, tugging at the hem of Daniel's sweatshirt. I don't want to admit that I spent most of the drive planning alternate timelines for award ceremony prep. "I mean, I tried, but my signal was kind of spotty."

"Did you catch the *Herald* article about his gallery almost going bankrupt?"

"What? No!" Mateo holds out his screen, and I quickly scan the article. It's from a year ago, about how Dominick Payne and a few other artists opened an ambitious, sprawling gallery on Newbury Street, only to run into financial problems almost immediately. They were saved from closing, Payne claimed in the article, by an "outside investor."

"Well, that was a convenient, and vague, influx of cash," I say when I finish reading.

"Right? The guy had money problems, and then all of a sudden, he didn't," Mateo says. "Sounds like Autumn on a bigger scale." His expression darkens. "Plus, what kind of person keeps using a studio they're not renting anymore?"

I manage not to remind him that I'd made that exact point when we first saw Boney entering the building this morning. "The kind of person who's doing something they shouldn't," I say instead. "And wants any fallout to land on the new owners."

"I'm gonna send this to Cal," Mateo says, swiping at his screen. "I think he's coming around about Ms. Jamison being involved, don't you?"

"I hope so," I say, chewing the inside of my cheek. "Ceramics class, my ass. That anonymous tip has to be about her. I never got anywhere near Boney."

Mateo rubs a hand over his jaw, his expression thoughtful. "Maybe you didn't have to."

I tilt my head, confused. "Huh?"

"You said you heard something that led you to Boney, right? Well, maybe whoever killed him caught a glimpse of you and decided to make you the fall guy." Mateo shrugs as I gape. "Maybe the anonymous tip is bullshit."

Before I can answer, a voice breaks in. "I'm so sorry for the wait."

I blink in surprise as the man who'd greeted us earlier emerges into the hallway; I'd been so caught up in my conversation with Mateo that I'd completely forgotten we were waiting for someone. The man is compact and white-haired, wearing a black smock with *Sorrento's* embroidered in white script across the front. "I'm Vin Sorrento. How can I help you?" he asks. A welcoming smile lights up his weathered face as he approaches, but dims once he gets a better look at Mateo. "My goodness, young man. What happened to you?"

Mateo touches the bandage at his temple. "Oh, it's nothing. I was, um, in a car accident. A minor one," he adds as Mr. Sorrento's expression grows more alarmed.

"I'm very sorry to hear that."

"It's fine. I'm Mateo Wojcik, we spoke earlier? And this is—" He catches himself before he says my name, and I wave while ducking my head. "This is my friend. You said I had to come in person to get my cousin Autumn's schedule."

"Yes, that's right. Can you show me some identification, please?"

"Sure thing." Mateo reaches for his wallet. "I really appreciate this. We've had a family emergency, and Autumn's not answering her phone."

"Oh dear. Was it the car accident?" Mr. Sorrento asks.

"Ah, no," Mateo says, handing over his driver's license. "Different emergency. Everyone's okay, I just need to talk to her."

"Of course." Mr. Sorrento takes Mateo's ID and holds it up to the light. "Your family must be very worried. Someone else called right after you."

Mateo goes rigid. "Excuse me?"

"Another gentleman," Mr. Sorrento says. "He sounded rather urgent as well. Wouldn't leave his name, though. This looks fine, thank you."

He tries to return the ID, but Mateo is too frozen to take it. I grab it for him, my heart pounding as I think back to the wreckage of Charlie's house. And oblivious Autumn, not answering her phone while she drives, having no idea what's been happening all day. "So can we get her schedule?" I ask. "Has she checked in at all?"

"I got an alert that she left her last customer about ten minutes ago," Mr. Sorrento says, wiping his hands on his apron. "I'll need to log into our system to get the rest of her route." He makes a sweeping gesture up the hallway. "The computer's in the main office. Would you like to wait here, or come along? We have coffee made."

I look to Mateo for guidance, but he's still not moving. "We'll wait here, thanks," I say.

"All right. Be back soon," Mr. Sorrento says. I watch him disappear around the corner, then give Mateo's arm a reassuring squeeze.

"See, she's fine. She's doing her route like normal."

"She's not *fine*." Mateo starts to pace. "Someone's after her."

"You don't know that. Whoever called could have a totally innocent reason for wanting to find her. Maybe it was . . ." I search my brain for a comforting alternative. "Your dad."

"Yeah, right," Mateo snorts, his strides lengthening. He curls one hand into a fist and slams it repeatedly into his palm. "Like he's gonna suddenly start giving a crap."

"Well, Mr. Sorrento didn't give whoever it was any information, did he? So they won't be able to track Autumn down." I clutch Mateo's arms to hold him still. "Look, I realize I'm the last person to give this particular piece of advice in a crisis, but—letting yourself spiral will only make things worse. Trust me on this."

That startles him enough that he huffs out a near laugh. "Well, you're the expert."

Mr. Sorrento appears at the end of the hallway then, waving

a piece of paper, and I release Mateo's arms. "See? He has her route. We'll find her. Everything will be okay."

"I'll believe that when I see it," Mateo says, but his tense expression softens. Then, unexpectedly, he brushes the edge of my hoodie away from my face, and leans down to kiss my cheek. "Thanks for talking me down," he says, tugging the hood back into place before heading toward Mr. Sorrento.

"Anytime," I say, resisting the urge to touch my fingertips to my cheek.

Mateo turns to give me a fleeting smile over his shoulder. "You know what? You're cute when you're incognito."

Despite everything, something that feels a lot like happiness starts to bubble through my veins. But then I watch Mateo confer with Mr. Sorrento in the hallway, and the emptiness of my earlier words hits me hard. *Everything will be okay,* I said. I'm praying that it's true for Autumn, but I know it's not true for Mateo and me.

The buzzing joy recedes as fast as it came, replaced with the same five-word drumbeat that keeps ruining the only bright spot in this disastrous day.

You have to tell him.

YOUTUBE, CARLTON SPEAKS CHANNEL

Ishaan and Zack are in the Carlton High parking lot.

ISHAAN, *panning to the crowd of students behind him:* This is Ishaan and Zack coming to you live from Carlton High, getting in-person reactions from fellow students to our *Hawkins Report* segment about the deadly feud between Boney Mahoney and Ivy Sterling-Shepard. Hey, Carmen! *(The camera focuses on a pretty brunette walking past.)* Do you have any comment?

CARMEN, *stopping:* My comment is, You suck.

ISHAAN: Come on, now. A kid died. We're just trying to get at the truth.

CARMEN: How about you let the police do that?

(Two boys appear over her shoulder, one in an athletic jacket and one with a buzz cut.)

BUZZ CUT: Ivy Sterling-Shepard, people. The classic story of a good girl gone bad.

ATHLETIC JACKET: Remember when she read porn at the talent show? Good times.

ZACK: Look, I think we can all agree that we're raising some important questions here, but this is getting a little off topic.

(Emily Zhang starts pushing her way through the crowd of students, calling out, "Excuse me, coming through! I have new information!" She puts her hands on her hips once she's in front of the camera.)

EMILY: First of all, I heard from Ivy. She says she had nothing to do with what happened to Boney.

ISHAAN: Yeah, well, she *would* say that. Where is she?

EMILY: Second of all, you guys refused to do basic research, so I did it for you. There were twelve absences in the Carlton High student body today, including two other seniors.

ISHAAN, *looking mildly interested:* Who were the seniors?

EMILY: Mateo Wojcik and Cal O'Shea-Wallace.

CARMEN: Oh, please. Mateo's not involved in this.

ISHAAN: Cal who?

194

ZACK: Yeah, Mateo's just, like . . . home sick or something.

EMILY: How do you know? Have you talked to him? *(She pauses, waiting for Zack to respond, but he doesn't.)* If Ivy is guilty by absence, then he should be, too. Especially since they used to be friends.

CARMEN: They did?

ISHAAN: Seriously, who's Cal?

ZACK: Okay, let's—wait a sec. Is that Daniel Sterling-Shepard? *(The camera zooms on a blond boy with an athletic bag slung over one shoulder.)*

ISHAAN: Yeah, it is. Heading for lacrosse practice like it's a normal day. Is he clinging to routine, or does he just not give a crap? Yo, Danny boy! Daniel, over here! *(The blond boy turns.)* You wanna make a statement about your sister?

(Daniel raises both middle fingers.)

ISHAAN: Powerful statement.

19

MATEO

I never fully appreciated Cal's driving skills until now. It's almost three-thirty in the afternoon, when greater Boston's early rush hour traffic starts filling up the roads, but we haven't seen any of it. He keeps overriding the GPS by taking back roads to get to Hyde Park, where Autumn is supposed to be in about fifteen minutes. When the system recalculates once again and posts a new estimated arrival time, it looks like we might actually make it.

"How do you know all these roads?" Ivy asks. She's been giving Cal the lowdown on everything we talked about in Sorrento's, and he's been absorbing all of it without arguing or defending Ms. Jamison. But he hasn't said much, either.

"My girlfriend before Noemi was a competitive fencer," he says. "I used to drive her to meets all over the place."

"Fencing? That's interesting," Ivy says, and bam—Cal jumps

at the chance to change the subject, launching into a monologue about his ex that I immediately tune out. I don't blame him for wanting to focus on something else for a few minutes, but I can't do the same. I keep flashing back to what Mr. Sorrento said in the hallway: *Someone else called right after you. He sounded rather urgent.*

Ever since Autumn started selling the Oxy, I've been mad at her. I was afraid she'd get into trouble, maybe even get Ma or me into trouble. But I never thought, until today, that she could get *hurt.*

My phone buzzes in my pocket. I pull it out, hoping for a message from Autumn, but it's from Ma. I get a quick jolt of apprehension—*she knows*—but it's just a picture of her and her friend Christy flanking my aunt Rose. They're sitting on Aunt Rose's rock-hard, floral upholstered couch, which has a bunch of silver and gold balloons tied around one arm. All three of them are beaming, cheerful and oblivious.

Don't forget to call Aunt Rose and wish her a happy birthday!

I won't, I text back, suppressing a sigh. Ma will know if I don't follow through, so at some point in this horrible, endless day, I'm going to have to yell birthday greetings so my ninety-year-old great-aunt will be able to hear me over the sounds of her party.

Which . . . huh. Gives me an idea, actually.

"Almost there," Cal calls.

I look out the window and frown, ready to protest, because we're still surrounded by trees, so there's no way we're close to a sports bar in the middle of downtown Hyde Park. Then he makes a sharp turn, and we're suddenly merging onto a two-lane highway. I spot the blinking red sign for Uncle Al's Sports Pub less than a quarter mile away.

"You're a miracle worker, Cal," I say, glancing at the clock on my phone before stuffing it into my pocket. It's 3:23, or about two minutes before Autumn is due to show up. Mr. Sorrento told us routes can vary depending on traffic, but she was on time for her last stop.

"The good thing is, if she's in there sharpening knives, we'll know right away," Cal says, turning into the parking lot for Uncle Al's. "You can't miss the murder van."

He's right, and she's not here. Cal pulls into an empty space and kills the engine. "Should we wait?" he asks.

"Yeah," I say, because we're still a minute early, but Ivy shakes her head.

"We should go inside and ask if she's already been here. That way, if she's ahead of schedule, we won't lose time heading for the next place."

"Good idea," I say. Ivy is still in full disguise mode, her over-sized hoodie covering half her face. "You want to come with?"

"Sure," she says, unbuckling.

We're both all business, not showing any trace that we hooked up an hour ago. If there's one good thing to come out of this mess, it's knowing I might have another shot with Ivy, but I can't shove my worries down far enough to think about that yet.

I'm not my father, after all.

The parking lot is right next to the road, and the sound of cars roaring by at high speed makes it impossible to talk as Ivy and I make our way inside Uncle Al's. The noise level is almost as high in there; a TV blares in the corner of the entryway, and loud conversation spills over from the bar. The air smells like fryer grease and stale beer. There's a woman my mom's age sitting at a stool beside a hutch with a stack of large menus, and she gives us a confused once-over as we approach. Uncle Al's is a restaurant, not just a bar, so theoretically we could be there to eat, but I doubt we fit the typical customer profile.

"Party of two?" the woman asks uncertainly.

"No. I'm looking for my cousin," I say. "She works for the knife-sharpening place, Sorrento's? She's supposed to be in your kitchen now, or soon."

"Hmm." The hostess purses her lips. "Can't say I know anything about that. Let me get a manager for you."

"Thanks," I say as she rounds the corner into the bar. Ivy turns her attention to the TV screen, which shows the Red Sox at batting practice.

"Gotta love sports bars," she murmurs. "They're not big on the news, so I probably won't have to see my face plastered on-screen while we're here." Her forehead knits up. "Do you really think that tip might've been called in by the person who killed Boney?"

"I don't see why we should trust someone who won't even give their name." I lean against the hutch and think back to when Cal and I first watched Dale Hawkins this morning. "Plus, it's weird how the tipster called the police *and* Dale's show, isn't it?" I say. "Not even the regular news, which might've fact-checked it a little better. Like they wanted that description out far and wide and fast."

"Yeah," Ivy says, her eyes still fixed on the television. "You're right. And it worked, didn't it? Everyone's talking about me instead of looking for the actual killer. I don't know, though." She scuffs the toe of her shoe against the floor. "Part of me still wants the tip to be about Ms. Jamison." I raise my eyebrows, and she scuffs harder. "I guess because if it is, then it's more her fault I got dragged into this than my own."

"None of this is your fault," I say. "Anyway, somebody sent Dale Hawkins links to Ishaan and Zack's YouTube videos, remember? You could blame her for that."

She rolls her eyes. "You know that had to be Ishaan."

The front door bursts open then, framing two red-haired figures against the bright sunshine outside: Cal and Autumn. "Found her," Cal says breathlessly.

Autumn's eyes widen when she catches sight of me. "What happened to your face? Did you get into a—"

Before she can finish, I've yanked my cousin into a bone-crushing hug. It's the first I've ever given her that's not casual and one-armed, and it surprises me as much as it does her. Relief floods my veins, and for a few seconds, all I can think is *She's okay. She's okay.*

As long as she's okay, we can figure out the rest.

"Mateo, what the hell?" Autumn's voice is muffled against my shoulder, and bewildered enough that I know Cal hasn't had a chance to explain anything. "Are you all right?"

"I am now," I say, releasing her. "But we have a lot to talk about."

20

MATEO

"Ow!" Autumn shrieks, shaking her wrist. "Goddamn it, that hurts."

"Stop punching the wall, then," I say as Ivy and Cal stare at my cousin with twin expressions of alarm. We're all sitting in the back of the murder van, surrounded by boxes of knives and sharpening tools, because the windowless interior feels safer than Cal's car.

And also so Autumn can lose her shit in private.

"I can't," Autumn grits out. "I'm too. Fucking. *Upset!*" The last word is a scream, and she lets her fist fly again with another yelp of pain. "Boney, oh my god, Boney." True to form, Autumn hadn't checked her phone all day, so we had to be the ones to break the news about Boney to her. She's not, to put it mildly, taking it well.

"That poor, stupid kid. Oh my God, I hate this. I hate myself. I hate *you*." Her voice rises on the last word as she turns and punches me in the arm, hard enough that I'll have a bruise to-morrow. "I hate you, you asshole! Why did you let me do this?"

I don't answer her, because she doesn't need an answer, but Ivy pipes up, "You can't blame Mateo for—"

"I know that, Ivy!" Autumn yells, hammering her fists on the floor.

"Seriously, you're gonna break something," I say. "Either your hands or the van."

Ivy and Cal are both gazing around as though they're try-ing to figure out how to escape while simultaneously hiding all the knives, but the thing is—this is how Autumn deals. Ma was constantly patching up the drywall in her room when she first moved in. It used to freak me out, too, until I realized that you have to let her get it out of her system.

"I tried so hard to be careful," Autumn says. Her voice chokes off on the last word, and she takes a few deep breaths before continuing. "I only have one customer. One of the guys I work with at Ziggy's Diner gets migraines that his doctor won't treat, so he takes the Oxy for that. I thought I could keep an eye on him, make sure nothing bad happened, and everything would be okay." She lets out a frustrated moan and pummels the floor again. "And I *told* Boney not to go to Boston. That deal was all kinds of sketchy. He promised he wouldn't!"

"Yeah, well, apparently the guy convinced him otherwise," I say. "According to Charlie, Boney said you were holding them back."

"Arghhhhh." Autumn finally stops punching things long enough to bury her face in her hands, muffling her voice. Not enough that I can't hear her next words, though. "I'm turning myself in."

Alarm hits me, fast and hard. "No you're not," I say.

"Yes I am!" She lifts her head to glare at me. "The police need to know what Boney was involved in if they're going to catch the creep who killed him."

I glare right back. "If you turn yourself in, you'll go to jail."

"I *should* go to jail!"

"And then what happens to Ma?" I ask, and that finally shuts her up for a second. "Listen. We've been doing things your way for a while now, and I think we can both agree that your way sucks. Right?"

Autumn scowls. "Shut up."

"I'll take that as a yes. So it's time to do things my way. Here's what you're going to do." I've been thinking this through the whole time she's been ranting. "You're going to drop off the murder van, Uber to South Station, and take a bus to the Bronx. Text Ma and tell her you want to surprise Aunt Rose for her birthday."

"That I want to . . ." Autumn stares at me in astonishment. "But the party will be over before I get there. Aunt Elena and Christy will be driving home by—"

"Tell her you want to stay overnight. You both need to be out of town, because whoever killed Boney probably knows where we live."

Autumn tries again. "But what if—"

"And you can't go home to pack," I interrupt. "Buy a toothbrush at South Station or whatever. See if you can convince Ma to stay a few days. Maybe by then, the police will have solved this thing."

"Not if they don't have any clues, they won't," Autumn protests. "Since you're sending the clues *out of town.*"

"I have to," I say. "Someone was looking for you."

"Maybe it was Gabe," Autumn says.

"Then why wouldn't he tell Mr. Sorrento his name? Check your phone. Do you have any messages from Gabe, saying he's trying to find you?"

She scrolls through the pileup of texts she's gotten all day. "I have a few from him . . . okay, he doesn't *specifically* mention calling Sorrento's, but that doesn't mean that he didn't. He might've just forgotten to mention it."

I glower at her. "Stop arguing. I'm serious about this. If some drug kingpin out there knows our names, then you need to keep Ma away." She inhales, like she's gathering steam to argue, so I go in for the kill. "You owe me, Autumn. *You owe me.* I've been telling you for weeks not to pull this Oxy bullshit, and you wouldn't listen. You got us into this mess. The least you can do is get Ma out of it."

Autumn falls silent, cradling her red, raw punching hand, and I can tell by the furtive expression on her face that she's looking for a way out. When she heaves a deep sigh, I know she hasn't found one. "All right. I'll go. But what about you? It's *your* name on that list. You're in more danger than anyone." A pleading tone creeps into her voice. "Come with me."

"I can't. I have to stay with these guys," I say, gesturing toward Ivy and Cal. "We need to . . ." And then I trail off, because I have no clue what we need to do next.

Ivy clears her throat. "I had a thought," she says, shifting her position on the van floor. "Our only lead, pretty much, is Ms. Jamison, right? And possibly Dominick Payne. But we're not sure how closely they're connected." She turns toward Cal. "What if we go to her classroom at school and check out that signed print? We can compare his signature to what's on the D card."

Cal frowns. "Why would we do that?"

"Because then we'd know whether they're more than just colleagues," Ivy says. "If they're in a romantic relationship, there's a lot more reason for her to protect him—or be working with him. Maybe we could call in an anonymous tip of our own."

"I don't know," Cal says doubtfully.

"Do you have another idea?" Ivy asks, then seems to think better of letting him answer. Now that Charlie's not here to blackmail him, he'd probably say, *Go home*. "Look, I think we just need to keep moving forward. Asking questions and getting information. I mean, what if we hadn't gone to Charlie's? We wouldn't know anything about Boney and the drugs."

"We would if Mateo had told us," Cal mutters.

"Again, so we're clear—wasn't in the loop on Boney," I say testily, shooting Autumn a hard look. "Since somebody decided to keep that to herself."

My cousin avoids my gaze. "How are you going to get into school? By the time you get back to Carlton, it'll be close to five o'clock. Everything will be locked."

"Yeah," Ivy says, and her determined expression dims. "I've been worrying about the time. I was hoping to be doing something else by five o'clock, but . . . you know what? It's fine. Adjustments can be made. I'll just wear a less complicated dress. One with fewer buttons."

She's lost me. I look down at her sweatshirt-and-skirt combo, which doesn't look all that complicated. "And that will unlock the building because . . . why?" I ask.

"It won't," Ivy says, flushing a little. "Sorry, different topic. I was thinking about getting ready for my mom's award ceremony. But if we make it to school by five, I can be home before five-thirty, which is plenty of time." She squares her shoulders. "The night can still be perfect, especially if we find something that takes the focus off me and puts it onto Ms. Jamison."

Cal and I exchange glances, and I can read my own thoughts reflected in his face: *Let her have this.* We stay silent as Ivy digs into her bag and pulls out a ring of keys, separating the biggest one from the others. "*This* will unlock the building," she says. "It's a master key. I needed it for the charity auction last week, and I never got around to giving it back."

"You're not worried about running into people?" Autumn asks. For the first time since we got into the murder van, a ghost of a smile flits across her face. "I mean, seeing as you're a fugitive and all, Ivy."

Ivy had pushed her hood off while we were talking, but now she pulls it back over her head. "I'm prepared," she says. "Besides, almost everyone should be cleared out by now."

"Okay, well . . . listen, you guys." Autumn twists her hands in her lap, her tone turning serious. "I know you must think I'm a piece of shit."

"No—" Ivy starts, but Autumn waves her words away.

"It's fine. You should. I did a horrible thing. I thought it wouldn't have any consequences, but it did, and I have to figure out how to live with that." Her voice thickens. "I want you to know that I never would have done something like this if I didn't feel so . . . hopeless. And helpless. The thing is, there are only two people in the world that I love with my whole heart and soul. That I'd kill for, or die for, or whatever qualifier you want to use."

Autumn punches me in the arm again, but more gently this time. "One of them is this jerk. The other is my aunt Elena. And the way my aunt fell apart when she lost her job and her health at the same time—it broke my heart. Smashed it to pieces, basically. I didn't even know I could still hurt like that. I thought my parents dying was the worst I could ever feel, but this—let me tell you, this was right up there." She brushes angrily at her eyes. "I'm not saying that to make excuses. I just want you to understand."

"God, yeah," Cal says. "Of course."

Ivy's eyes are wide and glassy. "I understand."

"Do you?" Autumn asks. It almost sounds like an accusation, and I'm about to ask her what she's getting at when she adds, "Good. Because you need to know that the only way I can even start to put this right is to make sure that nobody else gets hurt. I'm going to do what Mateo asks because, like he said, I owe him. But I want you guys to promise me something. Not *you*," she adds, cutting her eyes toward me. "I can't trust you with this. But Cal and Ivy—if you get to a point where you need to explain what happened to keep yourselves or anyone else safe, don't hold back on my account." Autumn lifts her chin, her voice firm. "Don't you dare let Mateo make you. Spill your guts and take me down. I mean it. I'm not going anywhere until the two of you promise me that."

The silence in the van is deafening. I open my mouth to fill it, but Autumn shoves her palm in front of my face before I can. "You shut up, Mateo. I'm talking to them."

Cal licks his lips. "Okay," he says. "I promise."

Ivy just nods, looking shell-shocked, until Autumn reaches over and shakes her shoulder. Not as hard as she's been manhandling me, but enough to show she means business. "Say it," she commands. "I need to hear you say it."

"Yes." Ivy gulps. She almost looks afraid, and I'd tell Autumn to dial it back if I weren't so desperate to keep things moving.

"The words, Ivy," Autumn presses. "Say the words."

"I promise," Ivy whispers. Then she swallows hard. "And I'm . . . I'm so sorry about everything that happened to your aunt." Her eyes flick toward me. "Your mom."

"It's awful. But it doesn't excuse what I did." Autumn moves past me to unlock the van's back door. "You guys better get going. Be careful."

I feel like I should say something now—something deep and meaningful and true. Like, *I don't blame you for any of this.* Or, *If I didn't agree with you on some level, I would've figured out a way to stop you.* Or maybe, *I'd die for you, too.* But all I can manage, as I climb out of the van, is "Keep Ma away from here."

"I will," Autumn says.

The sun's disorienting after the darkness of the van, and I squint as spots dance across my line of vision. "Cal, where'd you park the car again?" I ask.

"This way." I turn toward his voice and feel a hand on my arm, but it's smaller and lighter than his would be. I blink and Ivy's face, drawn and tight, comes into focus.

"I need to tell you something," she says.

21

MATEO

Ivy looks serious, but she's serious about everything. Besides, I'm pretty sure I'm immune to bad news at this point.

"What's up?" I ask, letting her guide me to Cal's car. We climb in and he fires up his GPS again, though I don't know why he's bothering when he'll probably just work his back-route magic to Carlton High.

"I . . ." Ivy glances at Cal as she settles herself into the passenger seat and turns to face me. "I feel like I should maybe tell you this privately, Mateo, but I don't see us being alone anytime soon, and I don't . . . I can't not tell you, any longer."

"Um, if this is a declaration of love, I'm happy for you," Cal says as he starts the car. "But it's going to get super awkward for me."

I snort. "Eyes on the road, Cal. Nobody needs your commentary." I expect Ivy to agree, maybe even laugh, but she just looks wretched. For the first time since she grabbed my arm, unease stirs in my gut.

"Fine," Cal says. "Let me activate invisible mode so the two of you can discuss nothing of importance in private." He mimes putting a shield over his head, like the giant nerd he is. I love the kid, but he should lay off the comics occasionally.

"You know you can still hear us if you're invisible, right?" I ask.

"Can't hear you! Invisible!" Cal says, and I can't help but laugh.

Ivy doesn't, though. She's gone silent, so I prod, "I think that's your cue."

"Yeah. Okay. So . . ." Ivy's facing me, but she's not really looking at me. Her eyes are on the window beside me as Cal merges onto the highway and cars start flashing past us. "It's hard to know where to start, but . . . I think it would be the junior talent show, last year," she says.

That's so unexpected that at first I have no reaction. Then I swallow a grin. "You mean your hot-firefighter monologue?" I knew what that was about as soon as I heard it. Every time one of her aunt's books arrived, Ivy used to read the back copy to Cal and me.

Ivy cringes. It's obvious that still bothers her, and I wish—just like I wished when I watched from the audience last year—that she'd listen to me if I told her to let it go. Yeah, she got owned by Daniel, and it was embarrassing. But the thing she doesn't get is that most people wanted to laugh *with* her, not at her. Ivy has a sense of humor, but she couldn't pull it out when she needed it. If she'd been able to brush it off, or maybe even run with it, she could've won yesterday's election by a landslide.

And none of us would be here right now.

"Yes," she says, twisting her hands in her lap. "I guess I don't need to tell you that I was really upset, and humiliated, and just . . . so mad at Daniel. He's always like that. He's the star of our family, but he still tears me down every chance he gets."

"Ivy, if you don't get that you're a star, too, I don't know what to tell you," I say.

I mean it as a compliment, so I'm surprised—and kind of horrified—when she blinks back tears. "Don't cry," I add urgently. "It's not that big a deal." I can almost hear my mother's voice in my head, saying the same thing she used to say back when Autumn first came to live with us and her rage would dissolve into tears: *Tears are healthy. I'd be more worried if she didn't cry.*

But that was over losing her parents. Not being embarrassed at school.

"I'm not upset about the talent show," Ivy says. "Not anymore. This is about . . . what I did after." She swallows hard. "When I tried to get back at Daniel."

"Get back at Daniel?" I echo. "What, like—revenge?"

"Yeah," Ivy says. "I wanted him to know what it's like to be the laughingstock of the school. I didn't know how, exactly, but I wanted to do *something.*"

I'd laugh if she didn't look so miserable. The idea of straight-laced Ivy Sterling-Shepard plotting against her jackass brother is pretty entertaining, even if I can't imagine why she thought it would work. Daniel's way too full of himself to care what other people think about him. "So what'd you land on?" I ask.

"Well, that's the problem. I was waiting for the right opportunity, but it never came, and then . . . I was supposed to pick him up at Patrick DeWitt's birthday party last June. The one he had at Spare Me."

The uneasy feeling comes back. Not just because that's our former bowling alley, but because that was *the* party. The one that ruined everything. "Yeah?" I say cautiously.

"Yeah." Ivy flushes brick red. "So Daniel texted me to pick him up early because he was bored. But by the time I got there, he'd decided that he didn't want to leave anymore. The guys had started filming themselves doing tricks, and they were posting the videos on Instagram. Daniel was getting all pumped up because he kept bowling strikes with his eyes closed, or backward, or hopping on one foot. He told me to leave, but I was like— what's the point? I'll just have to come back in an hour. So I sat there and felt annoyed, and started organizing bags from the errands I'd just run for my mom and . . . I got an idea."

I don't want to know. I'm positive, with every atom in my body, that I don't want to know what that idea was. So I don't say anything, but Ivy keeps going.

"They had a pretty big audience at that point. I thought . . . I guess I thought it would be poetic justice if I could make Daniel look like an idiot in front of everyone. And I'd bought some baby oil at CVS for my mom earlier. So when the guys took a break to get pizza right before Daniel's turn, I . . ." She's literally shaking now, vibrating in her seat like somebody flipped her on switch and set it to high. "I spilled some of it, on the lane. So Daniel would fall on his ass while he was showing off. Except . . ."

"Ivy. Holy shit." Cal speaks for the first time, which is good, because I can't. "Except he didn't. Patrick DeWitt did."

Hell yeah, Patrick DeWitt did. He went flying into the ball dispenser and dislocated his shoulder. The whole thing was captured on Instagram by half the lacrosse team, which turned out to be great news for Patrick's parents when they decided to sue my mother. Fury pulses through me, hot and white, and it's all I can do not to slam my fist through Cal's window.

Ivy's full-on crying now, and fuck that. Tears might be healthy, but she hasn't earned these. Other people suffered—*really* suffered—for what she did, not her. "So what you're telling me is, you set Patrick's accident up," I say in a low, deadly tone. "But instead of telling someone, you let my mother get sued for negligence."

"I didn't know!" Ivy says tearfully. "I mean, I knew about Patrick, of course I did, but everyone said he was going to be okay. I didn't know about the lawsuit. I was out of the country with my mother when it happened, and it was summer, so people weren't talking about it at home." She's still trembling like a terrified rabbit, but I don't care. I can't stand to look at her. I can't believe I *kissed* her. "And I tried . . . when I realized what happened," she goes on. "I tried to make up for it by asking my dad to give your mom a job—"

"Give her a job? To replace the one you took?" I'm yelling now, my voice too loud for the small car. It's a good thing I'm not driving because if I was, we'd all be dead. I'd have lost control and smashed into whatever was closest, burying Ivy's words in an explosion of glass and metal and shattered bodies. I'm angry enough for that to almost sound good. "My mother built that place up from the *ground*, Ivy. It was her life. It was all our lives. Now Autumn and I are working five jobs between us, and

Ma can barely work, and all day you've been acting like none of that has anything to do with you. Just *Oh, that's too bad, sucks to be you guys.*"

Ivy swipes fiercely at her wet cheeks. "I didn't mean—I feel horrible about it. It's why I told you, even though—"

"Even though what? Even though you turned my cousin into a drug dealer?"

Ivy's face crumples, and a corner of my raging brain knows that was too far. But all I can think about now is Ma's expression when she got slapped with the DeWitts' lawsuit. "Overwaxed lane," she'd said numbly, dropping heavily into a chair. Her knees had already started to bother her then, but we didn't know yet that it was going to be a permanent problem. "And the thing is—they're right. It was slippery. But I don't understand why. I didn't do anything different that day. I don't know what happened."

Ma wasn't mad about the lawsuit, even though Patrick's shoulder healed fine and the DeWitts were overreacting assholes with their *It's important to take a stand against irresponsible businesses* crap. She felt guilty. Like she deserved to lose everything.

Then she did, and my cousin got backed into a corner enough that she made the worst decision of her life. When I think about the domino effect of Ivy's stupidity, I almost can't breathe. My entire life would be different if she'd minded her damn business and kept that baby oil in her bag where it belonged.

Baby oil. Jesus. Of all the possible ways to get your world destroyed, that has to be the most pointless.

"I'll make it up to you—" Ivy starts.

"Oh yeah? How're you gonna do that? Build a time machine

and go back a few months to keep yourself from being an asshole?" I rub a hand across my forehead, hard, wishing I could scrub the entire story from my brain. "You know what the worst thing is, Ivy? It's not only that you basically ruined my mother and were too cowardly to admit it. It's that you were so goddamn *petty.* That was your big idea, huh? Your brilliant plan for getting back at Daniel. Who wouldn't even be a problem if you could've managed, just once, to get your head out of your ass and not treat a stupid joke like the end of the world."

The car falls silent. I can barely spare a thought for Cal, but the small part of me that's not consumed with rage pities him for being trapped in this car. Then again, if it weren't for Cal, none of us would be here, so fuck him, too.

"For what it's worth," Ivy finally says in a low voice, "I hate myself just as much as you hate me."

"Not possible," I spit out. "In case it's not clear, Ivy—I'm done with you. You're pathetic, and I don't want to see or speak to you again for the rest of my life."

She drops her head. "Oh, it's clear."

There's nothing else to say. I almost can't remember why we're headed to Carlton High anymore, but as soon as we get there, I'm out. Cal and Ivy can both go to hell.

And I hope she burns there.

22

CAL

I wish that invisibility shield had been real. And soundproof. You wouldn't think I'd need it anymore, since Mateo and Ivy have been silent since their fight. But it's the kind of silence that fills your ears with a dull roar that's somehow worse than screaming. By the time I pull into the parking lot at school, my head is throbbing from the pressure.

The lot is nearly empty except for Ivy's car and a few other stragglers. Before I can even shift into park, Mateo brusquely says, "Can you pop the trunk?" When I do, he gets out of the car, grabs his backpack, closes the trunk, and leans into the still-open rear-seat door. I'm half-afraid he's about to go off on Ivy again, but all he says is "Later, Cal." Then he slams the door and takes off across the parking lot toward the back fence.

"Well, shit," I say, gazing after him. "I didn't think he was going to *leave*."

Ivy slumps in her seat. "He can't stand the sight of me."

Fair point, but the day can't end like this. There's too much still hanging in the balance. "Stay here," I say, sliding out from behind the wheel. "Let me talk to him."

I have to practically run to catch him before he hops over the fence. "Mateo, wait. Stop," I say breathlessly, grabbing hold of his arm. "Aren't you gonna come in?"

He spins to face me. "For what?" he asks, pulling his arm away. "What are we here for, again? A fucking *painting*? Who cares. It's just another one of Ivy's stupid ideas, and you know what? I've had more than enough of those."

I'm not going to try to defend her to him. I still can't fully wrap my head around what she did, so I can only imagine how Mateo feels. "Look, I get it," I say. "I don't blame you for being pissed. But what are you going to do now?"

He shrugs. "Go home. Then go to work."

"But you can't go home!" I nearly yell. "You sent your cousin out of town because it's not safe. What if someone's waiting for you?"

"Don't worry about me, Cal," Mateo says. "I'm not your problem anymore. The Shittiest Day Ever is officially over."

He turns, and I catch his arm again. He pulls away, and this time his expression is verging on thunderous, so I talk fast. "But we don't even have our stories straight. What are you going to say if the police ask about Autumn? Or—"

"Nothing. Not a goddamn thing." Mateo crosses his arms. "They can't prove she did anything wrong. Boney's dead. Charlie's not talking. I'm washing my hands and walking away. I was home sick today, and that's it. I'm done." The steeliness in his voice recedes just a little as he adds, "Take care of yourself, okay, Cal?"

This time I don't try to stop him. He vaults easily over the fence, and with a sense of hopeless foreboding, I watch his back retreat into the woods. We're way past the point of pretending that none of this happened. If Mateo was thinking straight, he'd remember that it's not only up to him, or Charlie, whether the police find out about Autumn. And maybe he would've thought twice before ripping into Ivy.

"Cal?" Her voice snaps me back to reality. I turn to see Ivy walking slowly toward me, her gaze locked on the woods where Mateo disappeared. She's taken her backpack from my trunk, and it dangles loosely from one hand. "What did he say?"

"He said he's done. With everything."

"Oh," Ivy says quietly. It's a testament to how much the argument in the car devastated her that she doesn't point out the multiple flaws in that plan. Instead, she says, "My parents' plane is supposed to land at five-thirty. They probably have a million messages waiting for them from the school, and their friends, and quite possibly the police, so . . ." She takes a deep breath, then exhales slowly. "We need to fix all of this before then."

"Ivy," I say as gently as I can. "I'm not sure we can fix this." She doesn't reply, and I add, "We're in way over our heads. Like, this is our heads"—I press one palm toward the ground and stretch the other as far over my head as it will go—"and this is the situation we're in. Times infinity. You get that, right?"

She's silent for so long that I almost repeat the question. "Yeah, I get it," she finally says. "But I'm still going to do what we came for. Are you?"

What we came for. What was that, again? Mateo's words echo in my ears: *A fucking painting? Who cares?*

Ivy has already turned toward the building, pausing at her

car to toss her backpack into the passenger seat. Then she keeps walking, picking up her pace, and I watch her progress with a sense of inevitability. A thousand years ago this morning, I was willing to believe anything Lara told me. But the connections between her and Boney just keep growing. She's right in the middle of this disaster, and while I still don't know exactly what she's done, I do know this: there's no way she's acting alone.

Love you so much, angel. Let's make it happen, D.

Who cares? I guess I do.

I jog after Ivy to catch up to her at the back entrance, and wait as she pulls her key ring from her bag. She fits a large brass key into the rusted lock and turns, tugging at the door's handle. It opens with a loud creak of the hinges, revealing a long, dim hallway.

"Where are we?" I ask, stepping inside behind her.

"Near the gym," she says, and I should've guessed. The space has that distinctive gym smell, the harsh scent of ammonia failing to fully mask years of built-up sweat. News clippings about Carlton championships line the walls, and as we move farther into the hall, I know exactly where we are. Lara's classroom is down here, too; in fact, proximity to the athletic offices is probably what threw her and Coach Kendall together in the first place.

We're three doors from Lara's classroom when the sound of voices stops us short. ". . . But you really need to work on your split dodge," someone says.

"Yeah, I know," comes the response. "My timing was off."

A new voice chimes in. "Along with everything else."

"Well," says the first voice in a kindly tone, "you have a lot on your mind today. I don't expect perfection. But I know practice can be a good distraction, and maybe that's something you can work on at home while you wait to hear from your sister."

Ivy's eyes bug out. Before I'm fully aware of what's happening, she's grabbed my arm, yanked open the nearest door, and shoved me into a small, dark room. "What the hell?" I sputter, my shoulder banging against the nearest wall. I barely have time to register that we're in a closet full of mops and buckets before she's pulled the door closed behind us and darkness descends.

"That's Daniel and Coach Kendall," she hisses. "His office is next door. And Daniel's friend Trevor, I think. Lacrosse practice must've just let out."

"Oh shit," I mutter, my heart dropping as I listen to Coach Kendall's earnest voice go on about *protecting the ball on the run*. Ever since I started hanging out with Lara, I've done my best not to think about him; or if I do think about him, it's to tell myself that he and Lara are a bad fit and should break up. But now, listening to him talk with Daniel and Trevor, all I can think is that he's a nice guy staying late with a worried student while his fiancé runs around behind his back. With more than one person.

"Daniel, do you still have those extra gloves from the last game?" Coach Kendall asks.

"Yeah, in the front pocket of my bag," Daniel says.

"I'm gonna take them back, okay? Fitz might need them." A chuckle, then Coach Kendall asks, "What do you have in here? Rocks?" God. It's exactly the kind of dumb dad joke Wes would make, which only makes me feel worse.

"Just a lot of balls," Daniel says.

"Balls," Trevor repeats, snickering. "So many."

"All right, guys, I gotta head out. Rest up tonight, okay?"

"You got it, Coach."

A set of footsteps passes our door, then fades. Daniel and Trevor shove each other around for a few minutes, laughing about something I can't make out, and then their footsteps pass us as well, loud and echoing as they race down the empty hall. We wait until there's nothing but silence, and then we wait some more. Finally, Ivy opens the door a crack and peers into the hallway. "Coast is clear," she whispers, pulling her keys from her bag and holding them tightly in one hand so they won't jingle as she walks.

"You sure that key will open it?" I ask as we approach Lara's classroom. The door is closed, the interior dark.

Ivy rattles the knob; it doesn't budge. "We'll find out," she says. The same square key from before fits easily into the lock, and when she turns the knob again, the door swings open with a low creak.

"It's pretty crap security to have one key for everything," I say.

"Well, this is Carlton." Ivy steps through the doorway, and I follow. "Nothing bad is ever supposed to happen here, right?"

The classroom is dim until Ivy flicks the switch near the door, flooding it with light. It's weird, considering the circumstances, but I can feel myself starting to relax as I smell the familiar mixture of paint and pencil shavings. The room looks the same as always. A long table running against the far wall is covered with art supplies: thick stacks of paper, bright paint bottles, boxes of charcoal and colored pencils, and galvanized steel canisters to hold paintbrushes.

Even before Lara started teaching here, this classroom was my happy place—the one part of school where I always felt like I belonged. Come to think of it, though, I probably felt more at home here *before* she became my teacher. Because this room was just about the art then; my fingers itching to grab charcoal or a pencil as soon as I walked through the door, my mind buzzing with images I couldn't wait to translate onto a page. There was no desperate yearning to be noticed, no confusion and guilt when I finally was. A comic I drew sophomore year is framed on the back wall, from when my teacher, Mr. Levy, submitted my work for a contest. It won first place, and the whole class clapped when Mr. Levy hung it up.

"Well done, Cal," he said. "I hope you're as proud as we are." And I was.

A wave of something almost like homesickness washes over me, so strong that my knees feel weak and I have to lean against the wall for support. It hits me, suddenly, that I wasn't just feeling nostalgic for middle school in the parking lot this morning. I was nostalgic for *this*—the Before Lara version of Cal—because that's the last time I can remember liking myself.

Noemi could've put it more gently, maybe, but she was right. I'm a shell.

My phone rings, startling both Ivy and me. I answer in a panic to stop the noise, and barely register that it's Wes before holding it to my ear. "Hey, Dad."

"Cal?" His voice is tight and worried. "Are you all right?"

"Sure," I say quietly. "Why wouldn't I be?"

"Because of that podcast about you," another familiar voice says, and my heart sinks. Oh God, my dads are conference calling me. This can't be good.

"It wasn't a podcast, Henry. Those are audio only." I squeeze my eyes shut as Wes continues, "Cal, one of my students forwarded a YouTube video recorded by two of your classmates, talking about Brian Mahoney's death. There was some very unfortunate speculation about your old friend Ivy, but also . . . they said you were absent today?"

All of a sudden, Mateo's *deny everything* strategy doesn't look so bad. But even without knowing what Ishaan and Zack said about me on Carlton Speaks, I'm positive that won't work with my parents. "Um, yeah. I was sick. Am sick."

"Well, then why on earth . . ." The confused hurt in Wes's voice makes me feel about an inch tall. "Why didn't you tell me that when we spoke earlier?"

"I didn't want to worry you." I open my eyes and instantly feel worse. There's something uniquely terrible about having this conversation in Lara's classroom.

Henry breaks in. "Cal, I don't understand why we found out about your absence through a pod—pardon me, through an online video. Neither of us called to excuse you, so why didn't the school call us?"

Sweat starts to bead on my forehead. "Maybe they forgot."

Ivy is glaring at me; I'm making too much noise. I'm also about to get a bunch more questions I can't answer, so I quickly add, "I need to throw up. I'll call you back." Then I hang up and silence my phone. "I'm as screwed as you are," I tell Ivy.

"I highly doubt that." She's circling the room, eyes roving. "Where's the Dominick Payne painting?" I'm not recovered enough to answer her, but she spots it on the wall behind Lara's desk before she's taken another step. "Aha," Ivy says, approaching it.

The painting is an abstract cityscape with bold lines and

vibrant colors, and I hate the fact that I kind of like it. I'd even complimented it to Lara, though I'd never examined it closely enough to register what the signature looked like. But now that I'm barely a few feet away, I can see a scrawl of black on the bottom. And—

"They're nothing alike," Ivy says.

She's holding the D card up against the painting, and she's right. The *Let's make it happen* note is written in cramped, loopy handwriting, while Dominick Payne's signature is all tall, slashing letters. The D on the card doesn't even look like it's the same letter as the one in Dominick's signature.

"Huh. How anticlimactic," I offer. I'm more relieved than disappointed because I don't care, suddenly, who D is. It doesn't matter. Well, it matters to whatever case Ivy's trying to build, I guess, but not to me.

"Yeah," Ivy says. She looks lost as she stuffs the note back into her bag, and I realize she was counting on this: some kind of breakthrough to distract her from what happened in the car with Mateo. "I guess we can still look around," she says, stepping behind Lara's desk and opening the top drawer. Her heart doesn't seem in it, though.

I gaze out the window at the darkening sky. It's getting close to dinnertime, and even the late commuters will be crowding the roads soon—including my parents, who are probably worried sick after that last call. They have no idea how much worse it's going to get, and I need to figure out how to tell them. Not just about today, but about everything.

"Ivy, let's go, okay? Grab some coffee or something," I say. There are still things I need to tell her, even though it's probably too late for them to make a difference. "Maybe you should drop

Lara's day planner here. Let her think she left it in her office. You're going to have enough to explain soon without having to explain that, too."

"No." A hint of her usual stubbornness returns to Ivy's face as she continues rooting through Lara's desk. "She's still massively shady. Boney died in her studio. Charlie's house got torn apart. She had a list with both of their names circled, and she—" She tugs hard on the bottom drawer and frowns. "This is locked."

"Listen . . ." I pause, trying to come up with the right words to get her out of here. Then there's a loud rap on the half-open door and I jump back in surprise as a blond head pokes through, wearing an expression that's half-incredulous, half-angry.

"What are you guys doing here?" Daniel Sterling-Shepard demands.

23

IVY

"What are *you* doing here?" I counter, trying to buy time. "I heard you leave."

"You heard me leave?" Daniel repeats. "What are you, spying on me now?"

This isn't starting well. "No, I just—I heard you and Trevor in the hallway when I was coming in, and then I . . . I heard you leave."

"I came back to take a piss," my brother eloquently says. "And then I heard *you*. For the first time in hours." He's wearing a Carlton Lacrosse T-shirt and shorts, his hair sweaty against his forehead. His oversized lacrosse bag is slung over one shoulder, making his stance lopsided. He lowers it to the ground and leans against the doorframe, eyes narrowing. "Why are you wearing my sweatshirt?"

I tug on one of the hood's strings. "I, um. Was cold."

"You were cold," Daniel repeats. Then he shakes his head,

like he's trying to clear it. "Never mind. More importantly, where the hell have you been all day?"

"Oh, you know," I say as vaguely as possible. Cal inches closer to the wall, like he's trying to get out of the line of fire between Daniel and me. "Here and there."

It's an obnoxious response, fully deserving of my brother's answering glare. "Do you realize I had to miss half of lax practice to talk to the cops about you?" he asks.

Oh God. My legs are rubber bands, suddenly, barely keeping me upright until I can collapse into the nearest chair. "The cops?" I repeat. "What . . . why?"

"Why do you think?" Daniel snaps. "Maybe because you've been missing all day, and everyone's been talking about you, and nobody knew where you were? Except for that brief moment in time when you ran away from a news crew downtown, of course."

Here it is. This entire horrific day is about to come crashing down on me, and I'm nowhere near ready for it. "So they think . . . do they really think I killed Boney?" I whisper.

Daniel lets out a harsh laugh. "They don't know what to think. They'd like to talk to you, but you've been, you know." He puts his hands up in finger quotes. *"Here and there."*

I can't match his sarcasm right now. "What kind of questions did they ask?" I press.

"Oh, they ran the whole gamut. Where you were, why you weren't in school, why you were downtown today, were you angry with Boney about the student council election. Fun stuff like that. And they wanted your phone number."

"Did you give it to them?" I ask while simultaneously checking my phone for unknown calls. There are a few, but before I can listen to any of them, an alert flashes on my screen. *Flight 8802 is delayed due to air traffic, and is now scheduled to arrive at 5:45 p.m.* I glance at the clock on the wall and wince; even with the delay, that's less than half an hour from now.

Less than half an hour until they know everything. My stomach sinks, and I finally have to admit that I've been fooling myself for hours. For the entire day, really.

Cal was right. We can't fix anything.

"I gave them *a* number," Daniel says.

I frown. "What do you mean?"

He shrugs. "I might've transposed a couple of digits."

I blink. I can't have heard that right. "On purpose?" I ask, confused, and he rolls his eyes. "What did you tell them about me?"

"Nothing."

"What do you mean, nothing?" I ask, frustrated. I might deserve these vague answers after the ones I gave him, but that doesn't make them any easier to take.

"What I said. I told them I talked to you around one o'clock, and you seemed fine, and I hadn't heard from you since."

You seemed fine. I flash back to that conversation, which mainly consisted of Daniel yelling at me and refusing to give me Charlie St. Clair's phone number. "Did you tell them that I asked for Charlie's number?"

He shakes his head. "No."

I don't get it. This was his chance to show the world how much of a disaster I truly am, and nobody would have blamed him for taking it. So why didn't he? "How come?"

Daniel sucks in a frustrated breath. "Because I didn't know what was happening! You left me high and dry all day, and I had no clue if I'd be saying something that was going to screw you over."

My mind spins as I stare at him. "Why . . . why would you care about screwing me over?" And then, before he can answer, I add, "You hate me."

The words come out of the saddest, most insecure corner of my brain—the part of me that knows my relationship with Daniel hasn't been the same since he became *extraordinary* and I became *less than*. I've never said them before; I'm not sure I've even thought them before. And I'm terrified suddenly about what Daniel will say in return.

His mouth twists. "You really think that?"

"You humiliated me at the talent show—"

"It was a joke, Ivy!" Daniel cuts me off. "A stupid goddamn joke. I thought you might laugh, for a change. Like we used to whenever one of Aunt Helen's books showed up. I didn't think you'd read the thing in front of the entire auditorium."

"You know I'm not good at off-the-cuff speaking," I protest.

"I know zilch about you. Because that's what you tell me."

We stare at one another, and is that—*hurt* on my brother's face? How is it possible, when I'm the one who's been hurting all this time? I think back to that day at Spare Me, when Daniel was showing off in front of his friends, and the satisfaction I'd felt at plotting my revenge. I ruined Ms. Reyes's entire livelihood for that. It can't be because I've been wrong about my brother all this time.

"My Sugar Babies," I say abruptly. "You took them, you jerk. So don't try to pretend like you haven't been giving me a hard time for years."

"This again?" Daniel rubs a hand over his jaw. "Can you

please explain what you're talking about with the freaking Sugar Babies? Because I do *not* understand."

"The Sugar Babies that Mateo left for me on our porch in eighth grade," I say, folding my arms. Daniel still looks blank, so I add, "Come on, you remember. He left them with a note, inviting me to go see *Infinity War.* You took them before I had a chance to read it, and that's basically why Mateo and I stopped being friends. Or anything else."

A dawning understanding flits across Daniel's face. I feel a quick stab of satisfaction until he turns to Cal and says, "You gonna leave me hanging?"

When I look toward Cal, he's gone pale, his hands shoved into his pockets as he stares at the floor. "Huh?" I ask. Cal doesn't say anything, and I turn back to Daniel. "What are you talking about? What does Cal have to do with this?"

My brother waits a beat, eyes on Cal. When Cal still doesn't speak, Daniel huffs in annoyance. "Seriously? Okay then. Well, here's what I remember, Ivy. I came home one day and Cal was on the porch, holding a packet of Sugar Babies and a piece of paper. I asked what he was doing, and he said he was going to surprise you, but since you weren't around, he'd give them to you some other time. And he asked me not to say anything."

"Cal?" I feel almost woozy, my brain spinning in too many directions. "Is that true?"

Cal is pressing himself against the wall, like he's hoping he can fall right through it and wind up in some other dimension, far away from Daniel and me. Finally, when he realizes that isn't going to happen, he nods resignedly and says, "Yeah. It is."

24

MATEO

When I get home, I step into a disaster area.

I thought I was prepared for this, but it turns out nothing prepares you for seeing your house torn apart. I hardly recognize the rooms I grew up in; it's like someone built an alternate version for a postapocalyptic movie set. A sick sense of dread pulses through me as I survey the wreckage, and I have to remind myself that it could have been worse. Compared to what happened to Boney, we got off easy.

I close the door behind me and stand motionless for a few long minutes, listening. The house is silent, with a deserted stillness that tells me whoever did this is long gone. They probably came here right before, or after, they hit Charlie's.

What had Charlie said? *Houses get broken into all the time.* Maybe, but not like this: two in a row in the same town, on the same day one of our classmates died. I can't report this. All I can do is clean it up before Ma and Autumn get home.

I gaze around, trying to figure out where to start, and the enormity of the task overwhelms me instantly. Rather than admit it's impossible—half our dishes are smashed, for crying out loud—I head for the refrigerator. There's a quarter bottle of store-brand cola left, which I know is flat because I had a glass last night and there wasn't a bubble in sight. I don't care; I unscrew the top, tip it to my mouth, and drink the entire thing in under ten seconds. It tastes as bad as expected, but at least it soothes the dryness of my aching throat.

Maybe I'm getting strep, like Ivy said this morning. Wouldn't that be ironic.

No. I'm not thinking about Ivy. I wipe my mouth, leave the empty bottle on the counter with the rest of the mess, and pull out my phone before sitting down at our kitchen table. There's a new text from Autumn with a picture of a bus ticket: *Bronx-bound.*

Relief washes over me, but it's a smaller wave than expected. Mostly, I just feel alone.

I scroll past dozens of notifications until I see a new text from my dad. It's time-stamped for right around the time I was chasing Autumn's murder van around greater Boston. *It's official: I'm starting at White & West on Oct 1. See you soon!*

I huff out a humorless laugh. My father actually did it; left his roadie gig so he could take an assistant manager job at a music store nearby. *So I can help out more,* he'd said when he told me he was applying. I didn't pay much attention at the time, because I figured it was just a bunch of empty talk, like always.

Guess not. Too bad he couldn't have done it a month ago, before Autumn started her Oxy side hustle. I consider texting back *Too little, too late,* but penetrating my father's bubble of cheerful cluelessness requires a level of energy I don't have.

My mother's last text is right after my dad's. I study the picture she sent of my beaming great-aunt, her day made because Ma cared enough to show up for her party. *Don't forget to call Aunt Rose and wish her a happy birthday!* There's not much I can do to make today less of a disaster, but at least I can do that.

Aunt Rose only has a landline and I have no idea what the number is, so I scroll to Contacts and call my grandmother. I can't deal with using Ma as a go-between right now.

Gram picks up on the first ring. "Mateo, mi amor. We're missing you today."

The words put a lump in my throat, and I have to swallow before I can reply. "Hey, Gram. Sorry I couldn't be there, but I wanted to wish Aunt Rose a happy birthday."

"Ah, well, she went upstairs for a nap about ten minutes ago. She might be done for the night, to be honest. All the excitement wore her out. Do you want to talk to your mother? Elena!" she calls before I can protest.

"Gram, no—" I start, but my grandmother is already back.

"She's on the phone with Autumn," she reports.

Good. Making plans to stay the night, I hope. "It's fine. I need to go to work, but I'll try to catch Aunt Rose later."

"Don't worry, I'll tell her you called. You're so busy." A familiar note of exasperated concern enters my grandmother's voice. "You work too hard. I told Elena that as soon as I saw her. Every time I speak to you, you sound so tired."

"I'm not tired," I say automatically, even though every cell in my body feels heavy with exhausted misery. "I'm fine."

"Oh, Mateo. You're not fine, but you'll never admit it, will you?" She sighs, then adds the same thing she always does. "You'll be the death of me."

"I gotta go, Gram. Love you," I say, then disconnect before she can kill me with more kindness.

I glance at the clock on our microwave. I'm supposed to be at Garrett's in an hour, but obviously that's not going to happen. I'll need all night to clean up this mess, and besides, I can't imagine showing up there like it's a typical Tuesday. I try to picture myself busing the table where I sat with Cal this morning, or wiping down the booth where I put Ivy after she fainted, but—no. I'm not thinking about Ivy.

Except that I am. I kind of can't stop. All of the things I said to her in Cal's car keep running through my head in one long, poisonous loop. In that moment, I was so full of rage that all I wanted to do was hurt her. And I did a great job.

"She deserved it," I say out loud, testing the words. They sound right. They *are* right. Ivy did a stupid, selfish thing that shut my mother's business down, and then she didn't even have the guts to come clean when it might've made a difference.

"She deserved it," I repeat, but it sounds less convincing the second time around. When I'd admitted I knew Autumn was dealing drugs, Ivy didn't judge me for it. And yeah, that's at least partly because she felt guilty—but it was guilt over unintended consequences. *We all make mistakes, right? And almost never see the fallout coming.*

I lift a hand to massage my sore temple, and my fingers make contact with the Band-Aid Ivy put on. I'm tempted to yank it off, but even I'm not dumb enough to bleed out of spite. I know

I should call Garrett's, but before I can, a new text from Autumn flashes across my screen. *I'm not going to the Bronx.*

Wait. What?

I start typing, but Autumn is faster. *I told Aunt Elena. I had to. She knew something was wrong and she wouldn't let up. You know how she is.*

My throat tightens. Yeah, I do, but *come on*, Autumn. You had one job.

I couldn't keep lying to her with Boney dead, she adds.

No, no, no. She wasn't supposed to do this. And told Ma what, exactly?

Autumn's next text answers the question. *She wants me to go to the police.*

And then: *I'm sorry. I tried.*

I don't want to read anything else. I shut my phone down and shove it across the table before it can ring with a panicked call from my mother. My heart pounds as I stand and leave the kitchen, circling our wreck of a living room. Anger, worry, and shame are all coursing through me, fighting for dominance, and for the first few laps around the room, shame wins. Because now my mother knows everything—including what I'm capable of keeping from her.

Then worry takes over, crushing my chest with thoughts of my cousin. What the hell is Autumn thinking, turning herself in like this? Boney's gone, and Charlie's only seventeen, so she'll wind up taking the fall for this entire mess.

I can't just torture myself with what-ifs; I need to *do* something. There's no point in trying to clean the house up anymore, but I can check out how bad the rest of it is. I make my way upstairs, steeling myself to survey the damage to our bedrooms. It's as bad as downstairs, although at least our laptops look okay. Still, the idea of someone going through my personal stuff— tossing everything I own aside like it's nothing—makes me want to put a fist through the wall. I can't stand being in my room, so I go back into Autumn's.

The bulletin board above her desk has been torn off, as if somebody thought it might be concealing a wall safe, and tossed to the floor on top of a pile of clothes. I pick it up and place it carefully on the desk, studying the collage of pictures that represent Autumn's life.

Everything about that life will change after tonight. Autumn will probably be arrested, turned into a warning and an example for other Carlton kids, and people will say she deserved it. They won't care about any of the reasons behind what she did.

She deserved it.

The biggest picture on Autumn's bulletin board is of her mom and dad, the aunt and uncle I barely knew, holding my toddler cousin between them. The second-biggest is of me and Ma flanking Autumn at her high school graduation last spring. There's one of Autumn and me at the New England Aquarium from the summer she first got here, posed stiffly next to an exhibit about the biggest and smallest fish in the world. I know the whale shark is the biggest, but I have to squint at the sign next to Autumn to remember what the smallest fish was called. *Paedocypris progenetica,* barely a third of an inch long.

That's Autumn, I think, my eyes drifting to the twelve-year-old version of my cousin. She's the small fish in this whole mess. There's somebody a lot bigger involved, somebody who moves enough pills that they can store thousands of them in an abandoned shed. Somebody with the knowledge, the resources, and the cold-blooded will to kill Boney. If the police could find that person, Autumn wouldn't matter anymore. They'd have their whale shark.

It makes me wish I'd never left Cal and Ivy. You can say what you will about Ivy—and God knows I did—but she doesn't give up. And she has a knack for figuring things out. If Ivy believes there's something important in Ms. Jamison's classroom, she's probably right.

As soon as I start thinking about Ivy, her face leaps out at me from Autumn's bulletin board. The picture was taken in Carlton Middle School's streamer-decorated gym, at the only dance I'd ever gone to there. We moved around all night as a group: me, Autumn, Ivy, Cal, and Daniel. In the photo our arms are slung across each other's shoulders, our smiles wide and full of braces. Across from that picture is one of Autumn at last year's senior bonfire in the woods, her face pressed close to Loser Gabe as Stefan St. Clair grins over their shoulders. Beneath that is my mother and father's wedding picture, and I swear to God, Ma already looks like she knows she just signed up for taking care of an adult kid.

My eyes flick between the photos as my brain catalogs everything that happened today. Boney's death. Dale Hawkins's news coverage. Stealing Ms. Jamison's day planner. Finding the kill list. Learning about Charlie's involvement. Talking to Autumn in the murder van. Fighting with Ivy. There's something running through it all—not a common thread, exactly, but a loose one. It keeps dangling right outside my line of vision, taunting me with the fact that if I only knew where to tug, I could start to unravel everything.

The thought enters my head before I have time to push it away: *What would Ivy do?* And I'm pretty sure I know.

I pull a phone from my pocket. Not mine, the one I tossed aside like a coward downstairs, but Boney's. *Maybe it's his name,* Ivy said when she was trying to guess his passcode at Crave Doughnuts. She'd entered *B-O-N-E-Y,* which hadn't worked, so I type in *B-R-I-A-N.*

"Holy shit," I mutter when the screen unlocks. My pulse accelerates as I pull up Boney's messages; the last one is just a number. *5832.* The code to Ms. Jamison's studio. There's no name attached to the phone number that sent it, but I hit audio and hold it to my ear, scanning Autumn's bulletin board while it rings.

I zero in on one of the pictures and think, *Maybe.*

Then the call goes to voicemail, and I almost drop the phone as a familiar voice fills my ear. There's no *maybe* about it. My heart starts to pound as my vision narrows to a pinprick, until I can't see anything except the picture that caught my eye. I could kick myself for all the signs I missed, but at least I finally grabbed hold of the thread.

And for the first time all day, I know what I have to do.

YOUTUBE, CARLTON SPEAKS CHANNEL

Ishaan and Zack are in someone's house, surrounded by students holding cups. Some are talking intently, some seem shell-shocked, and others are mugging for the camera.

> **ISHAAN:** Hey, everyone, it's Ishaan and Zack continuing our round-the-clock coverage of Boney Mahoney's death. We're live at Stefan St. Clair's house, where current and former Carlton High students have come together after today's tragic news.

> **ZACK,** *looking nervous:* Technically, we weren't invited to this.

> **ISHAAN:** It's practically a memorial service. Everyone's invited. Anyway, we've been flooded with questions from our viewers, so we're gonna address a few of them now. *(Looks down at something in his hand.)* First up: Jen from Carlton asks, *Is this Ivy girl actually a suspect, or just a person of interest?* Great question, Jen. Keeping in mind that we have absolutely no legal training—

> **ZACK:** Or knowledge.

ISHAAN: I would say that she's probably both. Plus a fugitive. But again, those may not be the exact terms that law enforcement would use.

ZACK, *under his breath:* Where is Emily when we need her?

ISHAAN: Emily is, quote, *not talking to either of you for the rest of my life.* Unquote. Next question comes from Sully in Dorchester, who says, *Don't you rich pricks have anything better to do than . . .* Okay, that's more of a comment than a question, Sully.

(A girl pushes her way in front of the camera, breathless.) You guys. My best friend's cousin's dad works for a guy who knows a guy who bought the building Boney died in, and she said he said there might be *drugs* involved.

ZACK: I mean—yeah, that's how Boney died, right? Drugs.

GIRL: Not just that. There were drugs found where he died. Like it was a literal den of drugs or something.

ISHAAN: Den of drugs. That's good. That's what we should title this episode.

(A boy with white-blond hair steps into the edge of the frame. He looks a lot like Charlie St. Clair, except taller and more clean-cut.)

BLOND BOY, *scowling:* What's going on here?

ISHAAN: Oh hey, Stefan. Great party. You remember me? Ishaan Mittal, we were in the same media technology class—

STEFAN: That's not what I asked. What's going on? *(His scowl deepens.)* Are you filming something?

ZACK: Yeah, we're with the Carlton Speaks Channel, and we've been reporting on Boney's death all day, so—

(The camera suddenly goes dark. Over the sound of confused protests, one voice emerges clearly before the sound cuts off.)

STEFAN: Get the fuck out of here.

25

CAL

"*You* took the Sugar Babies?" Ivy gapes at me, betrayal written all over her face. "Why, Cal? Why would you do something like that?"

I wish I could use a bottle of paint remover to wipe off Daniel's smug grin. I was going to tell Ivy—I even tried, briefly, when we were outside Crave Doughnuts—but not like this. "It's complicated," I say, rolling up my sleeves as my eyes dart to the hallway. "Hey, did you guys hear that?" I'm almost positive I heard footsteps, and grab hold of the distraction like a drowning man with a life preserver. "I think somebody might be coming."

Daniel leans out the door, looking left and right. "Nope," he says succinctly.

Ivy narrows her eyes. "Stop trying to change the subject and explain yourself."

"I'm sure this is a fascinating story," Daniel says, picking up his lacrosse bag. "But I don't need to hear it. Trevor and I are going to Olive Garden."

"Of course you are," Ivy sighs, but not like she's actually mad about it.

He lifts his eyebrows. "You coming home later, or what?"

"I . . . yeah," Ivy says, getting slowly to her feet. "I'll explain everything then."

"Trevor has his mom's car, so you can take ours," Daniel says. His expression gets even more smug as he glances between us. "If Cal was your ride, I'm guessing you're gonna need it." He backs out of the doorway, and I give him the finger in my head.

"Okay," Ivy says. It's bad news for me that she's letting him go like that, because it means all the laser-like attention that was focused on Daniel a second ago has shifted firmly to me. "Start talking," she says, folding her arms across her chest. Then, before I can say a word, her eyes go wide and almost sympathetic. "Oh my God. Were you in love with me?"

"No! Come on, Ivy. Just because you and Mateo picked up right where you left off, and Charlie's developed some kind of weird fixation, doesn't mean the whole world is in love with you." I say it with the force of complete certainty, and it's not until the words are out of my mouth that I realize I just trashed the only excuse she might have been willing to accept.

She scowls. "Then why?"

It's not like I went to her house with the intention of taking anything. I wanted to hang out, because we hadn't done that in a while, even though we had plenty of free time. I didn't text, because she'd started taking hours to return my texts, and I didn't feel like waiting for company. When I entered the porch, I saw the Sugar Babies straightaway, but I didn't look at them until my knock on the door went unanswered. Then I picked up the note, unfolded it, and read Mateo's words.

I didn't know, then, that the two of them had kissed. Ivy didn't tell me until after she thought he'd ghosted her. But I realized in a flash why I'd started feeling like the odd man out.

"Because I didn't want things to change," I tell Ivy now.

"You didn't want things to change," she echoes.

"Yeah. For two years, you guys were my best friends. And then suddenly, you're a couple? You'd already started to ignore me. You *did*," I emphasize when she starts to protest. "You'd been leaving me out of stuff for weeks. And we were about to start high school, and I thought . . . I thought if you guys were going out, I'd be completely on my own. Or you'd have a bad breakup and want me to take sides. Either way, everything was going to change. And I liked things the way they were."

The irony, of course, is that the three of us fell apart anyway. If I hadn't been a scared, stupid thirteen-year-old, I might have seen that coming. It was naive to think that ripping up a note, and tossing a gift, would end the attraction between Ivy and Mateo. They were still magnets vibrating in each other's presence, but—I flipped them. All the things that used to draw them together started pushing them apart, until they were so far away from one another that I was left standing alone in the middle.

Ivy's face droops, her lips turning downward. "I liked him," she says quietly, tugging at the hem of Daniel's sweatshirt. "I liked him so, so much."

"I know." I did, but I also didn't. I didn't understand, back then, what that kind of liking felt like. My middle school crushes were infrequent and unreciprocated. There hadn't been a Noemi, and there definitely hadn't been a Lara. I thought what I'd done was a ripple on a pond, something that would be barely noticed and easily forgotten.

An apology is on my lips, but then Ivy's brows shoot up and her hands fly to her cheeks. "That is—that's the most selfish thing I've ever heard!" she says.

And with that, my temper spikes. Maybe it's a defense mechanism, a refusal to accept that what I did was so bad after all, but—considering the day we've had, you'd think she might realize the irony of that statement. "Oh, really?" I ask. "The *most* selfish? The absolute most? Sorry, have you already forgotten the car ride over here? Do I need to remind you that you shut down Spare Me with a bottle of baby oil?"

"That's not what we're talking about right now!" Ivy hisses.

"Still relevant!" I hiss back.

Ivy flexes her hands, like she's getting ready to shove me against the wall. "My whole life could've been different if I'd gotten that note! We probably wouldn't even be in this mess right now. And Spare Me would never have happened."

Oh, hell no. "You don't get to blame me for that," I snap. "That was all you."

"And Daniel . . . I've been awful to Daniel . . ."

"Not over this," I remind her. "You didn't even know about the Sugar Babies until this afternoon. You've been awful to Daniel on your own." She doesn't have a good answer for that, and my face burns at the memory of Daniel's self-satisfied smirk. "Anyway, were you seriously buying all of that back there?" I continue. "Daniel is suddenly your pal, looking out for you, running interference with the cops out of the goodness of his heart? Come on."

Ivy furrows her brow and lifts her phone, alternating between stabbing the screen and holding it to her ear. "It's true, though," she says after a few minutes. "I didn't get any calls from them. He must've actually given them the wrong number."

"If he did, I'm sure he had his own reasons." Lara's card is sticking out of Ivy's bag, and a sudden, unwelcome thought lands with a sickening thud. Daniel has, as Lara would say, an *interesting face*. And even though he doesn't take art, as far as I know, he's down in this corridor all the time for lacrosse. "Maybe he's D. Maybe he didn't come into Lara's classroom because he heard your voice. Maybe he came looking for her."

"What?" Ivy's face is a mask of confusion until she follows my gaze. "Oh no," she says instantly. "No way."

"Why not?" I ask. Now that the idea has entered my brain, I can't seem to shake it loose. "Does it look like his handwriting?"

"I . . ." Ivy pulls the note out of her bag and opens it. She doesn't look as though the contents reassure her. "I don't know. Daniel doesn't *write* stuff. He texts, or types. But there's no way . . ." She narrows her eyes. "You're just saying this to distract me."

"No, I'm not. All day, you've been insisting that Lara's part of this drug scheme. You keep looking for ways to make her fit, but you're gonna ignore the fact that your brother kept his mouth shut today in a *very* uncharacteristic way? Not to mention that he was sporting thousand-dollar sneakers just now?"

"What?" Ivy recoils. "That's ridiculous. He was not."

"He was. I've seen those limited-edition Nikes on the news. They're a grand, easy."

"Well, he . . . he has a job," Ivy stammers.

"Busing tables, right?" I ask. She nods. "Mateo does that, too. You ever seen *him* in thousand-dollar sneakers?" She doesn't

246

respond, and I add, "Maybe Daniel isn't D. Maybe he's the Weasel. Think about it. He's everyone's friend, he's invited to all the parties, he *really* doesn't want the cops involved—"

"Stop it!" Ivy cuts in. "You're being horrible."

"Yeah, well, so are you."

We regard each other in silence for a few seconds, and then Ivy stuffs Lara's card far enough into her bag that she can zip it shut. "I'm done talking with you about this," she says stiffly. "I'm done talking with you, period."

"Fine by me," I say. It seems impossible, suddenly, that I ever could have cared enough about Ivy's friendship to sabotage things between her and Mateo. Mateo, who stalked off like an angry toddler the second things stopped going his way. The two of them deserve one another.

"I'm leaving," Ivy says.

I shrug with pretend nonchalance. "This isn't Logan Airport. You don't have to announce your departure."

"Ughhhh," she growls, spinning on her heel and flouncing away. A second later she's gone, leaving me with the satisfaction of a solid parting shot.

It fades fast, though, and a feeling of gloom settles over me as I look around Lara's classroom. Now what? Mateo's gone, Ivy's gone, and there's nothing left for me to do except go home and explain myself to my parents. The thought doesn't fill me with glee, to say the least. I find myself backing farther into Lara's classroom, letting my eyes linger over the workstations, the supplies, the student creations on the wall.

The desk.

Ivy tried to open Lara's bottom drawer earlier, but she couldn't. It's locked, which I know because Lara keeps her inhaler in there. "Can't have this going missing," she told me once, before dropping it inside and turning a key in the lock.

Then she slipped the key somewhere beneath her desk.

I cross the room to sit at the desk, sliding my hand beneath it. At first all I feel is cool metal and then—something raised. I tug at it, and pull a small, rectangular box from under the desk. It's a magnetic case, and when I push against the top, a key pops out.

I fit the key into the bottom-drawer lock. It turns easily, and I pull the drawer open. Only I don't see Lara's inhaler.

Inside are dozens of plastic freezer bags filled with pill bottles. I don't have to check the labels to know what they are, but I do it anyway.

You're afraid of the wrong things. Ivy told me that once, a long time ago. I brushed her off, but maybe it's true after all. These bags should scare the hell out of me—what they are, what they represent, what they mean in terms of what has to come next—but they don't.

I stare at them in silence for a few seconds, thinking. Then I pick up one of the plastic bags, stuff it under my shirt, and head for the door.

26

IVY

I sit in my car in the empty Carlton High parking lot, put the key in the ignition, and turn over the engine. Just like I've done hundreds of times before. After that, though, it's not an exaggeration to say that I have absolutely no idea what to do next.

My phone dings, startling me, and I look down. *Flight 8802 is delayed due to air traffic, and is now scheduled to arrive at 6:00 p.m.*

I rest my forehead against the steering wheel, imagining an alternate universe where my biggest worry would be the fact that I have to bring Mom's outfit to the award ceremony. Instead of the very real possibility that the whole thing will be canceled once I'm arrested at the door.

I wonder if I should be proactive and call my parents. Will hearing from me as soon as they land make any of this better? Or should I catch up with Carlton Speaks first, and see how much worse the rumors have gotten since we left Charlie's house? Or maybe I should call Mateo, and leave a long, rambling voicemail apology since there's no way he'd pick up.

I'm not calling Cal. To hell with him.

And Daniel . . . I don't even know what to think about Daniel.

There's something on Reddit called *Am I the Asshole?*, where people write in about personal conflicts and ask others to tell them who's in the wrong. Sometimes it's horrifying, sometimes it's funny, but a lot of times it's someone who's genuinely confused about whether or not they're the bad guy in a given situation. Now I'm running the last four years between me and Daniel through an AITA filter, wondering if all the things he did that I thought were deliberate and malicious were actually reactions. Or is Cal right, and Daniel was just manipulating me back there?

It's tempting to think that—comfortable and familiar—but it's not like I'm the world's nicest person. I was just spite-voted out of student council office, after all, in favor of somebody who ran as a joke.

Boney. Oh my God, Boney.

I haven't let myself cry about Boney all day, but the tears come now. I wrap my arms around the steering wheel and sob until my throat aches. I wish I could go back to yesterday afternoon, when the election results were announced, and congratulate Boney the way I should have. If I'd been a gracious loser, I would have insisted we meet this morning to discuss a transition plan, and he might never have gone to Boston. For once in my life, I could've used my infamous pushiness for good. Boney would be eating dinner with his parents right now, not lying cold in a morgue.

"I'm sorry, Boney," I choke out, the words a ragged gasp. "I'm so sorry."

I'm almost cried out when my phone chimes again in my lap. I wipe at my eyes, and take a few long, deep breaths before picking it up. *Whatever or whoever this is,* I think, *I'm going to do the right thing.*

The text is from my brother. *Hey, we broke down. Can you pick us up?*

I blink at my screen as Daniel sends his location. He's not far from here; somewhere on the edge of Carlton, it looks like.

I rub a palm across my still-wet cheeks. Cal really rattled me back in the classroom, tossing out all those wild theories about Daniel. It's ridiculous; there's no possible way my brother is involved with Ms. Jamison, or with drugs. He'd have to be a true master manipulator to pull that off, and I'd have to be a complete fool not to have seen it.

It's weird about the sneakers, though. I had no idea they cost that much.

Ugh. No. I give myself a mental slap. *Do the right thing, Ivy. Don't sit here coming up with conspiracy theories while your brother needs help.* I've been frozen with indecision since I got into my car, but here, finally, is something I can do.

On my way, I text back.

27

MATEO

It's not even dark yet, but the party's already in full swing when I park Mrs. Ferrara's pristine 1980s Buick in front of the neat ranch house. All those years of shoveling out my elderly neighbor's driveway finally paid off with an emergency loaner car. And thank God for that, because this would've been a hell of a walk and there wasn't time for that.

Music spills from open windows, and the front yard is full of familiar faces. Carlton High students past and present are standing in clusters, some looking subdued and serious, others laughing like it's just another night at Stefan St. Clair's. The house is small for Carlton, and from what I've heard, Stefan has multiple roommates, but still. It's a pretty great setup for a college freshman.

As I head for the front door, two girls with black ribbons in their hair wrap their arms around one another while a third girl snaps their picture with her phone.

"Make sure you hashtag it *RIP Boney*," one of the girls says.

I open the door and step inside, the loud beat of rap music washing over me as I scan the crowd for familiar faces. Charlie St. Clair lifts a bottle in greeting, and I wait while he makes his way toward me. He's still wearing the puka shell necklace I almost strangled him with, but he's changed his shirt for something less blood-spattered.

"You made it," he says, gazing over my shoulder. "Where's Ivy and Cal?"

"Not here," I say. "How's your house?"

"Empty. My parents are totally freaked. They went to a hotel and they're gonna, like, have a whole new security system installed. They're talking bars on the windows, even." Charlie rubs his eyes, which look a few shades clearer than they did in Ivy's living room.

"You sober yet?" I ask.

"Yeah. Pretty much." Charlie scratches his chin. "I don't usually drink that much. But I was so freaked about Boney, and then I saw what happened to my house, and I—I needed something to take the edge off, you know?" He raises his bottle again, twisting it to reveal the Poland Spring label. "Nothing but water tonight."

"Good idea." I contemplate telling him about Autumn heading for the police station, but before I can, Charlie adds, "I can't stop thinking about it, though. Like, this morning Boney must've figured it was gonna be a normal day, and now he's gone." He takes a long sip of water. "Could've been me who got the call about that deal. Could've been you, right? If somebody mixed you up with Autumn."

I wouldn't have gone, I almost say. But maybe I would have;

if I'd gotten a random message about some big deal in Boston, I might've shown up to see how bad of a mess my cousin had gotten herself into. Besides, I know that's not Charlie's point. His point is that Boney got the rawest of all possible deals today, and on that we fully agree.

"Boney didn't deserve this," I say.

Charlie lowers his voice so that I can barely hear him over the music. "I know Cal wanted to tell someone about the drugs and everything. Maybe that was the right call. I don't know." He scrapes a hand over his jaw. "I told Stefan what's been going on, and he says no way. He says I just need to lie low and keep my head down for a while. And everything will work itself out."

That sounds exactly like something Stefan St. Clair would say. "Is Stefan around?"

"Outside," Charlie says, jerking his head over his shoulder. "There's a deck off the kitchen." I go to leave, but he steps in front of me. "Hey, listen. Is there something going on with you and Ivy?"

God. We don't have time for that conversation, and even if we did, I wouldn't know what to tell him. "Later, Charlie, okay?" I say, pushing past him.

I make my way into the kitchen, where bottles crowd every square inch of the counter and a line for the keg snakes into the dining room. "I didn't really know him all that well," the guy manning the keg is saying to the girl beside him. "But we have to celebrate life, right?"

"Right," the girl says somberly, tipping her cup against his. The sleeve of her shirt lifts just enough to display the black ribbon on her wrist. "Boney taught us that."

A sliding glass door leads to the deck. In the distance, I see both actual pine trees and their reflections mirrored in the glassy shine of a pond. I knew this neighborhood looked familiar; Stefan's backyard runs up against the new golf course. Ma laughed when she saw listings for these houses online. "They're calling them *waterfront*," she said. "I guess a pond is as close as you'll get in Carlton."

Stefan St. Clair is sitting on the edge of the porch railing, holding court with half of Carlton High's dance squad. He ignores me as I approach, because of course he does. Stefan might have graduated last spring, but he still considers himself the king of the school. The guy who knows everyone and everything, who'll throw a party every night of the week. Even the night that his former classmate died.

Stefan shakes his hair out of his face the same way his younger brother does when he laughs at something one of the girls says. I wind my way through his audience, until I'm so close that he can't ignore me any longer. "Hey, man," he says, tilting his head to guzzle the last of his beer. "What's good?"

"Have you seen—" I start, and then I break off as I catch sight of someone hovering at the edge of Charlie's yard, near the bushes that separate it from the golf course. Someone who's taking a leak, from the looks of it. "Never mind."

"Good talk," Stefan calls as I turn abruptly and head for the stairs that lead from the deck into the backyard.

I don't try to be stealthy about it. I want him to see me coming, because I need to see his face. He's weaving a little, though, and doesn't notice me until I'm almost halfway across the lawn. Then he stops in his tracks and snorts out an irritated half laugh. "Well, look who it is. What the hell are you doing here?"

"Hey, Gabe," I say, closing the last few feet of space between me and my cousin's loser boyfriend. "Or should I say, 'Hey, Weasel'?"

Startled alarm flickers in Gabe's eyes. "Dígame," I add, echoing the voicemail greeting I heard over Boney's phone while staring at Autumn's bulletin board.

And then I take a swing at him.

28

CAL

I've only been here once before—last week, when I gave Lara a ride home from school while her car was in the shop. "You want to come in and see my new charcoal pencils?" she asked with a flirty smile when I pulled into her driveway. I thought that was a euphemism, maybe, for taking the next step in our relationship, but I was wrong. All we did was sketch until she had to leave for a date with Coach Kendall.

After weeks of anticipation, I'm glad now that she never did anything except string me along. It makes all of this easier to deal with.

There's no sign of her car in the driveway, but she has a garage, so that doesn't mean she isn't home. I go to the front door and ring the bell, first lightly, and then I press hard on the buzzer. "Hello?" I yell. "Lara?" I'm not worried about the neighbors; Lara doesn't have much in the way of those. "I need to talk to you." There's no response, so I grab the doorknob and twist. First left, then right, but no luck.

I stand on the front step, considering. The last time I was here, Lara complained about a back door lock that didn't work properly. "I should get it fixed, but why bother?" she said. "I'm going to move soon anyway." I didn't want to talk about that; about the house she kept saying she was going to buy with Coach Kendall. I couldn't believe she'd actually go through with marrying him. She was avoiding a lot of stuff the whole time we were hanging out, and I hope that still includes home repairs.

I jog to the back of the house, which is ringed by trees that form the edge of dense woods. It's getting darker now, and cooler, and crickets are out in full force. Their chirping is all I can hear as I follow an overgrown stone path to Lara's back door. I grab the scratched brass handle and tug—first lightly, then harder as I can feel the flimsiness of the lock. I jiggle the handle every which way, tugging with ever-increasing force until the door finally pops open.

I slip inside and shut the door behind me. I've never been back here—it's like an indoor porch, with a bright green rug and wicker furniture everywhere—but Lara's house isn't big. I follow the only exit—a narrow hallway—until I see the familiar yellow paint of Lara's living room. And then I see . . .

Lara's scream is so deafening that I let out a yell, too, and back into the wall with my hands up. "I'm sorry!" I call as she continues to shriek. "I didn't mean . . . I just . . . the door was open. I'm sorry!"

"Oh my God," Lara says as recognition finally sparks in her eyes. Her face is flushed, one hand over her heart. "Oh my God,

Cal. You scared the life out of me. I thought for sure that you were . . ." She inhales a deep breath. "Oh my God. Okay."

I drop my hands as my heart rate starts to slow, and then I notice the oversized suitcase beside her. "Are you . . . where are you going?"

Lara looks down at the suitcase like she forgot it was there, then back at me. "Leaving town," she says.

It shouldn't surprise me, I guess, but it still does. I reach under my shirt and pull out the bag of Oxy. "Because of this?"

"What is . . ." Lara peers at the bag, her expression hardening. "Where did you get that?"

"Your desk drawer, at school. The one you keep locked. This was one of, like, twenty plastic bags stuffed in there."

I'm not sure what kind of reaction I was expecting, but a bitter laugh wasn't it. "Of course," Lara says. "Of *course* it was."

"Of course?" Anger starts to prick at my already-overstimulated nerves. "Sure. Right. Just like you of course put Boney's name on your *kill list,* and now he's dead."

"I did what?" Her brow creases with what looks like genuine confusion. "What are you talking about?"

"The Carlton High class roster, with Boney's name circled? Ivy found it in your day planner. Which she took, by the way. While we were in Second Street Café."

"Ivy took . . ." Lara's red bag is on the couch, and she grabs it by the strap and hauls it toward her. She roots through it for a few seconds, her expression darkening at what she doesn't find. "Ugh, that sneaky little bitch! I'm glad I sent those Carlton Speaks videos to the media. She deserves every bit of shit she's getting."

"You sent . . . so you . . ." I trail off, frowning. Something isn't adding up. "Why were you trying to get Ivy in trouble if you didn't know she'd taken this? What do you have against her?"

"Nothing. I just needed a distraction." Lara hoists the bag on her shoulder. "I needed time to get a few things together so I can make, shall we say, a fresh start. Because once I leave here, I'm never coming back."

I should be scared of her, probably, since I'm standing between her and whatever escape plan she's hatched. But for some reason, I'm not. All I can think about is how badly I need answers, and how easy it would be for her to slip away before she gives them.

"So you killed Boney?" I say. "Or had him killed? Which is it?"

Lara lets out another short, humorless laugh. "That's what you think? Really? And here I thought you knew me, Cal." I stare at her, wordless. "Whatever your sneaky little friend found in my planner—it wasn't mine." She gestures toward the plastic bag still dangling from my fingertips. "And *those* aren't mine. But you bought into it, didn't you? You thought they were. Which is exactly what he wanted you to think."

"Who?" I ask. "Dominick Payne?"

I take a step back and wait for her reaction, almost eager to see how stunned she is that we figured it out. And she does look shocked, but not in the way I expected. "Dominick?" Lara asks, almost choking on the name before her mouth settles into an incredulous half smirk. "You think *Dominick Payne* is some kind of drug lord? How do you even—no."

"No?" I hate the uncertainty in my tone, but I'm not ready to give up on Dominick Payne. Partly because he fits so well, but also because . . . who the hell else is there?

"No." Her lip curls. "So you've been playing detective, huh? I'm disappointed, Cal. I would've expected a better guess."

"Why?" I ask, frustrated.

Lara zips the top of her bag and fixes me with a disdainful look. "Because the answer is right in front of your face."

29

IVY

Gravel crunches beneath my tires as I turn left onto a private way. "Arrived," my GPS informs me, and I'm confused. Why would Daniel and Trevor be here? There's only one house that I can see. It's lit up, but there's no car in the driveway. Ahead of me, parallel parked on the side of the road, is another car with its headlights on. Beyond that, everything looks deserted.

Unease flutters in my stomach, and I pull out my phone to text Daniel. *I'm here. I think?*

His reply is near instant, and the headlights flash on the car in front of me. *I see you.*

What are you guys doing here?

Trevor needed to drop stuff off for a friend, but they're not home, and now the car won't start. We think it's the battery.

My nerves fade as I text back, *I'll get the jumper cables.*

Park closer first, OK? I'll pop the hood.

OK, I reply, before dropping my phone onto the seat beside me so I can inch the car forward. Trevor has his brights on, and I can't see beyond the glare. I stop when I'm a few feet away and shift into park, leaving the ignition running as I open the door.

"Is this close enough?" I call as I step outside, but the other car's doors haven't opened. I wait a beat, tapping my foot on the gravel. Daniel doesn't answer, probably too busy laughing it up with Trevor about something inane, and all the sibling resentment I pushed aside earlier starts to trickle back. That didn't last long.

"Don't rush. I'll do it all myself," I mutter, spinning on my heel to head for the trunk. Then I make a concerted effort to tamp down my irritation. *I am a good person, doing a good and helpful thing,* I chant to myself as I open the trunk and start moving all the blankets and recyclable shopping bags aside. *I am a good person, doing a good and helpful thing.*

If I *weren't* such a good person, I'd probably be annoyed that nobody comes to help before I finally unearth the cables. It's more than a little galling that my inaugural selfless act benefits a couple of lazy ingrates like my brother and Trevor. "Found them!" I call, stepping beside my car and waving them at the still-blazing headlights.

And then, finally, the other car's door opens. The driver's side, not the passenger's side.

"Trevor?" I ask, squinting into the lights. It's definitely not my brother; the shape isn't tall or broad enough for him. "Where's Daniel?" He doesn't reply, and as he gets closer, I realize it's not Trevor, either. The lines of a face finally emerge, and I blink in confusion when I realize who it is. "Hi," I say. "What are you—"

His hand reaches out, lightning-quick, yanking the cables so

263

hard that I go sprawling at his feet. "Ow!" I yell as sharp pieces of gravel bite into my palms and my knees. "What is the *matter* with you?" I try to stand up then, but a hand reaches out, shoving me back down, and I realize I shouldn't be angry. I should be scared.

I open my mouth to scream, and a hand clamps over the bottom half of my face. Suddenly it's hard to breathe, and panic floods my entire body as I'm hauled roughly to my feet.

"Sorry about this, Ivy," says a familiar voice in my ear. "I really am. But I didn't have much of a choice."

30

MATEO

Gabe tries to fight back, but there's no point. I'm a lot bigger than him, and a *lot* angrier.

I duck all of his badly aimed punches and throw him flat on his back, straddling him and pinning his hands until all he can do is struggle helplessly like a trapped bug. "How did you know?" he wheezes.

I didn't, for sure, until I heard Gabe's signature greeting coming from the number that texted the security code to Boney. But right before then, when I zeroed in on Gabe's picture among Autumn's collage, I remembered what Charlie had said in Ivy's living room: *You probably got on their bad side, if they switched your name out with your cousin's. Don't antagonize the Weasel, man!* There's only one person who hates me that much—and, I guess, cares about Autumn that much—while also being some-one who's at every party, and somehow had the money to buy himself a show-off muscle car despite not having a job. And that's the guy pinned beneath me.

"You *named* me," I snarl. "You *asshole*."

"I had to!" Gabe chokes out. "I had to give . . . He knew there were three people, and I needed . . . I couldn't give her name."

"Yeah, well, someone went looking for her anyway. They called her boss, and if I hadn't found her first—"

"That was me," Gabe says, still flailing. "Trying to make sure she was okay. I wanted to—I wanted to get her out of town after what happened to Boney."

The idea that Gabe and I were working toward the same goal startles me enough that I almost loosen my grip on him. But not quite. "Real noble of you, Gabe. You're boyfriend of the year. But you hung Boney out to dry, huh?" I stare daggers at him, briefly fantasizing about letting loose the kind of punch that will break his face. "You sent him to that building. Did you kill him, too?"

"No! God, no! I don't fucking kill people, man!" Gabe twists back and forth, trying to break free. "I didn't know that was going to happen. I'm not . . . look, I'm not an enforcer, okay? I find stuff out, and sometimes I set up meetings. That's all I do."

"That's all, huh? Who do you do it for?" I ask. When he doesn't answer, I lift him briefly off the ground and then slam him back down, hard enough that I could swear I hear his teeth rattle. *"Who do you do it for?"*

Gabe lets out a groan. "I can't tell you. He'll kill me."

"I'll kill you if you don't," I threaten. I'm furious enough that I almost mean it, but Gabe's eyes glint in a way that's far too smug for a guy who can barely move.

"No you won't," he says.

We stare at each other for a couple of beats. He's right, obviously, but he doesn't have to know that. I grab hold of the front of his shirt and spring off him, hauling him to his feet so that I can start dragging him toward the pond.

"What are you doing?" he screams, spittle flying into my face as he bends and twists, trying to escape my grasp. "Help! Somebody help me!"

Good luck with that; Stefan's party is way too loud for anyone to hear, even if they cared about two guys fighting. Gabe keeps flailing, though, landing a couple of glancing blows that I don't feel. When we reach the water's edge, I half throw him in, then follow right behind him. Cold water seeps into my sneakers and soaks my jeans, and Gabe sputters when some of it goes up his nose. He tries to stand up, and I shove him back down.

"I don't want you going near Autumn ever again," I say through gritted teeth. "So I'm going to make sure you can't."

"You're bluffing," Gabe says, but any trace of smugness is gone from his eyes. He looks terrified, and that's almost enough to stop me. Almost.

I push his head underwater and hold it there. When Ma made Autumn and me take a lifeguarding class two years ago, one of the first things we learned is that most people can hold their breath for two minutes—but in a drowning situation, they'll often start to panic less than ten seconds in. I count to twenty, an agonizingly long time with Gabe thrashing for his life beneath me, before I let him up.

He gasps huge lungfuls of air, coughing and sputtering all the while. I let him breathe for a few seconds, and then I shove his head back toward the water until it covers one ear. "Last chance, Gabe," I say as his wheezing turns panicked. "Next time I won't let you up. Who do you give information to?"

He pants for a few seconds without saying a word. I'm about to admit defeat and let him up, because I can't make myself do that again, when he moans, "Okay. Okay." He takes a deep breath and lets it out in a strangled half sob before finishing, "It's Coach Kendall. I give information to Coach Kendall."

31

CAL

I stare at Lara, immobile with confusion, until she shakes her head in mock exasperation. "You seriously have no idea, huh? Well, I'll say this for him—he has all of you fooled. He's always been good at putting up a front."

Lara grabs hold of her suitcase handle and spins it. I unfreeze and sprint forward until I'm between her and the door. She tries to dart past me, but I move with her, my arms spread wide. "You can't leave until you tell me, Lara. I won't let you. People are in real trouble."

"Oh, for God's sake," Lara groans, but her eyes cut toward the clock on the mantel. She has to know I won't physically restrain her, but I'll dance like this for hours if I have to. "It's Tom, you idiot." The name means nothing to me, and it must show on my face, because she adds, "Tom Kendall. *Coach* Kendall. My fiancé, remember?"

That startles me into silence, and Lara tries again for the

door. "No, wait!" I say, blocking it once more. "Coach Kendall is a drug dealer? How? Since when?"

"Tom only told me about it six months ago, but it's been a couple of years," Lara says. "He was small-time at first, using stolen prescription pads. Then demand got high enough that he started involving more people, and bringing drugs in from other states. Now there's a whole network of suppliers and dealers."

That's a lot to take in, especially since I'm having a hard time moving past the first sentence. "He told you *six months ago*?" I repeat, feeling as though I'm suddenly looking at a total stranger. "And you didn't turn him in?"

"He's my fiancé," Lara says, like that's all the explanation I should require.

"So you—what? Just decided to go along with it?"

She makes an impatient noise in her throat. "I don't have time for this, Cal. Tom is framing me, don't you see that?"

My jaw drops, because I absolutely do not. "He is? Why?"

Despite the total lack of accountability she's shown so far, I'm hoping she'll tell me that she was about to go to the police. But she purses her lips and says, "If I had to hazard a guess, it's probably because my indiscretions caught up with me."

"Your indiscretions?" I repeat. "Do you mean . . ."

I'm about to finish that sentence with "me," but Lara cuts me off with a sigh. "I've been involved on and off with someone else, and it's possible Tom saw some texts he shouldn't have."

I stare at her suitcase. "So are you running away with—that guy?" I ask. I almost say D, but I'd rather not explain how I know the initial.

She wrinkles her nose. "God, no. It's not like I was serious about him. Ultimately, he was just another distraction."

Just another distraction. That would probably hurt if I had time to think about it, but follow-up questions are piling up too fast for me to dwell. "So how was Coach Kendall framing you? Did he put that list in your day planner?"

Lara heaves a sigh. "Probably, but that's the first I've known about that. Things started feeling strange a couple days ago, when Tom kept asking me if I was going to be at the studio this morning, at ten o'clock like usual. It was weird, how insistent he was about the *time*." She twists the engagement ring on her finger, and for the first time, I notice how big the diamond is. "I thought he was trying to spy on me. So I decided I wouldn't show up, even though all I was planning to do there was sketch. I actually did go to that ceramics class. I kept waiting for Tom to check in, to follow up with more questions about the studio since he'd been so goddamn interested, but he didn't." She cocks her head at me, appraising. "*You* did."

"So . . ." I think back to sitting across from her at Second Street Café this morning. "So you really didn't know about Boney?"

"I had no idea," Lara said. "I couldn't put any of it together at first. I didn't understand why Brian was there, or why he'd died. I even wondered if Tom might've meant to kill me instead, and Brian became collateral damage when I didn't show up. But then I talked to Dominick, who'd heard from a reporter friend that the police found drugs all over the studio. Dom was half-hysterical, wanting to know why I'd left them there. And, of course, I hadn't."

Her lips twist in a bitter smile. "Then I couldn't stop thinking about the anonymous tip about the blond woman. At first I thought it must've been Ivy, but the timing was too convenient.

The whole thing felt like a circus. A *performance*. So I asked myself: If I'd shown up like I was supposed to—like Tom wanted me to—what would the police have found? Me crouching over the body of a student in a room full of Oxy. With my fingerprints all over the murder weapon, I'm sure, since Tom asked for my help sorting syringes last week."

"Sorting syringes," I echo, my voice dull with disbelief. I can't believe how casual she is about all this; like running a drug ring is just some weird hobby of her fiancé's that she stumbled across and decided to support. "That's a thing you guys do together, huh?"

Lara keeps going like I haven't spoken, sweeping her hand toward me. "And now you come in here telling me there are more drugs stashed in my classroom, and a—what did you call it?—a *kill list* in my day planner. That's a lot of evidence, isn't it? I'd say that's more than circumstantial. And there's probably plenty we haven't seen yet."

"So Boney . . ." I don't know how to finish that sentence.

"Tom must have killed Brian," Lara says simply. "Or more likely, ordered somebody who works for him to do it, then made sure he was at school all day to keep his hands clean. I don't know *why* Brian—he must have done something to make Tom angry—"

"He stole a bunch of his drugs," I interrupt. "He found them in a shed last month and started selling them."

"Ahhhh, okay. That makes sense," Lara says. Her voice is matter-of-fact, like Boney is just another item on her *Why My Fiancé Framed Me* checklist. "Tom freaked out when the Oxy disappeared, and he almost lost his mind when Carlton College declared a war on drugs three weeks later. Your father doesn't waste any time, does he, Cal?" I feel a quick burst of pride, because he sure as hell does not, and she adds, "That's exactly the kind of spotlight Tom doesn't want. He's always been so careful to keep his home and his business separate. He even has a guy whose entire job is keeping an eye on drug activity around town, so Tom can shut it down before anyone official gets involved. But this time, everything happened too fast."

Jesus Christ, I think hazily. *Stefan was right. There really is a Weasel.*

I don't have time to ask who it is; Lara's talking too fast, like whatever nervous energy she's been running on all day is finally bubbling over. "Killing Brian, and framing me for both the murder and the drug operation, takes care of all his problems at once," she says.

Pieces are falling into place too fast for me to keep track of. "So Ivy was just . . ."

"Wrong place, wrong time, right color hair," Lara says. "Maybe whoever killed Brian was waiting for me to show up, making sure I was really there before they called the police, and they mistook her for me. The windows in that place have gotten filthy ever since maintenance stopped." She grabs hold of the suitcase handle again. "So there you have it. I hope I've satisfied your curiosity, because I'm getting out of here before I wind up in jail for something I didn't do."

"But Lara! Wait!" I throw my body across the door again. "You can't just leave. You have to go to the police—they'll believe you. Lots of people must have seen you this morning, right? They'll know you couldn't have killed Boney, and—"

"I'm not counting on the police," Lara says. "It doesn't matter that I have an alibi. You don't know Tom. He might've failed at what he was trying to do, but he's relentless. He always has a Plan B, and I'm not sticking around to find out what it is." She releases the suitcase and tries to physically shove me away from the door.

I hold my ground. "But the police will find you! *Coach Kendall* will find you."

Lara's lips curve into a grim smile. "One of the nice things about Tom is, he's gotten to know some interesting people in his line of work. The kind of people who can help you disappear if you pay them enough. Which I have." She pats the bag on her shoulder, then quirks her lips at me. "Don't look so horrified, Cal. Even if things hadn't imploded, I was never going to last as a small-town art teacher. This is better for everyone."

I'm finally too shell-shocked to resist when she brushes past me, opens the door, and steps outside. I wait for the sound of her suitcase rolling down the stairs, but it doesn't come. For a second there's nothing but silence, and then I hear something else: a scared, muffled, whimpering sound that makes my heart thump hard against my rib cage. That doesn't sound like Lara, but it almost sounds like . . .

I lean into the doorframe and look through it. Lara is standing perfectly still, the suitcase at her side, staring at the scene in front of her. It's Coach Kendall, still wearing his Carlton Lacrosse jacket, with his arm around Ivy's neck and his hand over her mouth. Her eyes, wide and terrified, get even bigger when she spots me.

"Oh shit," Lara says under her breath, so low that I'm probably the only one who can hear her. "This must be Plan B."

274

32

CAL

Minutes later we're all in the garage across from Lara's house, because Coach Kendall has a gun and he's not afraid to wave it at us. Lara sits first, settling herself delicately in one corner like she's a guest at an underfurnished house party. I drop like a stone on the hard cement floor, and Coach Kendall finally takes his hand from Ivy's mouth to shove her next to me.

"Where is Daniel?" she asks hoarsely as soon as she can speak. "What did you do with my brother?"

"Nothing," Coach Kendall says. He lowers the garage door and flicks a light switch beside it, illuminating the interior with the dim yellow glow of a single bulb. Then he puts down the duffel bag he'd had on his shoulder and crouches beside it. "All I did was take his phone."

Ivy shudders with relief as my brain tries to absorb all of this new information. "Daniel?" I parrot. "So I was right? Daniel is the Weasel?"

Coach Kendall's face twists. Holy hell, how did I ever think this guy was friendly? He looks like a serial killer. "The what? What are you talking about?" His eyes narrow. "And why are you here?"

"Um. No reason." I snap my mouth shut and try to keep the plastic bag of pills I shoved back under my shirt from sliding out, but it's too late. Coach Kendall gestures at me with his gun, and I reluctantly let the bag drop into my lap.

"Throw it," he orders, and I do. "Jesus Christ," he mutters, turning the bag over in one hand. "What are you up to, Lara?"

"That's a better question for you, Tom," Lara says. Considering the circumstances, she sounds remarkably composed. "What's with the gun and the . . ." She flicks her eyes to Ivy. "Hostage?"

"How could you do that to Boney?" Ivy cuts in, her voice shaking. "He was your *student*. He trusted you!" She almost looks as though she expects him to agree; like he's still the affable coach she thought she knew. Someone she can argue with, or reason with.

"He was a thief," Coach Kendall says dismissively. "And a small-time dealer who wanted to be bigger. That's why he came to the studio this morning. One of my guys told him that if he returned everything that was taken, we'd let him into the business. But that little piece of shit had the nerve to show up empty-handed." His nostrils flare. "He thought it would give him *leverage*."

Ivy and I exchange startled glances. Charlie hadn't told us that part, and it didn't seem like he was trying to hide anything. Boney must have hatched that plan on his own. Maybe he thought he'd dazzle Charlie with his negotiating prowess afterward. *We could be big-time.*

"Is that why you had him killed?" I ask, my throat dry.

"No." He meets my eyes with a predator's gaze: alert, deadly, and totally dispassionate. "He was always going to die. I needed a body for the police to find." He turns back to Lara. "And for *you* to get found with. But I was supposed to get my investment back first."

Jesus, I feel sick. That explains why Charlie's house was torn apart; Coach Kendall must've been furious when he learned Boney didn't bring the pills. I wonder if his crew hit Boney's house, too, and Mateo's, but I don't dare ask. Especially since, as far as Coach Kendall knows, we have no clue that Charlie or Autumn are involved.

"And what were you going to do with your *investment*?" Lara asks in the same calm voice she's been using since we got here. "I was supposed to go down as Carlton's drug lord, wasn't I? Wouldn't that make business as usual difficult?"

"Temporarily. I'm a patient man, though. And it's not like the demand is going anywhere." Coach Kendall gives her an ugly smile. "If you'd been at your studio this morning, everyone would've gotten what they deserve. I thought about the reverse, you know—having you killed, and framing him. But a few minutes of suffering didn't seem like enough when I could put you in jail for life."

She doesn't flinch. "So now what?"

"So now . . ." Coach Kendall passes a hand over his face. "I've been thinking about this ever since I realized you weren't at the studio. There's no good solution, Lara. You really tied my hands. But Ivy, for whatever reason, popped up where you were supposed to be this morning, and she's been missing ever since. I can't frame you for Brian's murder anymore. That ship has sailed. But I can frame you for hers."

"What? No!" I yelp, and Lara turns to me.

"And Cal?" she asks. "How do you plan to explain Cal?"

Coach Kendall's nostrils flare again. "Cal wasn't supposed to be here."

"But he is," she says in the manner of someone sharing a helpful tip.

I can't deal with this. I can't sit here with these two, a pawn in whatever sick game they're playing with one another. "My parents know I'm here," I offer up, but Lara immediately lets out a dismissive snort.

"Oh, please. They do not. Tom, let's get real. What's your Plan B?"

Coach Kendall shifts restlessly. "You were supposed to take the fall for everything, Lara. All the shit that's been giving me an ulcer for the past month. Kids stealing pills and handing them out like candy in my fucking *backyard*. Cops sniffing around asking questions, and you being a lying, cheating bitch." He glares at her, jaw twitching, but she doesn't react. "That's all gone to hell now, so Ivy can take the rap for killing Brian, and you take the rap for killing her. And Cal, I guess. All part of your drug empire, which . . ." He taps himself on the chest. "Shocked and horrified me more than anyone."

"Uh-huh. Okay." Lara runs a hand through her hair, gazing at Coach Kendall with a look that's almost flirtatious. No, it definitely is. What the hell is going on here? "Baby, listen. I'm not telling you how to do your job, but that is a *terrible* plan," she says, not unkindly. He scowls, and she quickly adds, "You've always been good at the numbers side of things, but you have to admit, you find the people side a little frustrating. Right?" He doesn't answer, but some of the anger slips from his face, and she presses her advantage. "You've been counting all day on people to be predictable and do what they're told, and they keep letting you down."

Especially you, I think, but whatever she's doing seems to be working—Coach Kendall's gun hand has been dropping steadily as she's been speaking—so I keep my mouth shut. I shift in place on the ground, my hand brushing Ivy's, and two of her fingers hook lightly onto mine. Even though her hands are shaking, it's comforting.

"You need help getting out of this mess," Lara continues, fluffing her hair again. "So let me help you. From what I can see, we have two options here."

He cocks his head, considering, then gestures at her with the gun. "Go on."

"One, we both disappear." She glances at the bag beside her. "I know you have ID already, and I just got mine—"

"You just got yours?" Coach Kendall's face hardens again. "There's no *just* about it. That shit takes time. How long have you been planning to take off, Lara?"

"I believe in being prepared. You're in a dangerous business," Lara says smoothly, but there's a flicker of apprehension in her eyes that I can't quite read—like she knows she has to tread lightly here. It occurs to me, suddenly, that maybe Lara was fine with her fiancé's side business because she realized she could use it to fund a new life for herself.

"Look, I was scared," Lara continues. "But I love you,

Tommy. You know I do." She gives him the kind of smile that would've wrapped me around her finger a day ago. "I understand why you're angry. I know I made mistakes, but you did, too. If we could get away from all the pressure in this pretentious little town, I think we could fix everything that's gone wrong between us. And you deserve a break, don't you think? You've worked so hard. So that's option one. We find a nice beach where we can enjoy ourselves and stop worrying all the time."

Coach Kendall flicks his eyes between Lara, Ivy, and me. He actually looks like he's buying her crap, and while that's good news, it's also kind of shocking. It's come to my attention, recently, that I'm a massive sucker, but this is a whole other level. "Interesting," he says. "Although it throws years of work down the drain. What's option two?"

I lean forward despite myself. I don't mind the idea of these two disappearing, but I'm hoping Lara comes up with something even better—like Coach Kendall turning himself in. Maybe that's wishful thinking, but he seems to be putty in her hands. If anyone can persuade him to do it, it'd be her.

Instead, she tilts her head toward Ivy and me and says, "Frame someone else. Like, these two."

No. No. No no no no no.

Lara is still talking, even though the world just spun on its axis and should've knocked her flat on her ass. "This one is supposed to be smart, right?" she asks, lifting her chin toward Ivy. "At least, she thinks she is. But really, she's a nasty, vindictive little thing. Half the town already believes she killed Brian. It wouldn't be that much of a stretch for them to believe she's a dealer, too, especially if we keep the scale realistic. She doesn't need to have been running a full operation; it could just be her,

Cal, and some stolen prescription pads." Lara's voice is all honey and sweetness, despite the poison rolling off her tongue. "All we'd need to do is move a few things to her house, give them both an overdose, and call it a day."

Ivy makes choking noises beside me as Lara flutters her lashes at Coach Kendall, twirling a strand of hair around her finger. "I mean, there's more to it than that, obviously, but we can figure out the details together. The important thing is, it keeps the situation contained. No one you work with is implicated. No one except the two of them"—she gestures at Ivy and me— "knows you're involved, or that I use the studio Brian died in. Besides Dominick, and he won't say a word. He has an airtight alibi since he was giving a lecture out of town, and he doesn't want any trouble."

Mateo and Charlie know, I think, but manage not to blurt it out. I told Lara I'd kept her use of the studio to myself, and it's better for everyone if she keeps thinking that.

Coach Kendall is silent for what feels like an eternity, and my entire being is focused on sending *Vote to Disappear* vibes his way. I know it's no guarantee that Ivy and I will get out of here alive, but it has a one hundred percent better chance than the alternative.

But then he smiles. Actually *smiles,* like the pathetic, gullible creep that he is. "I like the sound of option two," he says.

Ivy tugs at my fingers, hard. When I cut my eyes toward her, she jerks her head downward and to the left, like she's trying to call my attention to something. I look at the space between us, but there's nothing except our interlocked hands.

"No time to waste, then," Lara says. "What's in the duffel bag?"

Coach Kendall's smile hardens. "Everything we need to get started."

Ivy yanks my hand more insistently and jerks her head again. Frustration builds in me, because she's obviously trying to tell me something and I have no idea what. Her head dips more deeply to the left as she squeezes my hand, and then—I get it. *Your left.*

I glance down while letting my fingertips brush the floor, seeing and feeling in an instant what Ivy has been trying to point out. There's a crowbar on the ground beside me; I must have stepped right over it without noticing. But Ivy did.

Coach Kendall and Lara are still talking as I close my fingers around the metal bar. ". . . help you get it ready," Lara is saying.

Coach Kendall narrows his eyes at her. "I'm not trusting you with a syringe full of fentanyl, Lara. But you can restrain this one." He jerks his head toward me. "There's duct tape in the side pocket. Take it out."

My hand flexes on the crowbar as I gauge the distance between me and Coach Kendall. His gun hand is within reach, if I can get a good enough swing in. The thought freezes me with self-doubt and fear, and I really wish I'd used that baseball bat in my trunk for more than just a prop at some point. Even once would've helped.

Coach Kendall's attention is fully focused on Lara as she unzips one side of his duffel bag, the gun pointed toward the ground. Ivy is almost crushing my hand, her nails biting into my palm with rhythmic, frantic pressure like she's chanting the word out loud. *Now. Now. Now.*

She's right. There won't be a better time.

I lunge forward with the crowbar in my grasp and swing it with all my strength toward Coach Kendall's hand. Lara screams and ducks as I make contact, and a shocked thrill of triumph surges through me when the gun goes flying toward the wall and Coach Kendall howls with pain and rage. *I did it, I can't believe I actually did it, I—*

And then I'm flat on my back, the entire right side of my head on fire from the impact of Coach Kendall's fist. The element of surprise ended way too fast.

Out of the corner of my eye, I see Lara scrambling on the floor, going for the gun, until Ivy leaps at her and drags her back. They're a tangle of motion, all blond hair and flailing limbs. Ivy manages to sweep the gun away from them, and I watch it skitter beneath a rusted lawn mower. Then I can't pay attention to them anymore, because there's a fist headed my way again. If I could talk, I'd tell Coach Kendall to think twice about beating me senseless, since it doesn't fit the framing scenario all that well. But my mouth isn't working, and from the look on his face, he's snapped beyond the point of reason. So I try to squirm out of the way instead.

And fail.

My skull explodes in agony as Coach Kendall connects again, only I moved just enough that it's not quite the knockout punch he was going for. I reach a hand out convulsively, grasping for anything that might help me, and my fingers brush rough fabric. Despite the pain radiating across every inch of my head, my thoughts are clear enough to know it's Coach Kendall's duffel bag. And to remember that he has a syringe full of . . . something.

Something that would help, if I could only get to it.

I twist and thrash beneath Coach Kendall as his hands close around my neck, inching myself closer to the bag until my fingers brush the hard edge of a zipper. I tug at it and can feel it start to give way, creating a small opening at the top of the bag. It's getting difficult to breathe, but I strain harder until I can slip my hand into the top of the bag. I flex my fingers, searching for something, anything, inside, when suddenly the pressure on my neck eases, only to be replaced with an agonizing twist at my wrist as Coach Kendall yanks my hand out of the bag.

"Nice try," he says, and this time, I don't have enough strength to even try to move when he hauls his fist back.

Then I feel white-hot pain, and stars erupt in front of me. They're bright orange, flashing and dancing, and it occurs to me hazily as viselike pressure returns to my neck that they're the last thing I'll ever see.

I never did learn how to fight.

My hands curl into fists as I try anyway. I swing at whatever part of Coach Kendall I can reach, but it's like punching a wall—painful for me, and nothing to him.

"No!" Ivy's scream sounds like it's coming from a thousand miles away. "Let him go! Let him go!" The clawing pressure on my neck disappears for a second, but then returns worse than before. All the breath leaves my lungs, and my hands fall to my sides, twitching uselessly. The orange stars expand and spin across my line of vision, sparkling like gems, impossibly bright and burning.

And tinged, suddenly, with a flashing ring of blue.

A new sound fills my ears. It's not Ivy's screams, or Coach Kendall's grunts, or whatever the hell Lara is saying. It's loud and commanding, crisp and official, and even though I can't make out more than a word here or there—"surrounded" is one, and that seems like a good one—I cling to the sound, and the blue lights, and to whatever shreds of consciousness I have left, as I force my fingers beneath the slackening band at my neck. Air slips into my lungs and I suck it in, and then, suddenly, the crushing weight is gone.

"Get down! Get down! On the floor! Hands over your head!" someone barks. Footsteps are everywhere. I try to obey because I think whoever it is must be talking to me, but my limbs won't cooperate and I flounder on my back like a dying bug, weak and gasping, until a pair of gloved hands grasp mine.

"Okay, settle down. You're all right," someone says. It's an unfamiliar voice, gruff and authoritative, but not without kindness. "Can you hear me, son? Your captor is in custody, and you are safe."

"Ivy," I gasp, blinking as I try to clear my vision. It's no use, though. Lights are still dancing in front of my eyes, but all of them are blue now.

"Your friend is safe," the voice promises. And I believe them enough that I let myself pass out.

I wake up on the ground outside, wrapped in a blanket that I struggle against until I see Ivy among the circle of faces looming above me. "How?" I rasp, letting someone help me sit up. It's the only word I can manage to push out of my raw throat, but Ivy's eyes are bright with understanding as she takes hold of my hand.

"Someone sent the police here," she says.

"Who?" I ask.

"I don't know." She shrugs, dislodging the blanket around her own shoulders. "You were only out for a few minutes, and no one's told me anything yet."

The officer holding me up is no help. "How about you rest now," she suggests. "An ambulance is on its way."

I don't want an ambulance. I feel fine, sort of. I ignore the officer, my eyes trained on Ivy. "Was it Daniel, do you think?" I ask. "Did he use his super brain to figure things out?"

"Not this time," Ivy snorts. "I just talked to Trevor. They were at Olive Garden when Coach Kendall texted me, totally clueless. Daniel didn't even realize his phone was gone. It was easy to hack, since all the lax guys use the same passcode so they can take pictures with each other's phones during games." She rolls her eyes. "Bunch of dumbasses."

"Lara, maybe?" I hate the hopeful lilt in my voice. Ivy pretends not to notice, but there's no missing the way her face hardens.

"She didn't help us" is all she says.

A transmitter clipped to the officer's hip crackles beside us. "Witness family, incoming," it intones. I cut my eyes toward Ivy, questioning. She swallows and shakes her head. "Mine are in a cab, stuck in rush-hour traffic. Must be you."

I rise as quickly as I can, helped by the officer, and eagerly scan the area. Every police car on the scene has its lights flashing, illuminating the street so brightly that Lara's deserted neighborhood looks like a movie set. I don't see my parents, but I know they must be nearby, and that's almost as good. There are what look like a dozen police cars parked around us, plus Ivy's car, and then . . .

I blink at the unexpected sight of a boxy sedan a few hundred yards away. Not at the car, even though I don't recognize it, but at the figure leaning against it. We're too far away for me to be sure, but I'd swear on the grave we just avoided that it's Mateo.

"Is that . . . ," I start to ask Ivy. But then I hear Henry's frantic voice calling "Cal!", followed by a piercing shout of joy from Wes, and everything else will have to wait.

33

IVY

"This is ridiculous," Dad mutters, stabbing at his eggs with a fork.

Mom pours a glass of vegetable juice. "Just ignore them."

"I am," Dad says. Stab, stab, stab. Daniel and I exchange glances across the kitchen table, and my brother silently holds up three fingers. Then two, then one, and then . . .

"Enough!" Dad roars, getting to his feet. He marches into the hall as Daniel and I crane our necks to watch him. Dad flings open the front door, and is greeted by flashes from half a dozen cameras. Reporters loitering near the news vans parked in front of our house spring to life, stretching microphones toward my father as he leans out the door. "We have no further comment!" he yells before slamming the door and stalking back into the kitchen.

Mom sips her juice. "They're never going to leave if you keep doing that."

I swallow a smile. Dad is spiraling, just like me. I'm not sure I realized, until reporters started camping in front of our house all day, how much we're alike in that respect. He's just a whole lot better at managing it, usually.

It's been five days since the police pulled Cal and me out of Ms. Jamison's garage. Or Lara's garage, I guess. Once you've been through a hostage situation with someone, you might as well be on a first-name basis. Coach Kendall is in jail, but Lara isn't. She lawyered up fast, refusing to say a word until one of the state's top defense attorneys agreed to represent her. Now she's cooperating with the police, helping them build a case against her fiancé, and she insists that everything she said in the garage was just an attempt to disarm him. She says she was too afraid of Coach Kendall to come forward before now, and that the false ID in her bag was a last-ditch attempt to escape from a cold-blooded killer who'd never let her go. It would be believable, I guess, if you hadn't been in the room while she fantasized about running off to a beach with him.

Lara also says that Cal—poor Cal, who spent two days in the hospital being treated for a concussion—misunderstood their conversation in the house before Coach Kendall arrived.

That Cal misunderstood *everything*.

I'm not buying it for a second. I know exactly how hard she was fighting for the gun in the garage, and it wasn't, as she put it, to *keep me from hurting myself*. And I'll never forget the look on her face when she called me "a vindictive little thing." But other people—people who aren't related to me, anyway—are divided. Some seem to believe her, and others act like her cooperation against Coach Kendall is more important than anything that came before it.

The Carlton Citizen of the Year Award has been postponed indefinitely, and I still feel bad about that. Not to mention having to finally come clean about what I did at Spare Me last spring. But here's the thing about getting taken hostage by your brother's lacrosse coach–turned–drug dealer: it gives you *a lot* of leeway. Mom and Dad are so happy that I'm not dead, they barely blinked at the fact that I single-handedly brought down a business.

"We'll make this right," Dad said. He's been on the phone all week with Ms. Reyes, his insurance company, and Shepard Properties lawyers. I only eavesdropped once, when I heard Dad yelling at one of his lawyers. "I don't care about *minimizing my exposure*," he said. "I care about what's fair." And while I felt another wave of remorse about putting my dad in this position, I also felt relieved that he is who he is. The kind of person who *will* make this right. And also the kind of person I could have talked to a lot sooner, if I hadn't been too twisted up with fear and insecurity.

Autumn has a lawyer too—not as flashy as Lara's, but a friend of Mateo's mom who took the case pro bono. Her name is Christy something, and wow, does she like to talk. She's been all over the news, pushing hard for rehabilitation instead of punishment, and so far, at least, the local politicians weighing in seem to agree. There's more focus on unraveling Coach Kendall's network of suppliers and distributors than on prosecuting Autumn or Charlie. Gabe Prescott is a different case, though, since his association with Coach Kendall goes back more than a year. Stefan St. Clair had it right; Gabe's job was essentially to spy on his friends and classmates, and he got paid a small fortune to do it.

I guess Autumn is doing all right. But I'm not sure, since I've only spoken to Mateo twice since it all happened: once at the police station when we all gave statements, and once when I called to thank him for saving our lives. I was afraid he wouldn't pick up, but he did.

"I didn't know you guys were in trouble," he said. "It was the police's idea to raid Ms. Jamison's place. They thought it might be a drop-off point for Coach Kendall. Then they saw his car, and your car, and a light on in the garage, so . . . that was that. They escalated."

"Well, thanks anyway," I said limply. I'm not surprised that he felt the need to clarify; Mateo doesn't like getting credit that he doesn't think he's earned. But at the same time, it felt like he was saying, *I didn't do it for you.* Especially since he hung up as quickly as he could after that without being straight-up rude.

I tried to not let it bother me—*perspective, Ivy, perspective*—but it did. I'd wanted that call to go differently, so much so that I'd swallowed my pride and sent a follow-up text the next day. *Let me know if you ever want to talk.*

I will, he replied. That was three days ago.

I've been hoping for a fresh start, but maybe Mateo isn't where I'm going to get it.

"You wanna play archery?" Daniel asks me, getting up from the table and putting his plate into the dishwasher.

I follow suit. "Yeah, okay." That's something we've started doing since Coach Kendall was arrested; playing multiplayer games via messaging. I'm not sure what Daniel's motivation is, but for me it's a low-pressure way to hang out with my brother while I figure out how to relate to him in a way that doesn't include resenting everything he does.

It helps that he's surprisingly bad at all the games, which is satisfying in a way that I realize does nothing to kill my hyper-competitive spirit. Baby steps.

"Good," Mom says, finishing the last of her juice. "Lie low until the gauntlet out front gets bored. I'm sure they will once your father manages to contain himself for more than ten minutes at a time."

"It's harassment," Dad mutters. "And that bastard Dale Hawkins is front and center, loving every second of this. Even though it's his irresponsible reporting that put Ivy in the spotlight with false accusations in the first place."

"Not just *his* irresponsible reporting," Daniel points out. "Ishaan and Zack helped. And they're milking it for everything they can." The boys have their own YouTube channel now, with paid sponsors, and they've been analyzing the Coach Kendall case all week. The highlight of the show was when Emily agreed to appear—for a hefty fee—and corrected everything they'd gotten wrong so far. She even made them apologize to me.

The segment went semiviral, which is kind of great. Watching my best friend turn into a social-media star is the distraction I didn't know I needed.

"They're just kids," Dad huffs. "And they're not in front of our house."

"It's the Fourth Amendment, love," Mom says placidly. "Unless they step onto our lawn, in which case you have my permission to turn the hose on them. Especially Dale."

Daniel and I settle into opposite ends of the couch in the living room, and I wait while he takes the first turn at archery. When his scores flash across my screen, it's two misses and a bull's-eye. "You're all over the place," I say, taking aim. Our dog, Mila, who'd been napping in the sunny spot in front of the sliding glass door, wakes up with a rattle of tags. She stretches, eyes us from behind an enormous yawn, and goes right back to sleep.

"I'm an all-or-nothing kind of guy," Daniel says, propping his feet up on the couch.

I lower my phone to swat at them. "Take your sneakers off."

"Take your sneakers off," he mimics under his breath like a five-year-old. But a good-natured one. As he unlaces them, the brightly patterned Nike swoosh makes me pause. I'd nearly forgotten Cal's thousand-dollar-sneaker comment in Lara's classroom.

"Where did you get those?" I ask.

Daniel leans back on the couch in stocking feet. "Get what?"

"Those sneakers. Cal said they cost a thousand dollars. It's one of the reasons why he thought you might possibly be the Weasel."

Daniel rolls his eyes. "That was ridiculous."

"Okay, but for real. Do they cost a thousand dollars?"

Daniel's cheeks get a little pink. "Well, if you pay retail, sure."

"So you didn't?"

"Of course not."

"Where'd you get them, then?"

He pauses for a beat before saying, "On eBay."

"Oh." I score a nine before a thought hits me. "Wait. Are they *used*? Did you buy sneakers that were on someone else's feet?"

His face confirms it before he's even said a word. "They're gently worn," Daniel protests over my gagging noise. "The person who sold them said he only wore them once. With socks."

"You have absolutely no way of knowing whether that's true, and even if it is? Still gross," I say.

"Well, it's better than paying retail and being the Weasel."

"Not by much," I say as I score a bull's-eye and send the game back to Daniel.

He grins, and I rest my phone on my knees while I wait for him to take his turn. It's a small thing, playing games together, but it's also kind of huge. We haven't done anything like this in years. When my parents and I got ready to leave the police station on Tuesday night, I didn't expect that Daniel would be in the reception area. But he was—and when I saw him, I started bawling, because for a few terrifying minutes while Coach Kendall was dragging me around Lara's property, I really did think he'd done something to my brother.

Even though the police confirmed that he was okay, I didn't fully believe them until I saw him waiting for me. When he hugged me, he lifted me off the ground like I was no heavier than a lacrosse stick, and it reminded me of getting hugged by a much smaller, younger version of my brother. I think because of the fierceness behind it, which made me cry even harder.

We talked without arguing for the first time in a long time that night. I told him about Spare Me, and apologized for trying to hurt him and stream it to the entire school. He took it pretty well, considering. He told me how much pressure he's under all the time, and we agreed to try being less horrible to one another. It's only been a few days, but I think we're doing okay.

Daniel is lining up a shot, brow furrowed in concentration, when my father appears in the living room doorway. "It's nice to see the two of you hanging out," Dad says with a slight catch in his voice.

"Don't do it," Daniel warns without looking up.

"Don't do what?" Dad asks, sitting between us. "Appreciate the fact that my children, whom I love more than life itself, are safe and healthy and happy?" He sniffs, eyes glistening.

Daniel puts his phone down with a sigh. "Is it crying time?" he asks as Dad slings an arm around each of us and crushes us to his chest.

It is. Dad's been doing this at least once a day since he got back from San Francisco, and to be honest, I don't mind. There are much, much worse things that could happen.

"I'm so proud of you both," Dad chokes out. "You've been so brave."

"I literally did nothing except eat breadsticks at Olive Garden," Daniel reminds him, his voice muffled by Dad's shirt. But that's not true. Daniel had to deal with everything coming out about Coach Kendall, and it hasn't been easy. Our entire family trusted him, but my brother most of all. Still, he's been deflecting any attempts to give him credit. "That was all Ivy."

Dad clutches me tighter, and while it's getting a little hard to breathe, I'm not about to complain. I caused a huge amount of trouble for him and his company by what I did at Spare Me, and we're still not sure how it will be resolved. At the same time, I've been reprimanded more than once by the police, who took pains to remind my parents that my and Cal's need to be rescued could have been avoided entirely if we'd reported what we saw from the beginning. My parents have every right to be furious with me—and they have been, on a daily basis since they got home. But it's always balanced out by moments like this.

"I wish you'd been more careful, Ivy," Dad says now. Mila is awake again, trotting back and forth in front of the couch like she's searching for an opening into the group hug. "But the way you pieced things together, and kept your cool?" His voice wavers, tinged with wonder. "That was absolutely extraordinary."

Extraordinary, he said. It feels as good as I thought it would.

34

MATEO

I didn't fully appreciate how small our house is until it had to contain my mother's fury.

She'd never been yell-till-her-face-turns-red mad before—not at Autumn and me, anyway—until she got back from the Bronx late Tuesday night. But even that wasn't the worst part. It's the disappointment that really hurts, and the way she looks at us now. Like she doesn't know who we are anymore.

I understand the feeling. Sometimes I don't know, either.

Two and a half weeks after the Shittiest Day Ever, we're still trying to figure out what normal looks like. It's too early to tell what's going to happen to Autumn, but she's been cooperating with police and Christy's doing a great job as her lawyer, so we're cautiously optimistic that she'll end up with probation and community service. Which she's already started, at a shelter specializing in treating substance abuse.

Or I should say, *we've* already started.

"You're doing the exact same thing she does," Ma said angrily, and I wasn't about to argue. It could've been a lot worse; Charlie St. Clair's parents shipped him off to military school in New Hampshire.

Autumn and I volunteer at the shelter three afternoons a week, and if the goal was to get us to feel like absolute shit for being part of the opioid crisis—mission accomplished. I knew, in abstract, that Autumn, Charlie, and Boney selling a prescription drug to privileged Carlton kids was part of a bigger problem. But seeing it in real time is a whole other thing, especially since part of my job is coordinating activities for kids who live at the shelter. There's no way I'll go near anything stronger than aspirin again after playing basketball with an eight-year-old who, between free throws, told me about his mom's third relapse.

Autumn and I are both drained when our shifts at the shelter end Friday afternoon, and it's a relief to come home to a quiet house. Today Ma's meeting with James Shepard, like she has almost every day this week, so she's not around to give us the Glare of Doom.

"You working tonight?" Autumn asks, kicking off her sneakers before collapsing into a corner of the couch. Our house is back to normal; once we started cleaning up, I was relieved to see that most of the furniture was undamaged. We had to replace a few things, and a lot of kitchen stuff, but insurance took care of all that. Turns out Ma has much better coverage on our house than she did on her business.

I sink into the opposite end of the couch. "Yeah, but not till seven," I say. I don't have to tell her where. We're down to one job each now that we know there's going to be some kind of settlement from what Ivy did at Spare Me. I held on to Garrett's, even though it's the farthest away, and Autumn still drives the murder van. Mr. Sorrento has been really understanding about her whole situation. "You?"

"No," she yawns, rubbing her eyes. "I have the night off."

"What are you gonna do?" I ask.

Autumn snorts. "Oh, I have big plans. Netflix, ice cream, cutting Gabe out of all my pictures and burning his head. It's gonna be a whole thing."

"Sounds great. Let me know if you need help with the last part." My cousin dumped Gabe as soon as she learned he'd given my name to Coach Kendall. She might've stuck with him when he was outed as the Weasel, considering how guilty she feels about her own part in Coach Kendall's operation, but Gabe using my name sealed his fate. The silver lining to this disaster, I guess, is that we're finally free of Loser Gabe.

"How are you getting to Garrett's?" Autumn asks.

I suppress a sigh. "Dad's driving me."

True to his word—for once—Dad's back in Carlton, working at White & West Music Emporium and inserting himself into my life like the overgrown best friend I never asked for. Harsh, I know. Though it's hard not to resent the guy when his sudden attention, which is just kind of pointless and intrusive now, could've changed everything a few months ago.

But I go wherever he wants to take me, because Ma insists on it, and it's not like I'm about to cross her on anything right now.

"It's just—" I start, but I'm interrupted by the door opening. Ma comes in, and we instantly go silent. I try to gauge her expression as she walks toward us and sinks into an armchair. Does she look a little less grim than usual? Maybe?

"Were you two at the shelter earlier?" she asks, and we both nod like puppets. "Good." She massages one of her knees, but more absently than like it's really hurting her. Taking her medication regularly seems to be helping a lot with the pain. "It's time for the three of us to have a little talk."

Autumn and I exchange glances. "Okay," I say cautiously.

Ma gives us a tight-lipped smile. "I have been *beyond* angry with the two of you," she starts, and then pauses like she's not sure where to go from there.

"We noticed," I say. Autumn kicks me, hard, and I shut up.

"And I still am," Ma continues. "What you did was . . . okay, I told myself I wasn't going to get distracted with another lecture." She takes a deep breath. "Because the thing is—it's occurred to me, as I've been meeting with James Shepard and talking about next steps, that I've set a bad example for the two of you."

"What?" I lean forward, confused. "You set a *great* example."

"I've always liked to think that," Ma says. "But I've spent most of your lives doing everything myself. Never asking for help, as though there's something shameful about needing it. I wanted you both to be strong and independent, and you are—but you went overboard. And I did, too." She shifts in her chair. "I'm going to tell you something that's a little hard to admit. Before the lawsuit happened, I'd been thinking about closing Spare Me. I was worn down running a business by myself, and I wanted to try something new. But I didn't know how to tell the two of you that. It felt like admitting I'd failed. Then the DeWitts sued and—I didn't fight as hard as I could have. I was underinsured, yes, but I could've made it work. I chose not to. And I should have told you that."

She sits back in her chair like she's waiting for a response, so I grapple for one even though I'm having a hard time making sense of her words. Autumn looks equally confused, tugging on a strand of hair as she taps one foot on the ground. "So you . . . you *wanted* Spare Me to go under?" I finally ask.

"I don't think I would have put it that way at the time," Ma says. "But looking back, I think that I did." Her face softens as she takes in our blank expressions. "I know that place meant the world to the two of you. It was a big part of your lives for a long time. I was proud of it, and of having a family business, but I was also exhausted. And that's my entire point."

Autumn scrunches her forehead. "What is?"

"That I preferred extreme failure to admitting I needed help. Which is a problem, isn't it? Because I've passed that exact characteristic on to the two of you." Her dark eyes bore into mine. "It's not always a bad thing to be proud and stubborn. You get things done. But once I got sick, everything fell apart, and none of us had the tools to deal with that."

Autumn bites her lip. "Aunt Elena, it's not your fault that I—"

"I'm not saying it's my fault," Ma interrupts. "I'm saying I recognize I've modeled some unhealthy behaviors for the two of you. And that stops now." She leans forward, her face becoming more animated. "James has given me carte blanche on what to do with the Carlton Entertainment Complex, including shutting it down and rebuilding Spare Me exactly like it was before. But I don't want that. I like the plans for the CEC; they make sense. And I like James's overall vision, so I'm joining Shepard Properties as a managing director for the entertainment division."

She waits expectantly for our response. "So you're working for Ivy's dad?" I ask. I don't know why I called him that, instead of *James*. Might just be where my head's at lately.

"I am. It's a fantastic job with great benefits. The co-pay on my medication will *actually* be twenty dollars." She narrows her eyes at Autumn, who's suddenly very interested in a stray thread on the couch cushion. "Being part of a team is going to be a nice change, and it's exactly what I need at this point in life. It's also what *you* need, because supporting this family is not in your job description. I'm sorry I allowed you to think that it is."

We're all silent for a moment, letting the words sink in. I can't fully wrap my brain around everything she's saying yet—the idea that Spare Me wasn't so much the rock our family was built on as a rock around her neck—but there's a small sense of relief, suddenly, at letting it go. Because maybe then I can let some other things go, too.

"We're going to be fine. Better than fine," Ma says firmly. "I'm optimistic about your case, Autumn. It's early days, but I think your genuine remorse, and the fact that you turned yourself in, will make a difference. In the meantime, I have a chance to build something new, and please believe me when I say that I am happy about that." She gives me one last, shrewd look. "So I don't want either of you hanging on to resentment about what happened last spring with Patrick DeWitt's accident. We're in no position to cast stones. All right?"

We both mumble assent as Ma gets to her feet. "Good," she says. "I'm going to rest for a little while, and then I'll make dinner." She heads upstairs, and Autumn waits until we hear the sound of Ma's bedroom door clicking shut to speak.

"Well," she says. "That's a lot to process."

"I'll say," I mumble, massaging my temple. I have a small scar there now, from when Charlie hit me with the golf club.

"I think . . . I think it's good, though?" she says cautiously. "Aunt Elena seems happy."

"Yeah. She does."

Autumn braids the tassels of the couch pillow. "Managing director of the CEC. Who would've thought?"

"First order of business is changing that name," I say, and Autumn snort-laughs before shooting me a wry look.

"So . . . maybe you can text a certain somebody back now?" she says. "Instead of pretending like you don't want to, and walking around with a permafrown and a bad attitude?"

"That's my normal attitude," I object. She makes a face, and I add, "Anyway, it's not about what Ivy did at Spare Me. I stopped being mad when she almost died." Even now, just saying the words fills me with a sick sense of dread. Coach Kendall was out of control that night, and could've easily killed everyone within reach. My last words to Ivy would have been, *You're pathetic, and I don't want to see or speak to you again for the rest of my life.*

"Then why aren't you guys talking?" Autumn asks.

I sink lower into the couch. "The stuff I said to her in Cal's car. How do you unsay something like that?"

"You don't," Autumn says. "You apologize. It's up to her whether or not to accept it, but I think she will." I don't reply, and she taps a finger against her chin. "Hmm. I wish I could remember a recent example of everything going to hell because somebody in this family was—how did she put it?—proud and stubborn? It's on the tip of my tongue, almost like it *just happened,* and yet . . ."

"Shut up," I say, tossing a pillow at her to hide my grin.

* * *

Seeing as I have a ride to Garrett's tonight, I have time to do something else first.

Ivy's driveway is filled with her family's cars, so I park in the street. When I approach the house, I can see her perched in the window seat of her room, reading. Her hair is loose around her shoulders—Charlie was right, it looks great like that—and the sight of her makes my chest ache.

The front porch is only a few feet away, but I pause when I'm halfway along the stone path that leads to it, considering my options. Ivy's parents are clearly home, and I'm not sure I'm up for talking to them right now. I'm still trying to figure out how I feel about the CEC news, considering how much time I've spent hating that place. Plus, James Shepard is a lot to take lately. I've seen him twice since he got back from San Francisco, and both times he flung an arm around my neck and said, "This guy. Where would any of us be without this guy?" And the next thing I know, he's crying on my shoulder. He means well, I know, but I'd rather avoid that particular scenario before talking to Ivy.

The path I'm standing on is lined with small stones, and I contemplate picking one of them up and tossing it at Ivy's window to get her attention. That would be beyond cheesy, though, wouldn't it? Plus, the stones make up such a neat little pattern that a missing one would be noticeable. And what if I threw it too hard and broke her window, and—

"Are you going to stand there all day?" a voice calls.

I look up to see Ivy leaning out her now-open window. "Maybe," I call back, my pulse picking up at the lilt in her voice. She sounds happy to see me. "Still deciding."

"Okay," she says, crossing her arms over the windowsill. "Keep me posted."

"I will." I reach into my pocket and hold up the box I bought on the way over. "I brought you something."

"Are those Sugar Babies?" she asks.

"They are."

She smiles, and even from a distance it lights up her whole face. "That's your only move, huh?"

"Pretty much," I admit.

"It's a good one," she says. "Be right down."

35

CAL

Amid Swirling Rumors, Embattled Carlton Teacher Resigns.

I sit at my kitchen table on Saturday morning, almost a month after Coach Kendall tried to kill me in Lara's garage, staring at the headline on Boston.com and wondering if I'll ever get used to being a *swirling rumor.*

I thought it was cut-and-dried, what happened between Lara and me. But the only thing she'll admit to is becoming "overly close" with me, to the point of exchanging text messages and seeing me outside of school. She turned over her phone to investigators, and when I read back through our messages to brace myself for what they'd be seeing, I realized how careful she always was. I come off like a lovesick teenager—which, to be fair, I was—and Lara comes off like a caring but ultimately boundary-respecting adult.

My parents believe me, though. One hundred percent, and they're furious.

Wes sits across from me with a steaming mug of coffee, wearing the kind of thoughtful look that tells me he's carefully gauging my reaction to the article. "There's still a double standard when it comes to viewing women as predators," he finally says.

That's what he keeps calling Lara, and even though I resisted the term at first, I get it now. Especially the way she keeps twisting the truth to suit the image of herself that she's trying to present: the helpful witness, relieved and grateful to finally be away from her domineering ex-fiancé, doing everything she can to make up for his crimes.

"At least she resigned," I say.

For a while, Wes and Henry talked about bringing corruption-of-minor charges or something similar against Lara. Maybe that's the right call, but the idea of having our relationship dissected even more than it already had been horrified me so much that they backed off. Ultimately, at least for now, they decided to focus on getting her teaching license revoked. Carlton High had already suspended her, pending investigation, when she quit.

I read through the article again, but there's nothing much new there. Lara has admitted that she was having an affair while engaged to Coach Kendall, but she's refusing to give the guy's name, and since he's not involved in the investigation, police aren't making her. So I guess we might never know who D is, and I remind myself that I'm okay with that.

Wes frowns, wrapping his hands around his coffee mug. "I know she's providing the police with valuable information, but I wish that wasn't quite as much of a shield as it's turning out to be," he says.

I don't answer, because I could really use a subject change. We've already discussed this at length. Multiple times. And while

I appreciate his support—both my dads have been great, considering how much I lied to them—sometimes I need a break from being part of the news cycle. I flick the article away and pull up my messages, opening one that Ivy sent at two o'clock in the morning. "Did you know the average person spends six months of their life waiting for red lights to turn green?" I ask Wes.

He accepts the conversational shift with a smile. "Is that an Ivy factoid?"

"It is." She's sending them to me constantly again, which I enjoy. I send her back panels of my latest web comic, *The Shittiest Day Ever,* which is by far the darkest, angriest, most emotional thing I've ever created. It's also, at least according to Ivy, the best.

"It's nice to see you reconnecting with your old friends," Wes says, taking a long sip of coffee. "And making new ones."

I wasn't sure how people would treat me when I went back to school that first week after being released from the hospital. Whether I'd be viewed as a hero for making it out of the garage alive, even though I got my ass kicked in the process, or a loser thanks to Lara's denials about what happened between us. I found out pretty fast when I walked down the hallway toward homeroom and a couple of guys in my class started singing "Hot for Teacher" at the top of their lungs. Everyone laughed, and my face burned with the realization of just how much the rest of senior year was going to suck. Then I felt an arm sling around my neck.

"Don't even think about giving my boy Cal a hard time," Ishaan Mittal called out in a booming voice, pulling me down the hall with him. In the wrong direction from my homeroom, but whatever. The YouTube show has made Ishaan a celebrity at

Carlton High, and as soon as he decided I was his *boy*—which was a little ironic, considering their most-viewed episode to date is the one where he had no idea who I was—people stopped laughing. Now he keeps inviting me places, and while I don't often go, I have to admit that he's not bad company when he isn't trying to book me as a guest.

Plus, it's nice to have other people to hang out with occasionally. Ivy and Mateo have restarted their epic interrupted romance, and while I'm happy for them, I don't always want to be in the middle of it.

"You're welcome," I told Ivy yesterday while she floated down the hallway beside me after saying goodbye to Mateo at his locker.

"Hmm?" she asked dreamily.

"If you guys had started going out in eighth grade, you would've broken up a month later," I said. "My interference stalled you to a point in your lives when relationships aren't measured in weeks."

She didn't even try to argue with me, which just goes to show how much Ivy has mellowed lately.

Ivy and I have fallen right back into old patterns. With Mateo, I'm trying to start new ones. It occurred to me, when I reflected on my Sugar Babies sabotage from years ago, that I'd always been a little threatened by him. Not as a romantic rival, but a friend rival; I'd thought Ivy and I were the closest in our trio, and I didn't like finding out that I was wrong. So I tried to protect our twosome, instead of giving it room to expand. After everything the three of us went through with Coach Kendall, though, it couldn't have been clearer that while Ivy and I make an okay team, we're a lot better when we're balanced with Mateo.

So I'm disappointed when my next text is from him. *Couldn't find anyone to switch shifts at the shelter, so I can't make the exhibit after all. I'm really sorry.*

No worries, I text back with a sigh. *The shelter comes first.*

Wes, who's now hyperalert to even the slightest change in my mood, puts down his coffee mug and asks, "What's the matter?"

"Nothing major," I say. "Mateo can't come to the Kusama exhibit tonight. And Ivy has plans with Emily, so—I guess I'm going alone."

I got tickets to see the Yayoi Kusama exhibit at the Institute of Contemporary Art in South Boston back in early September, when I thought Lara might go with me. Kusama does these multimedia installations called mirror rooms where you walk through an exhibit filled with lights and mirrors and art. It's supposed to be a one-of-a-kind immersive experience. Just looking at images online has gotten my creativity flowing, and I've been excited to see it live. But the idea of not having anyone to talk about it with afterward makes me feel deflated.

"Could you get an extra ticket for Emily?" Wes asks.

"No way. They sold out almost as soon as they went on sale."

"Why don't you ask one of your new friends?"

"Um . . ." I glance at the last of my texts, which is from Ishaan. *You going to Lindsay's party tonight?* "I don't think my new friends would be interested."

"You never know until you try," Wes says brightly.

He has a point, I guess, so I text Ishaan a link to the ICA's Kusama page and say, *Can't, I'm going to this. I have an extra ticket, do you want to come?*

Ishaan texts back almost immediately. *Looks weird.*

I toss my phone onto the table, trying to push down the

restless anxiety that's been my constant companion lately. That kind of response almost makes me miss Lara, which I'd really rather not do. But even though my social circle has expanded in a positive way lately, sometimes I still feel like the odd man out.

Wes is eyeing me with concern, so I force a smile. "I think I'm gonna make chocolate chip pancakes. You want some?"

"I would love some," Wes says, getting to his feet. "And so would your father, who should've been up half an hour ago. Let me get him."

I wait for him to leave the kitchen before I go to the refrigerator. It's pointless to get down about going to the Kusama exhibit alone. It's not that big of a deal, especially when I stack it against everything that happened last month. But it's been hanging over me as an event I'd planned with Lara in mind, and it would've been nice—symbolic, in a way—to replace her toxic presence with someone else. *Anyone* else.

I put eggs and milk on our kitchen table and head for the stove, then pause and turn back when I hear my phone buzz. It's a follow-up text from Ishaan.

I'm into it. What time?

YOUTUBE, IZ CHANNEL

Ishaan and Zack are sitting on an overstuffed sofa in Ishaan's finished basement, using a wide shot that shows Emily perched at the edge of a chair to their left. Ishaan has a sharp new haircut, and Zack is wearing a trendy leather jacket.

ISHAAN: Emily, you know what we're gonna ask.

EMILY: The answer is no.

ZACK, *fussing with the cuffs of his jacket:* Did you even check with her?

EMILY: I don't have to. There's no way Ivy will ever agree to let you interview her.

ISHAAN: Can't you convince her? *(Clasps his hands together in a praying motion.)* Come on, Emily. It would be so badass if she did.

EMILY: Believe it or not, Ivy doesn't care whether you, or anyone else, thinks she's *badass*. Things are finally getting back to normal for her, and she doesn't need to be reminded of the worst day of her entire life.

ZACK: Views would go through the roof, though. *(Lowers his eyes while tugging on his cuffs* *again.)* These sleeves are too long but they're also . . . not long enough. It's so weird.

EMILY: I'm not sure why you keep expecting me to help you with this, when you can't even book your *own* friend as a guest.

ZACK, *not looking up:* Have you met Mateo?

EMILY, *turning to Ishaan:* What about Cal? Aren't you guys buddies now?

ISHAAN: Yeah, but Cal has a complicated relationship with the show.

EMILY: Is that because it only recently acknowledged his existence?

ZACK: Maybe we could try getting hold of Charlie again. *(Gives up on his cuffs and pushes his sleeves up.)* That boot camp school has to let him use a phone eventually.

ISHAAN: I don't know, man. The place is hardcore.

EMILY: Or—and I know this is a radical idea, but hear me out—you could talk about something that's *not* related to the Coach Kendall case.

ISHAAN, *blinking:* Why would we do that?

EMILY: Maybe because there's a whole other world out there? And what's even left to talk about? It's been six weeks since he was arrested. Everything is settling down, and people are moving on. I know Ivy is.

ZACK: There's still a trial to get through. Plus, coming on the show could be cathartic for Ivy. She has a lot of support from our viewers.

ISHAAN: Totally. It would be a lovefest, but not, you know, in a creepy way. In a very boundary-respecting, appropriate way.

EMILY: You're not selling it. At all.

ISHAAN: Look, here's the bottom line: don't give me that "moving on" crap. With a case this strange, people should be worried when things get quiet.

EMILY, *arching her brows:* And why is that?

ISHAAN: Because it's the calm before the storm.

36

IVY

"In conclusion, if such egregiously predatory behavior isn't punished to the fullest extent possible, then no student in Massachusetts can ever feel safe."

I lean against Mateo, who's been sitting beside me on his bed while I read from the letter to the Board of Education that I just wrote on his laptop. "What do you think?" I ask.

He twirls a strand of my hair around his finger. "I think *egregiously* is kind of a distracting word," he says. "But otherwise, it sounds great."

"Really? I thought it was powerful." I frown at my screen. "How about *shockingly*?"

"How about you take a break?" Mateo asks. He kisses my temple, then my cheek, and then trails his lips down to my neck. "You've been working on that since you got here."

I resist the urge to melt against him. "I want to get it right," I say.

"I know," Mateo murmurs, still kissing my neck. "But you're not single-handedly responsible for taking Ms. Jamison down, you know. That's someone else's job."

"Sure, except they're not *doing* it," I say, frustrated. It's the bane of my existence that the woman who tried to kill me two months ago hasn't even lost her teaching license. "Maybe I should get Aunt Helen involved."

That's enough to give Mateo pause. He stops kissing me, making me instantly regret my big mouth. "Aunt Helen? The romance author? Why?"

"She's friends with the Under Secretary of Education," I say, closing the laptop and placing it on the end table beside Mateo's bed.

He blinks. "What, of Massachusetts?"

"No, of the United States. Aunt Helen went to Harvard. She's connected." I flop onto my back and stare at his ceiling. "I'm trying to be better about letting go of stuff I can't control, but it drives me crazy that Lara gets away with everything."

Mateo stretches out next to me. "Karma will get her eventually," he says.

"Not soon enough. She probably has drug money stashed all over town while she waits for things to die down." I roll over on one elbow and raise my eyebrows at Mateo. "And some clueless guy trailing after her like a puppy, doing her dirty work without even realizing it. I bet if you, Cal, and I followed her around for half a day, we'd find out all kinds of stuff."

Alarm flashes in Mateo's eyes. "No," he says instantly.

"Why not? We're good at that kind of thing!"

"We're *terrible* at that kind of thing. If it was up to us, the cops would've arrested Dominick Payne."

"All right, that's a fair point," I concede. Turns out that after all our suspicions, Dominick Payne was just a run-of-the-mill struggling artist with poor judgment in business, real estate, and friends. "But we've learned a lot since then."

"Yeah, we've learned to mind our own business." Mateo pulls me closer until our faces are only inches apart. "Ivy, listen. *Do not* go scorched earth on Ms. Jamison," he whispers, his dark eyes serious. "She's not worth it. Okay?"

"Okay," I whisper back, just before his lips brush mine. For a few perfect minutes, I don't think about anything except him.

Then a persistent voice reaches my ears. "Mateo!" Ms. Reyes calls. For about the third time, from the sound of her.

I sit up instantly, smoothing my hair and looking anxiously toward the door. Ms. Reyes has that effect on me. Even though she's told me a half dozen times that she forgives me for Spare Me, and she's more than happy in her new job, I haven't shaken my guilt.

"What?" Mateo yells back. His hands are still on my hips, ready to pull me back as soon as he deals with his mother.

"Your father is here."

"He is?" This time, Mateo loosens his grip. "Why?"

"I'm coming up," Ms. Reyes says, because she's awesome like that. Always plenty of warning. By the time she appears in Mateo's doorway, he's leaning back against his headboard on a smoothed-out comforter, and I'm sitting at the edge of his desk chair.

"Hi, Ivy," Ms. Reyes says kindly.

"Hello. We were doing homework," I say, despite the fact that a) it's Saturday and b) nobody asked.

Mateo sits up and swings his legs over the edge of the bed. "Why is Dad here?"

"He wants to take you out to lunch," Ms. Reyes says.

Mateo stiffens, a muscle jumping in his cheek. He's slowly warming up to his father being around more often, but he still gets annoyed any time he perceives Mr. Wojcik as pushing for more than Mateo is prepared to give. "Tell him he should take Autumn," he says. "Ivy and I have plans."

"Autumn is at the shelter," Ms. Reyes says. Autumn volunteers at the homeless shelter almost full-time these days, and she's looking into getting a degree in social work now that it seems likely that she'll end up with a lengthy probation period instead of jail time. "And I'm sure your father won't mind if Ivy comes along."

"Why should Ivy have to suffer, though?" Mateo grumbles, looking so grouchy that I want to fling myself onto his lap and kiss the expression away. Although I generally feel that way no matter how he looks.

"I don't mind," I volunteer. It's true; I like Mr. Wojcik. He's friendly, if a little try-hard and goofy, and I have zero crushing guilt in his presence.

"Thank you, Ivy," Ms. Reyes says, giving me a smile before turning back to her son. "It seems important to him, baby, so I think you should go."

And that does it. Mateo can't say no to his mother any more than I can.

"All right, fine," he sighs. We follow Ms. Reyes downstairs, where Mr. Wojcik is waiting by the front door, his ever-present scally cap in hand. He's handsome in a different way from Mateo, with dark auburn hair, a neatly trimmed beard, and bright green eyes. I expect them to crinkle in welcome when he sees me, like usual, but instead he looks mildly alarmed. Which only gets worse when Mateo announces, "Ivy's coming."

"Oh." Mr. Wojcik twists his cap in his hands. "Oh, I didn't . . . well. This changes, um. Huh. I'm sorry, Ivy, I didn't realize you were here. So, hello."

"Hi?" I say uncertainly. That was a little hard to follow.

"Maybe we should do this another . . ." Mr. Wojcik trails off, then gives himself a little shake, like he's gathering his courage for something. "No, you know what? This is good. Why not, right? Has to happen eventually. This is fine. Glad to have you along, Ivy."

"Okay?" I say in the same unsure tone. Mateo rolls his eyes while grabbing both of our coats out of the hall closet. He seems to think Mr. Wojcik's odd stammering is just his dad being annoying, per usual, but it feels different to me.

"Try giving him some notice next time, okay, Darren?" Ms. Reyes murmurs in an aside to her ex-husband as we head out the door.

It's a crisp, sunny day in late November, the last of the fall leaves still clinging to their branches. Almost two months have passed since Boney died, and things are—sort of normal? Better, mostly, than they were those first few days afterward. Boney was laid to rest, and his funeral was so packed that people had to stand on the sidewalk. I said my last goodbye to him at his graveside, alone, with a final, silent apology. And a promise that I'd never be as petty with anyone else as I was about him the day he died.

I scroll through Instagram once I've buckled myself into the back seat, smiling at a picture of Cal and Ishaan Mittal mugging with some Marvel superhero at a comic festival at the Hynes Convention Center. "I love that Cal and Ishaan are, like, best friends now," I say, holding my phone out to Mateo so he can look. For a while, I thought Ishaan was only being nice to Cal to get him on the show, but it turns out they like a lot of the same stuff.

"They should go see some penguins next," Mateo says.

Mr. Wojcik babbles about sports the entire way to the restaurant, which turns out to be a really cute little Italian place in downtown Carlton that my parents love. It's expensive, and I start feeling nervous all over again as he shifts the car into park. "If this is a special occasion, I can maybe—" I start, but as soon as I'm out the door, Mateo grabs my hand and presses his lips to my ear.

"Please don't leave me," he breathes.

Well. Okay, then.

"Why are we here?" Mateo asks his father in a normal tone of voice as we approach the entrance. "This isn't your usual kind of place."

"True, true. Well . . ." Mr. Wojcik wore his scally cap while he was driving, but now he takes it off and twists it in his hands again. "I guess you were right back there, Ivy. Today is sort of a special occasion. You see, I've—I've met someone."

Oh God. If Mateo hadn't just begged me to stay, I would be *so* out of here. I can't believe I accidentally crashed a new girlfriend meet-and-greet. "That's great," I manage while Mateo's face gets stony.

"It might be a little misleading to say *met*," Mr. Wojcik adds, heading straight past the hostess and into the dining room. Soft music pipes overhead, easy to hear over the distinct lack of voices and clattering silverware. I've only ever been here for dinner; it's not nearly as crowded during lunch. "This is someone I've been interested in for a while, and to be honest, one of the reasons I made the move back to Carlton was because I hoped things might work out with her. And, well, I'm lucky that they did."

"There it is," Mateo mutters under his breath. I squeeze his hand, feeling a stab of disappointment on his behalf. He's always maintained that his father didn't come back just to help their family, and I've always told him to be less cynical. I wish he hadn't been proved right.

Mr. Wojcik is still talking, winding his way through empty, white-clothed tables. "I would have brought the two of you together sooner, but things have been kind of complicated. To be honest, they're still complicated, but this person is very special to me, and so . . . ah." His voice softens. "There she is."

I follow his gaze and stop in my tracks, my stomach dropping through the floor. I blink multiple times in quick succession, hoping desperately that she's a mirage who'll go away. She doesn't; and even worse, once she realizes we're rooted in place, she gets up from her table and starts walking toward us.

"No fucking way," Mateo growls, his arm curling protectively around me. "Have you lost your mind?"

Mr. Wojcik steps in front of us, tugging so hard on his cap that he's liable to tear it in two. "Look, if you could just keep an open mind—"

And then she's beside him, her blond hair gleaming as she smiles sweetly at Mateo. "Mateo, please come sit. I can't tell you how excited I am to get to know you better," Lara Jamison says. Then she turns to me. "Ivy, nice to see you again."

As though she hadn't been wrestling me for a gun the last

time we were in a room together. As though she weren't spewing lies about Cal every chance she gets. I gape at her, too horrified to fake even a sliver of politeness, and she lets out a light laugh. "Darren, from the look of things, you could have prepared them better," she says.

Darren. *Darren.* Oh my God. Mateo's father is D.

"Sorry, angel," Mr. Wojcik says, giving her a worshipful glance before turning his attention back to his son. "Mateo, I know this is going to take some getting used to. You kids have been through a rough time. But so has Lara, and you've all made it to the other side, so it seemed like the right time to let you know . . ."

Then he says some more things. But I don't hear them, because Lara lifts her left hand to tuck a wisp of hair behind her ear, and blood starts pounding in my ears as I see the flash of a new diamond on her finger.

She doesn't care about Mr. Wojcik. I know she doesn't, because Cal told us what she'd said in her house about D— *ultimately, he was just another distraction.* But now that she has to play nice with the police and buff up her image, he's useful. There's no better PR than getting engaged to the father of one of the kids involved in the Carlton drug bust. After all, if *he* believes her story, then it must be true.

Turns out I was almost exactly right when I'd told Mateo that Lara probably had some clueless guy trailing after her like a puppy. I just didn't realize it was his dad.

All of my senses sharpen as I take hold of Mateo's hand and spin on my heel, pulling him toward the door. "Come on," I say, ignoring the startled look of a passing server. "We're getting out of here."

"And going where?" Mateo asks. His voice is hoarse and ragged, like he just woke up from a nightmare and found reality even worse. "Do I need to remind you we don't have a car?"

"It doesn't matter," I say, even though it obviously does. But that's purely a logistical problem, and right now, we need to be thinking bigger than that. We reach the restaurant door and I shove it open with my free hand, every cell in my body thrumming with purpose.

"We're going scorched earth," I say.

ACKNOWLEDGMENTS

I turned in a first draft of this book to my editor in January 2020, and began revising it two months later—at the beginning of what would become a world-changing pandemic. Like every industry, publishing scrambled to adapt, and I have many people to thank for keeping *You'll Be the Death of Me* on track during so much upheaval.

My agents, Rosemary Stimola and Allison Remcheck, who are always guiding lights, shone especially bright during this uncertain year. Thank you for your wisdom, your support, and your steadfast faith in my books. Thanks also to Alli Hellegers for your work on the international side, to Pete Ryan and Nick Croce for your help in managing operations, and to Jason Dravis for your expertise in the film world.

I am grateful to the many people at Delacorte Press who carefully steered this book through the editorial and production process, especially my brilliant editor, Krista Marino, who finds hidden depths in every story, and my publishers, Beverly Horowitz, Judith Haut, and Barbara Marcus. Thank you also to

Kathy Dunn, Lydia Gregovic, Dominique Cimina, Kate Keating, Elizabeth Ward, Jules Kelly, Kelly McGauley, Jenn Inzetta, Adrienne Weintraub, Felicia Frazier, Becky Green, Enid Chaban, Kimberly Langus, Kerry Milliron, Colleen Fellingham, Heather Lockwood Hughes, Alison Impey, Ray Shappell, Kenneth Crossland, Martha Rago, Tracy Heydweiller, Linda Palladino, and Denise DeGennaro.

I didn't get to travel last year, but my books certainly did. Thank you to Clementine Gaisman and Alice Natali of Intercontinental Literary Agency, Bastian Schlueck and Frederike Belder at Thomas Schlueck Agency, and Charlotte Bodman at Rights People for finding homes around the world for *You'll Be the Death of Me*. Special thanks as well to all the international editors and publishers who have supported my books, and brought them to readers in more than forty countries.

Thanks to Erin Hahn and Kit Frick for your thoughtful feedback on this manuscript, and to all the wonderful friends who helped me feel connected this year, especially Samira Ahmed, Stephanie Garber, Kathleen Glasgow, Lisa Gilley, Aaron Proman, and Neil Cawley. Lots of love to my son, Jack, and the rest of my family—I'm so grateful that we made it through this year in reasonably good health, even though I've missed hanging out with you.

And finally, thank you to all the readers who spend time with my books—you're the reason that I get to keep writing more of them.

TRUST NO ONE.

#1 *NEW YORK TIMES* BESTSELLING AUTHOR OF *ONE OF US IS LYING*

KAREN M. McMANUS

NOTHING MORE to TELL

Keep reading for a sneak peek at
another Karen M. McManus thriller!

TRIPP

My head is pounding when I wake up at six a.m. on Wednesday morning. All I want to do is go back to sleep, but I force myself to toss the covers aside and climb out of bed. The only thing I hate more than running is how I feel when I *don't* run.

I dress quickly, unplug my phone from its charger, and root around in the top of my bureau for my earphones. No luck. They're not on my desk or the floor either, so I grab my sneakers and head for the living room, the shaggy green carpet muffling my footsteps. Our house is a split-level that my dad inherited from his parents, and it's barely been updated since the seventies. One of the last things my mother did before she left was strip away the loud floral wallpaper and paint every room a different, jewel-toned color. I can still remember her standing in the middle of the dining room when she'd finally finished, paintbrush in hand, gazing accusingly at the walls like they'd broken a promise. "This is no better," she said.

Even then, I knew she wasn't talking about wallpaper.

She never got around to yanking up the rug. Just as well. It's ugly but insulating, which matters when you're not allowed to set the thermostat any higher than sixty-five degrees. My steps slow as I near the kitchen, and I yawn so hard that my jaw cracks. The bitter smell of burnt coffee wafts toward me, which it shouldn't, since I'm the only one up in the—

"Morning," a voice calls, startling me so much that I drop my phone onto my foot. It hits on exactly the wrong spot, and pain radiates through my toe as I retrieve it.

"Jesus, Dad!" I hobble toward the kitchen and glare at him. "You scared the crap out of me. What are you doing here?"

He's wearing a T-shirt one of his buddies gave him as a joke that reads *Peaked in High School,* and I guess you have to give him credit for running with it. My father was a sort-of star football player when he was my age; good enough that his name is on a couple of plaques at Sturgis High, but not so good that anyone recruited him to play past that.

Dad rubs one hand over his thick, graying hair before taking a sip of black coffee. "I live here, remember?"

I spot the cord of my earphones beneath a jumble of silver on the table—Dad's key ring, which takes up way too much space because it's full of random discs that he calls his "lucky medallions." I used to like them when I was a kid, partly because there was something comforting about the jingling noise they made, and partly because I still believed in luck back then. Now I avoid looking at them as I tug my earphones free.

"Yeah, but why are you up?" I ask. Dad works the night shift as a security guard at Sturgis Hospital and comes home about an hour before I get up for school. He sleeps most of the day, and I don't usually see him until nearly dinnertime.

"Working at Home Depot later this morning," Dad says through a yawn. "No point in going to sleep for two hours."

"Back-to-back? Why?" Dad's occasional Home Depot shifts are usually on the weekend, to avoid exactly this scenario.

"Car needs a new transmission," he sighs.

That's life in the Talbot household. My father works hard, but at jobs that don't pay much and offer zero stability. He's been laid off more times than I can count. On the one hand, you have to give the guy credit for plugging along, always landing something right before things fall apart. On the other hand, it'd be nice not to have to choose which bills to pay every month.

We don't talk about that, though. There are a lot of things we don't talk about.

"I'm gonna run," I say, stuffing the buds into my ears. "See you." Whatever Dad says in return is drowned out by my playlist, and I pull the hood of my sweatshirt over my head as Rage Against the Machine propels me out the door.

My feet automatically carry me on my usual path: down my street, a half mile until I pass Sturgis High School, and then a left onto Main Street. The upper section of Main is the best part of Sturgis, full of old Victorians that look good no matter how badly their paint is peeling. I steadily increase my pace for the next mile until I reach the end of Main Street. I'm at top speed now, the fastest I can comfortably run for any length of time. My limbs pump, smooth and purposeful, as endorphins course through me and fill my veins with a buzzy sense of well-being.

This is why I run. Because it's the only time I ever feel that way.

At this hour almost everything on Main Street is closed, even Brightside Bakery. The streets are quiet and nearly deserted; I can only see one car in my peripheral vision as I near the crosswalk. I don't slow down, since pedestrians have the right of way, but whoever's driving decides to be a dick and speeds up to blow past me before I can cross. "Asshole," I mutter, pulling up short on the sidewalk.

Then I do a double take as I catch sight of the driver. They pass in a flash, and I blink at the bumper, confused and disoriented. *No. It can't be.* The car is a nondescript gray sedan I've never seen before, with a New Jersey license plate.

It can't be.

I keep going and turn onto Prospect Hill. My heart thumps harder as I struggle to maintain my pace against the incline, and my lungs start to burn. Music pounds in my ears, urging me forward even though everything in me wants to slow down, until all of a sudden it's interrupted by a text tone.

I shouldn't look in the middle of the hardest part of my run. But that flash of familiarity in the gray car makes me pull out my phone, because there's no one else who ever texts me this early. I stop abruptly, panting, and steel myself for what I might see. It's not what I was afraid of, though. It's actually worse.

The text is from an unknown number, and the message is a single word.

Murderer.